ACKNOWLEDGMENTS

Unusual

Irene M. Crowell 3/27/89

THE MIDAS TOUCH OF TERROR . . .

It turns innocence to evil, beauty into beastliness, the mundane into the macabre. It can make a man a monster, a home a house of horrors.

It is the masters' touch . . . and it transforms these simple stories into tales of heart-numbing fear.

"The premier magazine in its field casts back nearly to its first year to marshal . . . [the] flesh creepers it's pleased to call its best."

—*Booklist*

"MEMORABLE, ATMOSPHERIC TALES."
—*Publishers Weekly*

"This collection . . . pleases through both its quality and its range."

—*Kirkus Reviews*

"It's hard to pick out favorites: THEY'RE ALL GOOD!"

—*Locus*

EDWARD L. FERMAN, publisher of *The Magazine of Fantasy and Science Fiction* for twenty years, has edited many anthologies, most recently *The Best from Fantasy and Science Fiction #24*. **ANNE JORDAN** is the magazine's managing editor.

THE BEST
HORROR
STORIES Vol. 1

FROM

THE MAGAZINE OF
Fantasy & Science Fiction

Edward L. Ferman
and Anne Jordan, Editors

ST. MARTIN'S PRESS / NEW YORK

Volumes 1 and 2 of this series were first published in one volume, under the same title, in hardcover and trade paper by St. Martin's Press.

THE BEST HORROR STORIES FROM *THE MAGAZINE OF FANTASY AND SCIENCE FICTION*

Copyright © 1988 by Mercury Press Inc.

Library of Congress Catalog Card Number: 88-1987

ISBN: 0-312-91499-7   Can. ISBN: 0-312-91500-4

Printed in the United States of America

St. Martin's Press hardcover edition published 1988
St. Martin's Press trade paperback edition published 1988
First St. Martin's Press mass market edition/April 1989

10 9 8 7 6 5 4 3 2 1

CONTENTS

INTRODUCTION

A friend of mine—who is a writer of horror tales—becomes immobile with fear at the idea of having to ride in one of those glass-sided elevators. He has missed out on a number of things because he is literally unable to get into such an elevator. Me, I'm not too keen on snakes and bugs, and the larger they are, the faster I move—in the opposite direction. Do I *really* believe that the spider dangling before my windowpane, which is possibly one millimeter in size, will suddenly turn feral, charge toward me, and wipe me from the face of the earth? Intellectually, no. Well . . . maybe.

The engine of fear is relentless, subjective, and fueled by the imagination. We all can imagine "what if" situations, but it takes a true literary talent to craft that "what if" into a story of quality and worth. When it comes to horror stories, one person's nightmare is another's inspiration, and nowadays the subject of a tale of horror is constrained only by the limits of a writer's imagination.

The horror story has come of age in the twentieth century. It is no longer merely the recitation of an eerie event or ghostly happening, but rather it is a tale of people—people reacting to the dark and the dark side of the soul, where control has been eliminated and chaos threatens. Horace Walpole created the "Gothic" in 1765 with his ghostly tale, *The Castle of Otranto*, giving us the tone and mood of the modern horror story. Each successive writer of horror has added something more to the genre so that today we can be frightened anywhere, anytime, by anyone . . . or thing. Horror has crept out of the castle and into *any* shadowy corner.

But "it"—whatever "it" is in a story that frightens us—must be believable. That takes skill. Anyone can make a person shudder (picture sliding down a banister that transforms into a razor blade—small, internal shudder?) but to create a story around that shudder and bring the story and characters to life takes unusual talent. At *The Magazine of Fantasy & Science Fiction* we take great delight when we encounter such talent. When we read a manuscript we look first and foremost for quality writing, for craftsmanship; gore is not important. Too often a beginning writer, perhaps overly influenced by the slash and stab "horror" movies of today, equates rivers of blood with what makes horror work. The best horror stories make a play for our minds and fears, not our queasy stomachs.

Since its inception, *The Magazine of Fantasy & Science Fiction* has published tales of horror that have been among the best in the genre, and the stories chosen for this collection are the best of these best. In putting together this collection we have tried to include tales for every taste. Yet the primary thing the tales in this very diverse collection do have in common is that they are all of exceptional quality, written by extremely talented people, with the express purpose of scaring you out of your socks.

Horror tales, and these thirteen tales in particular, are artfully crafted reminders to "take care!" Even the tiniest thing in our world can turn on us, can black out the light, douse the fire, and leave us alone in the dark, waiting. . . .

So—lock the doors, turn on all the lights (keep that flashlight handy, though), get comfortable, turn the page, read . . . and enjoy the creeping shadow of fear.

Take care!

—ANNE DEVEREAUX JORDAN

THE BEST
HORROR
STORIES Vol. I

FROM

THE MAGAZINE OF
Fantasy & Science Fiction

WINDOW

BOB LEMAN

Bob Leman is one of *F & SF*'s most valued and interesting contributors; he often takes a realistic, contemporary narrative and introduces a chilling wrinkle, turning the usual into the unusual and, at times, the deadly. "Window" was first published in *F & SF* in May 1980 and is a fine example of Bob's technique. It is a gripping story about a military project that is investigating telekinesis and which experiences an incredible accident: the disappearance of an entire building, along with one researcher, and the appearance, in its place, of something terrifyingly different from what it appears to be.

"We don't know what the hell's going on out there," they told Gilson in Washington. "It may be pretty big. The nut in charge tried to keep it under wraps, but the army was furnishing routine security, and the commanding officer tipped us off. A screwball project. Apparently been funded for years without anyone paying much attention. Extrasensory perception, for God's sake. And maybe they've found something. The security colonel thinks so, anyway. Find out about it."

The Nut-in-Charge was a rumpled professor of psychology named Krantz. He and the colonel met Gilson at the airport, and they set off directly for the site in an army sedan. The colonel began talking immediately.

"You've got something mighty queer here, Gilson," he said. "I never saw anything like it, and neither did anybody else. Krantz here is as mystified as anybody. And it's his baby. We're just security. Not that they've needed any, up to now. Not even any need for secrecy, except to keep the public from laughing its head off. The setup we've got here is—"

"Dr. Krantz," Gilson said, "you'd better give me a complete rundown on the situation here. So far, I haven't any information at all."

Krantz was occupied with the lighting of a cigar. He blew a cloud of foul smoke, and through it he said, "We're missing one prefab building, one POBEC computer, some medical machinery, and one, uh, researcher named Culvergast."

"Explain 'missing,' " Gilson said.

"Gone. Disappeared. A building and everything in it. Just not there anymore. But we do have something in exchange."

"And what's that?"

"I think you'd better wait and see for yourself," Krantz said. "We'll be there in a few minutes." They were passing through the farther reaches of the metropolitan area, a series of decayed small towns. The highway wound down the valley beside the river, and the towns lay stretched along it, none of them more than a block or two wide, their side streets rising steeply toward the first ridge. In one of these moribund communities they left the highway and went bounding up the hillside on a crooked road whose surface changed from cobblestones to slag after the houses had been left behind. Beyond the crest of the ridge the road began to drop as steeply as it had risen, and after a quarter of a mile they turned into a lane whose entrance would have been missed by anyone not watching for it. They were in a forest now; it was second growth, but the logging had been done so long ago that it might almost have been a virgin stand, lofty, silent, and somewhat gloomy on this gray day.

"Pretty," Gilson said. "How does a project like this come to be way out here, anyhow?"

"The place was available," the colonel said. "Has been since World War Two. They set it up for some work on proximity fuzes. Shut it down in forty-eight. Was vacant until the professor took it over."

"Culvergast is a little bit eccentric," Krantz said. "He wouldn't work at the university—too many people, he said. When I heard this place was available, I put in for it, and got it—along with the colonel, here. Culvergast has been happy with the setup, but I guess he bothers the colonel a little."

"He's a certifiable loony," the colonel said, "and his little helpers are worse."

"Well, what the devil was he doing?" Gilson asked.

Before Krantz could answer, the driver braked at a chain-link gate that stood across the lane. It was fastened with a loop of heavy logging chain and manned by armed soldiers. One of them, machine pistol in hand, peered into the car. "Everything O.K., sir?" he said.

"O.K. with waffles, Sergeant," the colonel said. It was evidently a password. The noncom unlocked the enormous padlock that secured the chain. "Pretty primitive," the colonel said as they bumped through the gateway, "but it'll do until we get proper stuff in. We've got men with dogs patrolling the fence." He looked at Gilson. "We're just about there. Get a load of this, now."

It was a house. It stood in the center of the clearing in an island of sunshine, white, gleaming, and incongruous. All around was the dark loom of the forest under a sunless sky, but somehow sunlight lay on the house, sparkling in its polished windows and making brilliant the colors of massed flowers in carefully tended beds reflecting from the pristine whiteness of its siding out into the gray, littered clearing with its congeries of derelict buildings.

"You couldn't have picked a better time," the colonel said. "Shining there, cloudy here."

Gilson was not listening. He had climbed from the car and was staring in fascination. "Jesus," he said. "Like a goddamn Victorian postcard."

Lacy scrollwork foamed over the rambling wooden mansion, running riot at the eaves of the steep roof, climbing elaborately up towers and turrets, embellishing deep oriels and outlining a long, airy veranda. Tall windows showed by their spacing that the rooms were many and large. It seemed to be a new house, or perhaps just newly painted and supremely well-kept. A driveway of fine white gravel led under a high porte-cochère.

"How about that?" the colonel said. "Look like your grandpa's house?"

As a matter of fact, it did: like his grandfather's house enlarged and perfected and seen through a lens of romantic nostalgia, his grandfather's house groomed and pampered as the old farmhouse never had been. He said, "And you got this in exchange for a prefab, did you?"

"Just like that one," the colonel said, pointing to one of the seedy buildings. "Of course, we could use the prefab."

"What does that mean?"

"Watch," the colonel said. He picked up a small rock and tossed it in the direction of the house. The rock rose, topped its arc, and began to fall. Suddenly it was not there.

"Here," Gilson said. "Let me try that."

He threw the rock like a baseball, a high, hard one. It disappeared about fifty feet from the house. As he stared at the point of its disappearance, Gilson became aware that the smooth green of the lawn ended exactly below. Where the grass ended, there began the weeds and rocks that made up the floor of the clearing. The line of separation was absolutely straight, running at an angle across the lawn. Near the driveway it turned ninety degrees and sliced off lawn, driveway, and shrubbery with the same precise straightness.

"It's perfectly square," Krantz said. "About a hundred feet to a side. Probably a cube, actually. We know the top's about ninety feet in the air. I'd guess there are about ten feet of it underground."

" 'It'?" Gilson said. " 'It'? What's 'it'?"

"Name it and you can have it," Krantz said. "A three-dimensional television receiver a hundred feet to a side, maybe. A cubical crystal ball. Who knows?"

"The rocks we threw. They didn't hit the house. Where did the rocks go?"

"Ah. Where, indeed? Answer that and perhaps you answer all."

Gilson took a deep breath. "All right. I've seen it. Now tell me about it. From the beginning."

Krantz was silent for a moment; then, in a dry lecturer's voice he said, "Five days ago, June thirteenth, at eleven thirty A.M., give or take three minutes, Private Ellis Mulvihill, on duty at the gate, heard what he later described as 'an explosion that was quiet, like.' He entered the enclosure, locked the gate behind him, and ran up here to the clearing. He was staggered—'shook-up' was his expression—to see, instead of Culvergast's broken-down prefab, that house there. I gather that he stood gulping and blinking for a time, trying to come to terms with what his eyes told him. Then he ran over there to the guardhouse and called the colonel. Who called me. We came out here and found that a quarter of an acre of land and a building with a man in it had disappeared and been replaced by this, as neat as a peg in a pegboard."

"You think the prefab went where the rocks did," Gilson said. It was a statement.

"Why, we're not even absolutely sure it's gone. What we're seeing can't actually be where we're seeing it. It rains on that house when it's sunny here, and right now you can see the sunlight on it, on a day like this. It's a window."

"A window on what?"

"Well—that looks like a new house, doesn't it? When were they building houses like that?"

"Eighteen seventy or eighty, something like—oh."

"Yes," Krantz said. "I think we're looking at the past."

"Oh, for God's sake," Gilson said.

"I know how you feel. And I may be wrong. But I have to say it looks very much that way. I want you to hear what Reeves says about it. He's been here from the beginning. A graduate student, assisting here. Reeves!"

A very tall, very thin young man unfolded himself from a crouched position over an odd-looking machine that stood near the line between grass and rubble and ambled over to the three men. Reeves was an enthusiast. "Oh, it's the past, all right," he said. "Sometime in the eighties. My girl got some books on costume from the library, and the clothes check out for that decade. And the decorations on the horses' harnesses are a clue, too. I got that from—"

"Wait a minute," Gilson said. "*Clothes?* You mean there are people in there?"

"Oh, sure," Reeves said. "A fine little family. Mamma, poppa, little girl, little boy, old granny or auntie. A dog. Good people."

"How can you tell that?"

"I've been watching them for five days, you know? They're having—*were* having—fine weather there—or then, or whatever you'd say. They're nice to each other, they *like* each other. Good people. You'll see."

"When?"

"Well, they'll be eating dinner now. They usually come out after dinner. In an hour, maybe."

"I'll wait," Gilson said. "And while we wait, you will please tell me some more."

Krantz assumed his lecturing voice again. "As to the nature of it, nothing. We have a window, which we believe to open into the past. We can see into it, so we know that light passes through; but it passes in only one direction, as evidenced by the fact that the people over there are wholly unaware of us. Nothing else goes through. You saw what happened to the rocks. We've shoved poles through the interface there—there's no resistance at all—but anything that goes through is gone, God knows where. Whatever you put through stays there. Your pole is cut off clean. Fascinating. But wherever it is, it's not where the house is. That interface isn't between us and the past; it's between us and—someplace else. I think our window here is just an incidental side-effect, a—a twisting of time that resulted from whatever tensions exist along that interface."

Gilson sighed. "Krantz," he said, "what am I going to tell the secretary? You've lucked into what may be the biggest thing that ever happened, and you've kept it bottled up for five days. We wouldn't know about it now if it weren't for the colonel's report. Five days wasted. Who knows how long this thing will last? The whole goddamn scientific establishment ought to be here—should have been from day one. This needs the whole works. At this point the place should be a beehive. And what do I find? You and a graduate student throwing rocks and poking with sticks. And a girlfriend looking up the dates of costumes. It's damn near criminal."

Krantz did not look abashed. "I thought you'd say that," he said. "But look at it this way. Like it or not, this thing wasn't produced by technology or science. It was pure psi. If we can reconstruct Culvergast's work, we may be able to find out what happened; we may be able to repeat the phenomenon. But I don't like what's going to happen after you've called in your experimenters, Gilson. They'll measure and test and conjecture and theorize, and never once will they accept for a moment the real basis of what's happened. The day they arrive, I'll be out. And dammit, Gilson, this is *mine*."

"Not anymore," Gilson said. "It's too big."

"It's not as though we weren't doing some hard experiments of our own," Krantz said. "Reeves, tell him about your batting machine."

"Yes, *sir*," Reeves said. "You see, Mr. Gilson, what the professor said wasn't absolutely the whole truth, you know? Sometimes something *can* get through the window. We saw it on the first day. There was a temperature inversion over in the valley, and the stink from the chemical plant had been accumulating for about a week. It broke up that day, and the wind blew the gunk through the notch and right over here. A really rotten stench. We were watching our people over there, and all of a sudden they began to sniff and wrinkle their noses and make disgusted faces. We figured it had to be the chemical stink. We pushed a pole out right away, but the end just disappeared, as usual. The professor suggested that maybe there was a pulse, or something of the sort, in the interface, that it exists only intermittently. We cobbled up a gadget to test the idea. Come and have a look at it."

It was a horizontal flywheel with a paddle attached to its rim, like an extended cleat. As the wheel spun, the paddle swept around a table. There was a hopper hanging above, and at intervals something dropped from the hopper onto the table, where it was immediately banged by the paddle and sent flying. Gilson peered into the hopper and raised an interrogatory eyebrow. "Ice cubes," Reeves said. "Colored orange for visibility. That thing shoots an ice cube at the interface once a second. Somebody is always on duty with a stopwatch. We've established that every fifteen hours and twenty minutes the thing is open for five seconds. Five ice cubes go through and drop on the lawn in there. The rest of the time they just vanish at the interface."

"Ice cubes. Why ice cubes?"

"They melt and disappear. We can't be littering up the past with artifacts from our day. God knows what the effect might be. Then, too, they're cheap, and we're shooting a lot of them."

"Science," Gilson said heavily. "I can't wait to hear what they're going to say in Washington."

"Sneer all you like," Krantz said. "The house is there, the interface is there. We've by God turned up some kind of time travel. And Culvergast the screwball did it, not a physicist or an engineer."

"Now that you bring it up," Gilson said, "just what *was* your man Culvergast up to?"

"Good question. What he was doing was—well, not to put too fine a point upon it, he was trying to discover spells."

"Spells?"

"The kind you cast. Magic words. Don't look disgusted yet. It makes sense, in a way. We were funded to look into telekinesis—the manipulation of matter by the mind. It's obvious that telekinesis, if it could be applied with precision, would be a marvelous weapon. Culvergast's hypothesis was that there are in fact people who perform feats of telekinesis, and although they never seem to know or be able to explain how they do it, they nevertheless perform a specific mental action that enables them to tap some source of energy that apparently exists all around us, and to some degree to focus and direct that energy. Culvergast proposed to discover the common factor in their mental processes.

"He ran a lot of putative telekinecists through here, and he reported that he had found a pattern, a sort of mnemonic device functioning at the very bottom of, or below, the verbal level. In one of his people he found it as a set of musical notes, in several as gibberish of various sorts, and in one, he said, as mathematics at the primary arithmetic level. He was feeding all this into the computer, trying to eliminate simple noise and the personal idiosyncrasies of the subjects, trying to lay bare the actual, effective essence. He then proposed to organize this essence into *words*; words that would so shape the mental currents of a speaker of standard American English that they would channel and manipulate the telekinetic power at the will of the speaker. Magic words, you might say. Spells.

"He was evidently further along than I suspected. I think he must have arrived at some words, tried them out, and made an attempt at telekinesis—some small thing, like causing an ashtray to rise off his desk and float in the air, perhaps. And it worked, but what he got wasn't a dainty little ashtray-lifting force; he had opened the gate wide, and some kind of terrible power came through. It's pure conjecture, of course, but it must have been something like that to have had an effect like *this*."

Gilson had listened in silence. He said, "I won't say you're crazy because I can see that house and I'm watching what's happening to those ice cubes. How it happened isn't my problem, anyhow. My problem is what I'll recommend to the secretary that we do with it now that we've got it. One thing's sure, Krantz: this isn't going to be your private playpen much longer."

There was a yelp of pure pain from Reeves. "They can't *do* that," he said. "This is ours, it's the professor's. Look at it, look at that house. Do you want a bunch of damn engineers messing around with *that*?"

Gilson could understand how Reeves felt. The house was drenched now with the light of a red sunset; it seemed to glow from within with a deep rosy blush. But, Gilson reflected, the sunset wasn't really necessary; sentiment and the universal, unacknowledged yearning for a simpler, cleaner time would lend rosiness enough. He was quite aware that the surge of longing and nostalgia he felt was nostalgia for something he had never actually experienced, that the way of life the house epitomized for him was in tact his own creation, built from patches of novels and films; nonetheless he found himself hungry for that life, yearning for that time. It was a gentle and secure time, he thought, a time when the pace was unhurried and the air was clean; a time when there was grace and style, when young men in striped blazers and boater hats might pay decorous court to young ladies in long white dresses, whiling away the long, drowsy afternoons of summer in peaceable conversations on shady porches. There would be jolly bicycle tours over shade-dappled roads that twisted among the hills to arrive at cool glens where swift little streams ran; there would be long, sweet buggy rides behind somnolent, patient horses under a great white moon, lover whispering urgently to lover while nightbirds sang. There would be excursions down the broad, clean river, boats gentle on the current, floating toward the sound from across the water of a brass band playing at the landing.

Yes, thought Gilson, and there would probably be an old geezer with a trunkful of adjectives around somewhere, carrying on about how much better things had been a hundred years before. If he didn't watch himself, he'd be helping Krantz and Reeves try to keep things hidden. Young Reeves—oddly, for someone his age—seemed to be hopelessly mired in this bogus nostalgia. His description of the family in the house had been simple doting. Oh, it was definitely time that the cold-eyed boys were called in. High time.

"They ought to be coming out any minute now," Reeves was saying. "Wait till you see Martha."

"Martha," Gilson said.

"The little girl. She's a doll."

Gilson looked at him. Reeves reddened and said, "Well, I sort of gave them names. The children. Martha and Pete. And the dog's Alfie. They kind of look like those names, you know?" Gilson did not answer, and Reeves reddened further. "Well, you can see for yourself. Here they come."

A fine little family, as Reeves had said. After watching them for half an hour, Gilson was ready to concede that they were indeed most engaging, as perfect in their way as their house. They were just what it took to complete the picture, to make an authentic Victorian genre painting. Mama and Papa were good-looking and still in love, the children were healthy and merry and content with their world. Or so it seemed to him as he watched them in the darkening evening, imagining the comfortable, affectionate conversation of the parents as they sat on the porch swing, almost hearing the squeals of the children and the barking of the dog as they raced about the lawn. It was almost dark now; a mellow light of oil lamps glowed in the windows, and fireflies winked over the lawn. There was an arc of fire as the father tossed his cigar butt over the railing and rose to his feet. Then there followed a pretty little pantomime as he called the children, who duly protested, were duly permitted a few more minutes, and then were firmly commanded. They moved reluctantly to the porch and were shooed inside, and the dog, having delayed to give a shrub a final wetting, came scrambling up to join them. The children and the dog entered the house, then the mother and father. The door closed, and there was only the soft light from the windows.

Reeves exhaled a long breath. "Isn't that something," he said. "That's the way to live, you know? If a person could just say to hell with all this crap we live in today and go back there and live like that. . . . And Martha, you saw Martha. An angel, right? Man, what I'd give to—"

Gilson interrupted him. "When does the next batch of ice cubes go through?"

"—be able to— Uh, yeah. Let's see. The last penetration was at 3:15, just before you got here. Next one will be at 6:35 in the morning, if the pattern holds. And it has, so far."

"I want to see that. But right now I've got to do some telephoning. Colonel!"

Gilson did not sleep that night, nor, apparently, did Krantz
or Reeves. When he arrived at the clearing at five A.M. they
were still there, unshaven and red-eyed, drinking coffee
from thermos bottles. It was cloudy again, and the clearing
was in total darkness except for a pale light from beyond
the interface, where a sunny day was on the verge of breaking.

"Anything new?" Gilson said.

"I think that's my question," Krantz said. "What's going
to happen?"

"Just about what you expected, I'm afraid. I think that
by evening this place is going to be a real hive. And by
tomorrow night you'll be lucky if you can find a place to
stand. I imagine Bannon's been on the phone since I called
him at midnight, rounding up the scientists. And they'll
round up the technicians. Who'll bring their machines.
And the army's going to beef up the security. How about
some of that coffee?"

"Help yourself. You bring bad news, Gilson."

"Sorry," Gilson said, "but there it is."

"Goddamn!" Reeves said loudly. "Oh, goddamn!" He
seemed to be about to burst into tears. "That'll be the end
for me, you know? They won't even let me in. A damn
graduate student? In *psychology*? I won't get near the place.
Oh, dammit to hell!" He glared at Gilson in rage and
despair.

The sun had risen, bringing gray light to the clearing and
brilliance to the house across the interface. There was no
sound but the regular bang of the ice cube machine. The
three men stared quietly at the house. Gilson drank his
coffee.

"There's Martha," Reeves said. "Up there." A small face
had appeared between the curtains of a second-floor window, and bright blue eyes were surveying the morning. "She
does that every day," Reeves said. "Sits there and watches
the birds and squirrels until, I guess, they call her for break-

fast." They stood and watched the little girl, who was looking at something that lay beyond the scope of their window on her world, something that would have been to their rear had the worlds been the same. Gilson almost found himself turning around to see what it was that she stared at. Reeves apparently had the same impulse. "What's she looking at, do you think?" he said. "It's not necessarily forest, like now. I think this was logged out earlier. Maybe a meadow? Cattle or horses on it? Man, what I'd give to be there and see what it is."

Krantz looked at his watch and said, "We'd better go over there. Just a few minutes, now."

They moved to where the machine was monotonously batting ice cubes into the interface. A soldier with a stopwatch sat beside it, behind a table bearing a formidable chronometer and a sheaf of charts. He said, "Two minutes, Dr. Krantz."

Krantz said to Gilson, "Just keep your eye on the ice cubes. You can't miss it when it happens." Gilson watched the machine, mildly amused by the rhythm of its homely sounds: *plink*—a cube drops; *whuff*—the paddle sweeps around; *bang*—paddle strikes ice cube. And then a flat trajectory to the interface, where the small orange missile abruptly vanishes. A second later, another. Then another.

"Five seconds," the soldier called. "Four. Three. Two. One. *Now.*"

His timing was off by a second; the ice cube disappeared like its predecessors. But the next one continued its flight and dropped onto the lawn, where it lay glistening. It was really a fact, then, thought Gilson. Time travel for ice cubes.

Suddenly behind him there was an incomprehensible shout from Krantz and another from Reeves, and then a loud, clear, and anguished "Reeves, *no!*" from Krantz. Gilson heard a thud of running feet and caught a flash of swift movement at the edge of his vision. He whirled in time to see Reeves's gangling figure hurtle past, plunge through the interface, and land sprawling on the lawn. Krantz said, violently, *"Fool!"* An ice cube shot through and landed near Reeves. The machine banged again; an ice cube flew out and vanished. The five seconds of accessibility were over.

Reeves raised his head and stared for a moment at the grass on which he lay. He shifted his gaze to the house. He rose slowly to his feet, wearing a bemused expression. A grin came slowly over his face, then, and the men watching from the other side could almost read his thoughts: Well, I'll be damned. I made it. I'm really here.

Krantz was babbling uncontrollably. "We're still here, Gilson, we're still here, we still exist, everything seems the same. Maybe he didn't change things much, maybe the future is fixed and he didn't change anything at all. I was afraid of this, of something like this. Ever since you came out here, he's been—"

Gilson did not hear him. He was staring with shock and disbelief at the child in the window, trying to comprehend what he saw and did not believe he was seeing. Her behavior was wrong, it was very, very wrong. A man had materialized on her lawn, suddenly, out of thin air, on a sunny morning, and she had evinced no surprise or amazement or fear. Instead, she had smiled—instantly, spontaneously, a smile that broadened and broadened until it seemed to split the lower half of her face, a smile that showed too many teeth, a smile fixed and incongruous and terrible below her bright blue eyes. Gilson felt his stomach knot; he realized that he was dreadfully afraid.

The face abruptly disappeared from the window; a few seconds later the front door flew open and the little girl rushed through the doorway, making for Reeves with furious speed, moving in a curious, scuttling run. When she was a few feet away, she leapt at him with the agility and eye-dazzling quickness of a flea. Reeves's eyes had just begun to take on a puzzled look when the powerful little teeth tore out his throat.

She dropped away from him and sprang back. A geyser

of bright blood erupted from the ragged hole in his neck.
He looked at it in stupefaction for a long moment, then
brought up his hands to cover the wound; the blood boiled
through his fingers and ran down his forearms. He sank
gently to his knees, staring at the little girl with wide astonishment. He rocked, shivered, and pitched forward on
his face.

She watched with eyes as cold as a reptile's, the terrible
smile still on her face. She was naked, and it seemed to
Gilson that there was something wrong with her torso as
well as with her mouth. She turned and appeared to shout
toward the house.

In a moment they all came rushing out, mother, father,
little boy, and granny, all naked, all undergoing that hideous
transformation of the mouth. Without pause or diminution
of speed they scuttled to the body, crouched around it, and
frenziedly tore off its clothes. Then, squatting on the lawn
in the morning sunshine, the fine little family began horribly to feed.

Krantz's babbling had changed its tenor: "Holy Mary,
Mother of God, pray for us. . . ." The soldier with the
stopwatch was noisily sick. Someone emptied a clip of a
machine pistol into the interface, and the colonel cursed
luridly. When Gilson could no longer bear to watch the
grisly feast, he looked away and found himself staring at the
dog, which sat happily on the porch, thumping its tail.

"By God, it just can't be!" Krantz burst out. "It would
be in the histories, in the newspapers, if there'd been people
like that here. My God, something like that couldn't be
forgotten!"

"Oh, don't talk like a fool!" Gilson said angrily. "That's
not the past. I don't know what it is, but it's not the past.
Can't be. It's—I don't know—someplace else. Some
other—dimension? Universe? One of those theories. Al-
ternate worlds, worlds of If, probability worlds, whatever
you call 'em. They're in the present time, all right, that

filth over there. Culvergast's damn spell holed through to one of those parallels. Got to be something like that. And, my God, what the *hell* was its history to produce *those*? They're not human, Krantz, no way human, whatever they look like. 'Jolly bicycle tours.' How wrong can you be?"

It ended at last. The family lay on the grass with distended bellies, covered with blood and grease, their eyelids heavy in repletion. The two little ones fell asleep. The large male appeared to be deep in thought. After a time he rose, gathered up Reeves's clothes, and examined them carefully. Then he woke the small female and apparently questioned her at some length. She gestured, pointed, and pantomimed Reeves's headlong arrival. He stared thoughtfully at the place where Reeves had materialized, and for a moment it seemed to Gilson that the pitiless eyes were glaring directly into his. He turned, walked slowly and reflectively to the house, and went inside.

It was silent in the clearing except for the thump of the machine. Krantz began to weep, and the colonel to swear in a monotone. The soldiers seemed dazed. And we're all afraid, Gilson thought. Scared to death.

On the lawn they were enacting a grotesque parody of making things tidy after a picnic. The small ones had brought a basket and, under the meticulous supervision of the adult females, went about gathering up the debris of their feeding. One of them tossed a bone to the dog, and the timekeeper vomited again. When the lawn was once again immaculate, they carried off the basket to the rear, and the adults returned to the house. A moment later the male emerged, now dressed in a white linen suit. He carried a book.

"A Bible," said Krantz in amazement. "It's a Bible."

"Not a Bible," Gilson said. "There's no way those—things could have Bibles. Something else. Got to be."

It looked like a Bible; its binding was limp black leather, and when the male began to leaf through it, evidently in search of a particular passage, they could see that the paper was the thin, tough paper Bibles are printed on. He found his page and began, as it appeared to Gilson, to read aloud in a declamatory manner, mouthing the words.

"What the hell do you suppose he's up to?" Gilson said. He was still speaking when the window ceased to exist.

House and lawn and white-suited declaimer vanished. Gilson caught a swift glimpse of trees across a broad pit between him and the trees. Then he was knocked off his feet by a blast of wind, and the air was full of dust and flying trash and the wind's howl. The wind stopped as suddenly as it had come, and there was a patter of falling small objects that had momentarily been windborne. The site of the house was entirely obscured by an eddying cloud of dust.

The dust settled slowly. Where the window had been, there was a great hole in the ground, a perfectly square hole a hundred feet across and perhaps ten feet deep, its bottom as flat as a table. Gilson's glimpse of it before the wind had rushed in to fill the vacuum had shown the sides to be as smooth and straight as if sliced through cheese with a sharp knife; but now small landslides were occurring all around the perimeter, as topsoil and gravel caved and slid to the bottom and the edges were becoming ragged and irregular.

Gilson and Krantz slowly rose to their feet. "And that seems to be that," Gilson said. "It was here and now it's gone. But where's the prefab? Where's Culvergast?"

"God knows," Krantz said. He was not being irreverent. "But I think he's gone for good. And at least he's not where those things are."

"What are they, do you think?"

"As you said, certainly not human. Less human than a spider or an oyster. But, Gilson, the way they look and dress, that house—"

"If there's an infinite number of possible worlds, then every possible sort of world will exist."

Krantz looked doubtful. "Yes, well, perhaps. We don't know anything, do we?" He was silent for a moment. "Those things were pretty frightening, Gilson. It didn't take even a fraction of a second for her to react to Reeves. She knew instantly that he was alien, and she moved instantly to destroy him. And that's a baby one. I think maybe we can feel safer with the window gone."

"Amen to that. What do you think happened to it?"

"It's obvious, isn't it? They know how to *use* the energies Culvergast was blundering around with. The book—it has to be a book of spells. They must have a science of it— tried-and-true stuff, part of their received wisdom. That thing used the book like a routine, everyday tool. After it got over the excitement of its big feed, it didn't need more than twenty minutes to figure out how Reeves got there, and what to do about it. It just got its book of spells, picked the one it needed (I'd like to see the index of that book) and said the words. Poof! Window gone and Culvergast stranded, God knows where."

"It's possible, I guess. Hell, maybe even likely. You're right, we don't really know a thing about all this."

Krantz suddenly looked frightened. "Gilson, what if— look. If it was that easy for him to cancel out the window, if he has that kind of control of telekinetic power, what's to prevent him from getting a window on *us*? Maybe they're watching us now, the way we were watching them. They know we're here now. What kind of ideas might they get? Maybe they need meat. Maybe they—my God."

"No," Gilson said. "Impossible. It was pure, blind chance that located the window in that world. Culvergast had no more idea what he was doing than a chimp at a computer console does. If the Possible-Worlds Theory is the explanation of this thing, then the world he hit is one of an infinite number. Even if the things over there do know how to make these windows, the odds are infinite against their finding us. That is to say, it's impossible."

"Yes, yes, of course," Krantz said gratefully. "Of course. They could try forever and never find us. Even if they wanted to." He thought for a moment. "And I think they do want to. It was pure reflex, their destroying Reeves, as involuntary as a knee jerk by the look of it. Now that they know we're here, they'll have to try to get at us; if I've sized them up right, it wouldn't be possible for them to do anything else."

Gilson remembered the eyes. "I wouldn't be a bit surprised," he said. "But now we both better—"

"*Dr. Krantz!*" someone screamed. "*Dr. Krantz!*" There was absolute terror in the voice.

The two men spun around. The soldier with the stopwatch was pointing with a trembling hand. As they looked, something white materialized in the air above the rim of the pit and sailed out and downward to land beside a similar object already lying on the ground. Another came; then another, and another. Five in all, scattered over an area perhaps a yard square.

"It's bones!" Krantz said. "Oh, my God, Gilson, it's bones!" His voice shuddered on the edge of hysteria.

Gilson said, "Stop it, now. Stop it! Come on!" They ran to the spot. The soldier was already there, squatting, his face made strange by nausea and terror. "That one," he said, pointing. "That one there. That's the one they threw to the dog. You can see the teeth marks. Oh, Jesus. It's the one they threw to the dog."

They've already made a window, then, Gilson thought. They must know a lot about these matters, to have done it so quickly. And they're watching us now. But why the bones? To warn us off? Or just a test? But if a test, then still why the bones? Why not a pebble—or an ice cube? To gauge our reactions, perhaps. To see what we'll do.

And what *will* we do? How do we protect ourselves against *this*? If it is in the nature of these creatures to cooperate among themselves, the fine little family will no doubt lose no time in spreading the word over their whole world, so that one of these days we'll find that a million million of them have leapt simultaneously through such windows all over the earth, suddenly materializing like a cloud of huge carnivorous locusts, swarming in to feed with that insensate voracity of theirs until they have left the planet a desert of bones. Is there any protection against that?

Krantz had been thinking along the same track. He said shakily, "We're in a spot, Gilson, but we've got one little thing on our side. We know when the damn thing opens up, we've got it timed exactly. Washington will have to go all out, warn the whole world, do it through the U.N. or something. We know right down to the second when the window can be penetrated. We set up a warning system, every community on earth blows a whistle or rings a bell when it's time. Bell rings, everybody grabs a weapon and stands ready. If the things haven't come in five seconds, bell rings again, and everybody goes about his business until time for the next opening. It could work, Gilson, but we've got to work fast. In fifteen hours and, uh, a couple of minutes it'll be open again."

Fifteen hours and a couple of minutes, Gilson thought, then five seconds of awful vulnerability, and then fifteen hours and twenty minutes of safety before terror arrives again. And so on for—how long? Presumably until the things come, which might be never (who knew how their minds worked?), or until Culvergast's accident could be duplicated, which, again, might be never. He questioned whether human beings could exist under those conditions without going mad; it was doubtful if the psyche could cohere when its sole foreseeable future was an interminable roller coaster down into long valleys of terror and suspense and thence violently up to brief peaks of relief. Will a mind continue to function when its only alternatives are ghastly death or unbearable tension endlessly protracted? Is there any way, Gilson asked himself, that the race can live with the knowledge that it has no assured future beyond the next fifteen hours and twenty minutes?

And then he saw, hopelessly and with despair, that it was not fifteen hours and twenty minutes, that it was not even

one hour, that it was no time at all. The window was not,
it seemed, intermittent. Materializing out of the air was a
confusion of bones and rent clothing, a flurry of contemp-
tuously flung garbage that clattered to the ground and lay
there in an untidy heap, noisome and foreboding.

INSECTS IN AMBER

TOM REAMY

Tom Reamy (1935–1977) first began publishing in
1974, when his story "Twilla" appeared in *F & SF*.
By the time of his death in 1977, his writings had
earned him considerable stature in the field of science fiction and fantasy and established him as a
writer of immense talent. His story "San Diego
Lightfoot Sue" garnered him the Nebula Award in
1976, the same year in which he received the John
W. Campbell Award for best new science fiction
writer. After his death his short fiction was collected
and published along with his only novel, *Blind Voices*
(1978). "Insects in Amber" is a fine example of Tom
Reamy's imaginative style. It is a gripping story that
opens with a haunted house scenario and then turns
into something quite different. . . .

The storm built in the southwest, turning the air to underwater blue, making the flat land look like the bottom of the sea. Lightning flickered in the approaching darkness and threw fleeting shimmers on the rolling clouds. Thunder that had been distant rumbles soon crackled across the Kansas prairie unhindered.

Tannie and I watched the spectacular display through the rear window of the new Buick station wagon. The rain followed us like a vague, miles-long curtain. It caught us in minutes and turned the late afternoon to night.

My father grunted and flipped on the lights and windshield wipers. He braked the station wagon carefully and hunched over the steering wheel peering into the downpour. Thunder crashed and rattled around us. The lightning flashes were so brilliant that they left a white streak floating before your eyes. The windshield wipers snicked away merrily, but futilely.

Tannie sat beside me bright-eyed with excitement. She was seven and had one of those inquisitive minds that drove certain adults up the wall.

We were starting out on one of those vacations the auto manufacturers, the motel owners, the resort owners, the tire companies, Howard Johnson's and the curio sellers on Route 66 like to promote. We had piled into the station wagon for three weeks of butt-numbing travel. We left Lubbock that morning (my father was an associate professor of English at Texas Tech) planning to go up through Kansas, Nebraska, South Dakota, over to Wyoming and Yellowstone, then back through Colorado and home. It wasn't the kind of vacation I would have initiated, though I didn't mind it that much.

I was fifteen, not too far from sixteen, and if given a guilt-free choice, I would have probably stayed in Lubbock to goof around with my friends. But since I had a special relationship with my family, the trip was no sacrifice.

We had planned to make it to Dodge City by nightfall, but the rain seemed to have put the kibosh on that. Dad was creeping along about twenty miles an hour, barely able to see the road. It went like that for a while until we came up behind a couple of other cars going even slower. We were behind a red Firebird with Arizona plates, and it was behind an old pickup truck. Dad didn't try to pass, and the Firebird seemed content to stay where it was too.

Mom squinted at an Exxon roadmap. "The next town is Hawley, but it looks pretty small," she said. "It's an open circle, which means"—she shuffled the map, "ah . . . under a thousand."

"Let's hope it's not too small to have a motel," Dad said, giving up on Dodge City.

"I don't care about a motel," Tannie chirped. "I just hope there's someplace to eat." She sat with her nose pressed against the window, fogging up the glass with her breath and then drawing pictures in it.

"Eat?" I laughed. "You've eaten enough today to kill a horse." I knew she really was hungry, but she liked me to tease her.

Tannie turned from the window and surveyed me coolly, but with a twinkle in her eye. I knew she was about to devastate me. She leaned back in the seat and crossed her arms. "There's a little too much sibling rivalry in this seat," she said with an ultra-ladylike air.

I groaned. She was always saying something like that. Mom and Dad laughed. I could see Tannie's mouth beginning to twitch. She wouldn't be able to hold that lofty expression very long.

"It's your own fault, Ben." Dad chuckled. "You should never have told her she was precocious."

"Yeah." Tannie grinned. "I looked it up."

"Uh-oh," Dad said. He stopped laughing and slowed the station wagon. I leaned on the back of the front seat and looked over Mom's shoulder. Wooden barricades with amber flashers were in the road ahead. Two cars were already stopped: a yellow Volkswagen and a dark, sedate sedan that may have been a Chevrolet. The pickup stopped behind the sedan, the Firebird stopped behind the pickup, and we stopped behind the Firebird. Everyone sat there for a bit in a neck-craning session; then a man in a raincoat got out of the passenger side of the VW.

He hurried around to the driver's side of the sedan, apparently intending to get in without comment, but the guy in the pickup stuck his head out the window and said something. The man in the raincoat hesitated, rather reluctantly, I thought, then came back to the pickup and stood there talking.

"Guess I'd better get out and see what's going on," Dad said with a resigned sigh.

"Charles, you're gonna get soaked."

Dad twisted around in the seat. "Ben, can you get to the umbrella back there?"

I got on my knees in the seat and dug around in the back among the suitcases, blankets, cardboard boxes full of who knows what, and all kinds of vacation gear. I finally found it and handed it to him. As Dad got out in the rain, a girl got out of the VW, also with an umbrella. They met at the pickup. Then a guy got out of the Firebird and joined them. It was turning into a convention.

They stood there in the pouring rain, all four of them, talking and waving their arms and pointing this way and that. Mostly it was the man from the sedan and the guy in the pickup. He was the smart one—he was in out of the rain. Then, after a while, they dispersed.

"We gotta take a detour," Dad said when he got back in.

"What's wrong?" Mom asked.

"Highway's underwater up ahead."

"Could you see it?" Tannie perked up at the first sign of disaster.

"No. The girl in the VW said a highway patrolman in a yellow slicker told her the road was flooded. He stopped her, and then the old gentleman in the sedan came along. Seems they know each other."

"Did he say the detour was safe?" Mom asked, looking at the rain with a little frown.

"I don't know. The patrolman seems to have disappeared. The guy in the pickup lives around here. He said it was okay."

Tannie bounced in the seat. "Isn't this exciting?" she squeaked.

"You won't think so if we have to spend the night in the car stuck in the mud somewhere," I said.

Dad grimaced. "Hold that thought, Cheerful Charlie," he said, and started the motor.

The sedan pulled around the VW and turned left onto a gravel road that cut off the highway at the barricades. The VW followed him, then the pickup, then the Firebird, and then us. Just like a camel caravan. The road wasn't bad, a little rough with lots of standing puddles.

I turned around in the seat and looked back at the highway, but I couldn't see the flashers anymore. We must have gone over a rise, although I hadn't noticed doing so. I also thought I saw the headlights of a car go by on the highway, but with the rain I wasn't sure. It must have been lightning.

Mom and Dad didn't talk. The farther we traveled from the highway, the darker it seemed to get. Mom watched the road nervously, and Dad kept his attention on his driving. Even Tannie was quiet for a change. She had her nose against the window again, trying to see by the frequent flashes of lightning. I don't know how far we had gone. It probably seemed farther than it was because we were moving so slowly.

Then I pressed my nose against the window and looked out. I don't know if it was coincidence or not, but it couldn't have been better if it had been staged by Alfred Hitchcock. There was a tremendous rattle of thunder and a flash of lightning that lingered for an unaccountably long time. I saw a house some fifty yards from the road on top of a low hill. It looked quite old, a big, boxy shape with lots of tall

chimneys and gables and a tower on one corner. The lightning faded slowly, and I turned my head to follow it, but
the lightning wasn't repeated.

I turned as Dad braked the station wagon to a stop. The
other cars in the caravan were stopped also, their brake lights
flicking on and off.

"You think somebody got stuck in the mud?" Tannie
asked with a faint current of desire under the question. I
think she would gladly be attacked by tigers just to find out
what it was like.

"Let's hope not," Dad grunted.

Somebody up the row honked his horn. "Looks like they're
calling another conference," I said.

"Looks like you're right." Dad pulled out the umbrella.

I leaned my arms on the back of the seat and watched
them gather around the pickup truck again. Then the rain
slacked or something, and I could see by the headlights of
the sedan a sheet of muddy water flowing across the road.
Trash and debris swirled around on it, weeds and tree limbs.

After a bit they disbanded and Dad got back in, wrestling
with the umbrella. "This road is flooded too," he said in a
discouraged voice. "We'll have to turn around and go back."

"Doesn't look like there's room to turn around. You might
get stuck in the ditch," Mom said matter-of-factly. She was
worried but wouldn't show it; she didn't want to frighten
Tannie and me.

"According to the guy in the pickup, we just passed,
quote, the old Weatherly place, unquote. We're supposed
to back up and turn around in the drive."

"Yeah," I said, "I saw it. Looked like something out of
a horror movie."

"Terrific," Dad groaned.

"I want to see!" Tannie squealed, and scrambled on top
of me, pasting her face against the damply cool window.

"Watch it!" I grunted. "You've got bony knees."

"Okay. Hold it down back there," Dad said, but he was

smiling. He backed the car slowly, looking over his shoulder.

"Can you see where you're going?" Mom asked.

"Actually, no." He grimaced.

Dad had it the worst. The others could see by the headlights of the car behind them. Tannie and I had our noses against the window again, watching for the house. A flash of lightning came right on cue. Tannie let out a little sigh of appreciation.

Dad stopped the station wagon with a lurch. Brake lights flashed on sequentially down the row. Dad raised up in the seat and examined the drive critically with a little frown on his face. A culvert crossed the ditch of rushing water, though more water seemed to be going over the drive than under it. He looked at Mom. She looked at the water. Dad shrugged, rippled a tattoo on the steering wheel with his fingernails, and pulled slowly in.

The front end had nosed in about three feet, when it lurched suddenly sideways and slipped into the ditch.

"Are we stuck in the mud?" Tannie asked with cloying innocence.

"I wouldn't be at all surprised." Dad put the station wagon in reverse and tried to back out. The tires whined and the rear end slithered farther into the road. Dad cut the engine and settled back in the seat with a snort.

"Looks like it's time for another conference," I said when I saw the others converging on us.

"Don't be a wiseacre," he groaned. He grabbed the umbrella and got out. I scooted over to the other side and rolled down the window so I could hear.

"Sorry, folks," Dad said.

"Tough luck, Mr. Henderson." That was the guy from the Firebird. They had apparently introduced themselves at a previous conference.

The girl in the yellow Volkswagen was Ann Callahan. She was twenty and absolutely lovely. That was the first time I had had a good look at her. When I did, I couldn't keep my eyes off her.

The old guy in the sedan was Professor Philip Weatherly. That's right: Weatherly, as in "the old Weatherly place." He was sixty, with a kindly but slightly befuddled expression. I also caught, inadvertently, a certain amount of nervous strain, but I didn't think much about it under the circumstances.

Carl Willingham was the driver of the pickup. He was about fifty, with a slightly protuberant beer belly and a cigar that he worried about in his mouth. He was wearing boots and a sweat-darkened Stetson. I think he had been sent over by central casting.

The guy from the Firebird was Poe McNeal. He was about twenty-five, with a cheerful face and a quick smile. He had a stocky, muscular build and a pleasant rather than handsome face. I liked him immediately.

Ann Callahan and Carl Willingham went to the front of the car, as close as they could get without wading, and examined the mired wheels.

"It wasn't your fault, Mr. Henderson," she said with a voice that did funny things to me. "The pipe is clogged and the drive was badly undercut."

The others moved up to check on it. "Maybe we could put something under the wheels to give it some traction," Poe McNeal suggested.

"Won't do no good," Carl Willingham grunted. "Car's too heavy and in too deep. Have to get a tow truck." The brown water swirled around the bumper.

"Great," Dad said. "How do we do that?"

"I guess we could wait till another car comes along and send them," Poe said without much conviction.

"How will they turn around?" Trust Dad to put his finger on it. "We may have three hundred cars piled up here before the night's over."

Poe grinned. "The tow truck drivers will love it."

"What about that house there?" Dad asked, squinting through the rain. A flash of lightning and a roll of thunder punctuated his question. Much too convenient; more like William Castle than Alfred Hitchcock.

"I noticed some chimneys. Maybe there's a fireplace where we can dry out and get warm." That was Ann.

Carl looked up the hill with displeasure. "Nobody lived in that house for fifty years. Like as not, it's about to fall down."

"Guess we could check it out," Poe said doubtfully. "Do you think the owner would mind a band of pilgrims taking refuge?"

Professor Weatherly spoke for the first time. "I suppose I'm the owner. You have my permission." His voice had a tenseness in it, like somebody with a pat hand.

Carl's frown grew deeper. "Don't know that I'd fancy spending the night in that house."

"Don't tell me it's haunted!" Poe cried with suppressed excitement.

"Don't rightly know," Carl answered with no trace of humor, "though I've heard folks talk."

The professor looked at Carl with a little frown, as if he'd misread one of his cards.

"I'll get a flashlight," Dad said, and opened the door of the station wagon. He leaned in, trying to keep himself covered with the umbrella. "Ben, hand me the flashlight." He looked at Mom. "We're gonna check out that house to see if it's fit to spend the night in." Mom nodded and looked through the darkness, trying to see it.

I dug the flashlight out from behind the seat. "May I go with you?"

"No, you can't. If it's not fit, there's no point in your getting wet."

"Heck!" I said.

"Heck, yourself." Then he grinned. "Come on."

I got another umbrella from the backseat cornucopia and

scrambled out. Poe was leaning in the window of the Firebird telling the other people what was happening. Then we all traipsed up the hill to the house.

With the darkness and the rain and trying to see where we were putting our feet, none of us really paid much attention to the house until we made it to the old-fashioned porch around three sides. Once out of the rain, we looked about without saying anything. The house was a little weather-beaten and badly needed paint, but it wasn't what one would call dilapidated. A few pieces of gingerbread were missing from around the top of the porch, and a few boards squeaked when stepped on, but I've seen people living in a lot worse.

Dad looked at the others and opened the wide front door with a fanlight over it. He shined the flashlight around, and the rest of us crowded in behind him. My arm bumped Ann's. She smiled at me. It was just one of those friendly but noncommittal smiles you give to strangers, but I felt my face getting warm.

We were in a large entry hall—I finally noticed. A wide stairway ascended to a second floor landing at the rear. We looked at each other with no small amount of bewilderment. Everything was clean and free of dust. The carpet running down the middle of the hall and up the stairs was faded but in good condition. The lace curtains over the windows on either side of the door, though somewhat yellowed with age, were clean. A tall grandfather clock at the top of the stairs suddenly rattled and struck six times. We all stared at it, hardly breathing, until it finished.

"When does Vincent Price arrive?" Poe muttered.

"What?" Ann said, turning her head suddenly toward him.

"Nothing." He grinned.

Dad looked at Carl. "Are you sure this has been empty for fifty years?"

He shrugged stoically. "Always thought it was. Musta been wrong."

We wandered into the living room (though I imagine it

was called a parlor in its day) which opened to the left off
the entry hall. "If this belongs to you, Professor," Ann said
softly, "you should know if anyone's been living here."

He was genuinely confused. "Mr. Willingham's right.
No one *has* lived here for fifty years. When I was last here,
thirty-five years ago, I hired a man to look after the place.
Apparently he's doing his job very well."

The living room/parlor was completely and neatly fur-
nished in that blocky, ungainly style of the early twenties.
Even so, it didn't actually look as if someone lived there;
more like a display; the Sunday parlor kept spotlessly unused
for company that never came.

"There's wood for the fireplace." Dad brightened. "I was
afraid we might have to burn the furniture."

Poe wrinkled his nose. "Wouldn't hurt."

The professor came out of his mood. "Why don't you
get the others from the cars and whatever else you might
need while Mr. Willingham and I get a fire going?"

So we reentered the downpour and slogged back to the
cars. Ann smiled at me as we went down the porch steps.
I missed one with my foot and had to grab the railing.
Damnation!

When we returned with the suitcases, blankets, and everything else we could carry, Weatherly and Carl had a crackling fire going. That and the half-dozen kerosene lamps
scattered around the room made it almost cheerful. We all
trooped in, bustling around, shedding raincoats and um-
brellas, and looking around tentatively. Everyone was happily excited and seemed to regard the whole thing as an
adventure.

"This is terrific," Linda McNeal said with delight. "I was
expecting spiders and rats." Poe's wife was twenty-two, blond,
pink, and pretty—and very pregnant. Poe helped with her
raincoat. I liked Linda as much as I did Poe.

"Either that, or some farmer would be using it to store
hay." That was Judson Bradley Ledbetter, known profes-
sionally as Jud Bradley—he thought Ledbetter sounded a

bit too hayseed. It was easy enough to tell he was Linda's brother. He was also blond, pink, and pretty, but with a dark undercurrent missing in Linda. I thought he was a bit overdressed and had obviously swiped his shoes from Carmen Miranda.

"Where are the ghosts?" Tannie asked, ready to get down to business.

"They don't show up till midnight," I said with a straight face.

"Stop it, Ben," Mom said. "You know she believes everything you tell her."

"You okay, hon?" Poe said to his wife. "You oughtn't to catch cold."

"You're the one who looks like you've been swimming with your clothes on."

He grinned. "I was expecting Fred MacMurray to paddle by in a rowboat."

"*The Rains of Ranchipur*!" Linda cried gleefully.

"Right!"

Mom wasn't one to let things go untended. "I have some towels in the suitcases," she said, and fished out several. She handed one to Linda.

"Thank you." Linda smiled. "Just my hair and feet are wet."

"Is this your first?" Mom asked.

"Yes. It's all sorta terrific, isn't it?"

"Yes, it is." Mom laughed. "I felt the same way when I had my two. Here, sit by the fire and take off your shoes." She and Poe pushed one of the chairs closer to the fire and fussed over Linda. Then she gave Tannie and me each a towel with instructions to dry everything that was wet.

Mom was in high gear now that she had something to do. I guess that's one of the reasons she made such a good faculty wife. There are a lot of women who can't hack it. I've seen perfectly level-headed women go glassy-eyed at the thought of one more faculty tea, and assistant professors' wives seriously consider sticking their heads in the oven after being cut down by a *full* professor's wife—delicately and with no visible wounds, of course.

Mom says a faculty wife has to be one-quarter hostess, one-quarter scullery maid, one-quarter diplomat, one-quarter secret agent, and one hundred percent saint.

"If everyone is getting settled," the professor said in his role as reluctant leader of the castaways, "I'll get my suitcases. I also have some food."

"I'll go with you," Dad volunteered. "We have some coffee in the car."

"Thank you," Weatherly replied. "There's a stove in the kitchen but, I'm afraid, no hot water."

"Clare, will you put some water on?" Dad asked. "We'll be right back."

"Of course."

They left and everyone was snuggling in quite comfortably. I got dry socks for myself and Tannie from the suitcase. Mom and Poe still hovered over Linda. Carl Willingham and Judson Bradley Ledbetter rotated themselves in front of the fire, drying off. Jud soon gave it up and went into another room to put on dry clothes, after fussing around in several matched pieces of luggage.

"When is it due?" Mom asked, not quite having exhausted the topic of babies.

"Five weeks," Linda said.

"We were on our way to visit Linda's parents in Wichita before she got too big to travel." Poe smiled a proud and slightly mystified father-to-be smile. "We live in Flagstaff."

"Oh, Poe," Linda moaned. "They're gonna be so worried when we don't show up. We were supposed to be there by eight."

"I know, hon, but there's nothing we can do about it."

"Would you like a blanket?" Mom handed her one before she could answer.

"Thank you, Mrs.—" She laughed. "I don't know your name."

"Clare Henderson. I guess that's the first thing we ought

to do. That was my husband, Charles, who just went for coffee. My son, Ben, and my daughter, Tannie."

Everyone had the slightly nervous fidgets you get when you introduce yourself to strangers. Except me. I was looking at Ann Callahan just coming into the room from an exploration foray.

"My name is Tania Henderson," Tannie announced proudly. "After my grandmother."

"That's a terrific name," Ann said as she joined us.

"Thank you very much." Tannie smiled at her.

"You're welcome," Ann beamed back at her. "I'm Ann Callahan. From Albuquerque."

"Poe McNeal. I won't mention what the Poe is short for. My wife, Linda."

"That's my brother in there," Linda said, inclining her head toward the closed door, "Jud Ledbetter. He lives in Hollywood."

Mom raised her eyebrows questioningly. "Is he an actor? He's handsome enough to be."

Linda's mouth quivered with a suppressed grin. "He'll probably tell you he is," she said, "but he's a model. You may recognize the back of his head." The grin broke through and Poe chuckled. "He's been in a lot of commercials, but the camera is always on the girl's shiny hair or her gleaming white cavity-free bicuspids. All you ever see of Jud is the back of his head. If you'd like to hear a choice account of the doubtful ancestry of TV commercial producers and directors, bring the subject up." She and Poe both smothered laughter.

"Why are you laughing?" Mom asked in confusion. "He seems fortunate to me."

"Oh, he is," Poe controlled himself. "He makes money hand over fist—a lot more than I'll ever make. You see, Mrs. Henderson, Jud and Linda and I grew up together in Wichita. Jud and I were in the same grade. It's just hard for us to take him seriously. We know too much about him."

Poe plucked at his sodden clothes, unsticking the fabric from his skin. "If you'll excuse me, I'll follow my beautiful brother-in-law's example and put on some dry clothes." He rummaged around in a suitcase and followed Jud.

"I take it your husband and brother don't get on too well," Mom said.

"No, it isn't that," Linda said, hitching the blanket higher around her shoulders. "They've seen very little of each other since high school, and Jud's changed a lot since then. I think the term is gone Hollywood. It's nothing serious. Jud's airs amuse Poe and Poe's amusement irritates Jud."

"Would you care to join me in the water-boiling detail?" Mom asked Ann, suddenly remembering.

"Sure," she said. They took a lamp and went in the direction opposite Jud and Poe.

"I wonder when they read the will," Poe said when they came back.

"Huh?" I asked, because my mind was still on Ann.

"In the movies," he explained, "when a bunch of people are gathered in a spooky old house like this, they generally read the will. But there's always the stipulation that they spend the night. And then the beneficiaries are murdered one by one."

"Poe." Linda frowned. "Don't talk that way. You'll scare Tannie."

"Nothing scares her," I said.

"Does too!" Tannie asserted.

"Either that," Poe continued, undaunted, "or they're lured there by a mysterious host, who then murders 'em one by one."

"*And Then There Were None* and *The Thirteenth Guest*," I supplied.

"Uh-oh." Linda laughed. "Poe's found a kindred spirit."

"Huh?" I said with another example of my brilliant re-partee.

"Poe and Linda ask each other questions about old movies," Jud explained with no small amount of condescension. "If one can stump the other, he gets a point."

"It's a game we play on trips to pass the time," Poe said with a slight narrowing of his eyes.

"May I play?" I asked.

"Sure." Linda laughed. "I'm not much of a challenge."

"Be warned, young man." Poe grinned. "You are opposing a master."

"Okay, my turn," Linda said, and looked studious. "Let's see. Ah—how many times was Scarlett O'Hara married?"

Poe turned to me with mock exasperation. "You can see the kind of competition I have. You know the answer to that one?"

"Sure." I grinned. "Three."

"No points for Linda," he crowed. She made a face at him. "All right," he continued, preparing a zinger, "what famous star of B westerns once played the romantic lead opposite Greta Garbo?" He settled back with a satisfied smirk.

Linda looked at him suspiciously. "You're making that up."

"No, I'm not." He laughed.

"Johnny Mack Brown," Jud muttered.

An expression of abject betrayal settled on Poe's face. "How did you know?" he groaned.

Jud raised his pale eyebrows. "You mean that's right? I just said the most unlikely name I could think of."

"I was gonna say Lash LaRue," Linda said with a straight face. We were all laughing when Dad and Professor Weatherly came back. The professor had a suitcase and a picnic hamper. Dad had a cardboard box with instant coffee, Styrofoam cups, sugar, powdered cream, and a bunch of other stuff. We were helping them unpack it all, when Mom and Ann returned, looking smug.

"Water's on," Mom announced. "With a little native ingenuity, feminine intuition, and a lot of luck, we figured out how to work that antique kerosene stove."

"Professor," Ann said with a slight frown, "does your caretaker live here in the house? There's food in the kitchen. Not much, mostly canned stuff."

"I don't know," he said with a befuddled look. "The man I hired lived in Hawley with his wife."

"Maybe some hobo has taken squatters' rights," Jud said.

"Wouldn't be nobody from around here," Carl said with assurance. "Folks in Hawley stay away from this place."

"You're here, Mr. Willingham," Mom pointed out. "Have you changed your mind about the place being haunted?"

"Never said it was haunted," he stated phlegmatically. "Just said folks talk."

What happened then is difficult to explain. Poe and I had gone back to Linda at the fireplace. I was sitting in a chair next to Linda while Poe sat on the floor with his arms around his knees. Everyone else was at a table about ten feet away unpacking the professor's picnic hamper. I was thinking that he surely had brought a lot of food for some reason.

I felt it coming before it hit me, but I was so startled I didn't do anything to protect myself.

There was an impact. Then pressure, pressure that knocked the breath out of me. If I'd been standing, I think I would have fallen.

My head flopped back against the chair. It couldn't have lasted more than a second, but the residue of cold fear was overpowering. The sweet chill of fear, drenched, infused with icy sugar water.

My eyes closed and I shivered uncontrollably. My arms were so weak, I couldn't lift them. I never knew so much fear.

But not my fear.

One eternal second and it was gone, the pressure and the presence gone as suddenly as it came.

I could hear what everyone was saying, their tiny voices far away; and I knew what everyone was doing, not seeing them with my eyes.

In that chill second Ann gasped and looked around quickly, seeking a source. Of what? Everyone stopped talking and looked at Ann, Professor Weatherly with more interest than I could explain.

Then Linda looked at me. "Mrs. Henderson!" she shouted. "Something's wrong with Ben!"

Everyone gathered around me except Jud and Carl. Ann was shaken. They helped her to a chair. Tannie stared at me with eyes like saucers. Mom and Dad knelt beside me. Mom put her hands on my clammy face.

"Darling, what's the matter?"

I tried to open my eyes, but my eyelids fluttered like moth wings, and I couldn't focus.

"Ben!" Dad said, strain and worry harsh in his voice. "Son, say something."

"Mom?" I whimpered. I wasn't ashamed of whimpering. I was thankful I didn't scream.

Mom put her arms around my shoulders and pulled me against her breast, holding me like I was two years old. Dad had his hand on the back of my head. I opened up all the way, let down all the barriers. I sopped up their love and concern and compassion. I bathed in it, swam in it, drowned in it. I let the warmth of it wash over me, let it drive out the chill of that fear.

"What is it, Ben? Are you ill?" Mom asked softly.

"Oh, Mom, it was so scared," I moaned against her shoulder.

"What was scared?" Dad asked in confusion.

My eyes focused on Ann over Mom's shoulder. She was staring at me, staring with surprised recognition. But she was no more surprised than I. Professor Weatherly was looking from Ann to me and back again like a startled owl. Then I saw everyone else was staring at me, too, and I got a little embarrassed. I disengaged Mom's arms and leaned back in the chair because I wasn't sure I could stand up. But I didn't take my eyes off Ann.

"I don't know, Dad," I said, trying to answer his question.

"Suddenly, I felt . . . I felt . . . it was like I had my breath knocked out . . . and . . . there was so much fear."

"That's what I felt . . . only not so strongly," Ann said calmly.

Tannie slowly and tentatively took my hand in hers and looked at me with big round scared eyes. I grinned at her and winked. Her little face sort of exploded and she grinned back. Mom turned to Ann.

"Are you feeling better, Ann?"

"Yes, I'm fine."

Tannie suddenly perked up and piped, "It must have been the ghost." A little wave of nervous laughter rippled around the room.

"I think she's right." Poe grinned. "I've seen enough movies to know a haunted house."

"I've heard folks talk," Carl said with a nod of his head.

"You keep saying that," Jud grumbled. "Exactly what do folks talk *about*?"

"This house and what happened here fifty years ago."

"I knew it!" Poe cried, and clapped his hands together sharply. "A house doesn't get a reputation for being haunted unless there's a story to go with it. What happened fifty years ago, a juicy murder?"

"First time I been in this place," Carl said, a little abashed at being the focus of attention. "Nobody I know's ever been inside. Seen it lots of times from the road. Used to be the main road before they built the highway."

"Well, what happened?" Poe squirmed.

Professor Weatherly was distinctly uncomfortable and wished he were somewhere else.

"Happened before I was born, but I've heard folks talk," Carl continued, warming to his subject. "The Weatherlys lived here. Had a right nice farm, folks say. That was before the Depression. Man, wife, two girls, and a boy. Real well liked, I hear, though folks say there was something peculiar about the boy. One night folks livin' close by saw the house all lit up kinda funny. Lights dancin' all over it and flames in one of the upstairs rooms. Thought the place was burning and rushed over to help. When they got here, there was nothin'. No fire, nothin'. They called. Nobody answered. They went inside and looked all over. Didn't find nobody. Just found that upstairs room where the fire was. They say it was the boy's room. The inside was all burned, but the fire was cold out. Nobody ever saw the Weatherlys or heard tell of 'em since."

"Hey!" Poe exhaled slowly. "That's even better than a juicy murder."

"Didn't they ever find out what happened?" Dad asked.

"Nope." Carl shrugged. "Not that I ever heard."

"Professor?" Ann turned to him. "You told me when we were stopped on the highway you used to live around here. In this house?"

"Yes, for a time." He fidgeted, then changed the subject. "Do you suppose the water's boiling, Mrs. Henderson? I'm ready for a cup of coffee."

"Oops!" Mom laughed. "I forgot about the water." She looked questioningly at me and I nodded. She hurried from the room. Ann continued to look speculatively at the professor but decided to let it drop for the moment.

"You said there were people living close by," Poe said hopefully. "Maybe we could walk to one of them and phone for a tow truck."

"And my parents," Linda added.

Carl shook his head. "Ain't there no more. Not many small farms anymore. Reckon there's not another house for four, five miles."

"Forget I mentioned it," Poe grunted, and settled back.

Mom returned with a steaming kettle and put it beside the coffee stuff. We made coffee and sandwiches from the copious picnic hamper and went back to the fireplace.

All of us except Carl; he was standing at the window looking through the rain toward the cars. He was more worried and nervous than the rest of us. Then he turned from the window and joined us. He was frowning and worrying his cigar to a frazzle.

"It's real funny," he said. "I've been kinda keepin' an eye on the road. Hasn't been another car along since we got here."

"Maybe the water went down," Jud said in a bored voice.

"Not likely." Dad frowned also. "It's still raining."

"The answer's very simple," Poe pronounced in mock gloom. "The ghosts lured us here for some diabolical reasons of their own and are now keeping everyone else away."

Professor Weatherly gave him a startled owl look. Well, well, the professor seemed to concur with that opinion. Linda laughed and shivered.

"Poe, stop! You're scaring *me* now."

"Not at all, young man." Weatherly rushed in to repair the breach. "Obviously, they've discovered the detour is also flooded and are turning the cars around."

Poe grimaced and laughed. "Spoilsport!"

Ann picked up the kettle and looked at me. "I'll put on some more water," she said, and left the room. I followed her, kicking myself for not getting her alone sooner.

The door to the kitchen was open. I leaned against the doorjamb and watched her fill the kettle from the hand pump. She had short dark hair—actually not much longer than mine. She was tall, with long, very good legs. With high heels she would be taller than I, but she was wearing sneakers. I was five-ten, but I hoped to make it to six feet in a couple of years. I know I didn't make a sound, and she had her back to me.

"Hello, Ben Henderson," she said without turning around.

The kitchen was dark and gloomy even though one of the kerosene lamps was burning. I had her alone and I didn't know what to say. So I pretended interest in the lamp.

"It's a wonder people didn't go blind with no more light than these things make." I gritted my teeth.

"They probably did," she said, and lit the burner under

the kettle. Then she turned and looked at me. She had a faint, slightly impudent smile on her lips. I felt as if I were standing there stark naked. It came so suddenly and unexpectedly, I blushed like a virgin. Then I blushed because I was blushing. The sensation was so erotic, I had to do some fancy mental footwork to keep from really embarrassing myself.

She laughed, but there was only fondness in it. "I'm sorry. I didn't mean to embarrass you. I only wanted to see if you could pick it up."

"Loud and clear," I said, fighting the tingle in the pit of my stomach.

"You're a very good-looking young man," she said matter-of-factly. "You should be used to it."

"It was a little different this time. You *knew* I was picking it up."

She leaned back against the kitchen cabinets. Her voice was wistful. "Don't you sometimes wish you were like everyone else? Do you get sick to death of always knowing?"

"Yeah. Sometimes."

"You're very lucky, you know. Your family loves you very much."

"You don't have a family, do you?"

"No. My parents were both killed when I was little. I was adopted by an aunt. Did you see that?"

"No, not really. I felt sadness and a sense of loss when you mentioned my family. It had to've been something like that."

"My aunt and uncle are very good to me, but, unlike you, there's no warm, comfortable glow into which I can retreat when things get a bit overwhelming."

So I did something I'd been wanting to do since I'd found out Ann was like me. She looked at me with pleased surprise. "Thank you, Ben," she said softly, like white velvet flowing over burnished gold.

"Think nothing of it. Warm, comfortable glows supplied on demand."

"You're an idiot." She chuckled.

"It was real, you know."

"Yes, of course I know," she said simply. Then she laughed. "And watch it, I've picked up that one before."

"Sorry." I grinned. "Involuntary reflex. Besides, you started it."

"You're not a child to me, Ben." I had again that feel of white velvet.

"I know. It takes a little getting used to, I guess. I thought I was all alone."

"Seeing yourself as others see you is true with a vengeance in our case. I guess the worst part of it is so many things are boring."

"Like card games."

"And school. Did you skip a grade?"

"Yeah."

"Me too. I'm in my last year of college."

"One more year of high school. What will you do when you finish?"

She shrugged. "I'll probably do postgrad work and get my doctorate in psychology." A smile. "That's one field we're very good in." I looked at her and she looked at me. It was good, so good. But we had a problem.

"What do you think Professor Weatherly is up to?"

She frowned. "I don't know. I have a feeling all this has been contrived somehow." I felt the same thing, but I didn't say so. She knew. "He's my psychology professor at the University of New Mexico. When I stopped at that road-block and he pulled in behind me, I was surprised, to say the least. He said he was on his way to Hawley, that he had lived near there as a child, that he owned some property and had come to settle some affairs." She looked around the room. "This seems to be the property and we seem to be enmeshed in his affairs."

"How did you happen to be here?"

She shrugged. "No reason in particular. After classes yesterday I just decided to take a drive over the weekend. I don't know why. It seemed a good idea at the time, though I'm not so sure now." She looked at me and smiled. I felt the hum of violin strings. "No. It was a good idea." She lowered her eyes. "The water's boiling. We'd better go back."

She turned toward the stove with her back to me. "Ben? What you were thinking a moment ago. I didn't mind."

"I know," I said, and took the kettle. She turned off the burner and looked at me. It never even occurred to me to blush.

On the way back to the parlor we found Tannie sitting on the bottom step of the stairway with one of the kerosene lamps beside her. She had her elbows on her knees and her chin in her hands. She had that perplexed expression she would get when she ran up against something too complex for her to understand. She was obviously waiting for me to help her out.

"Tannie, what are you doing wandering around?" I asked.

"I wanted to see the burned room," she mumbled with her mind still on something else.

"Did you find it?" Ann asked.

"Yes, thank you," she said politely, then looked up at me with a little frown. "Ben, what do ghosts look like?"

"I don't know," I said, and laughed because she was so serious. "I've never seen one."

She looked at her toes and absently scratched her leg. "I always thought they wore sheets, or that you could see right through them. Now I think they look just like people."

"What did you see?" I asked seriously, because I knew she'd seen something.

"There was a lady in the burned room. She was about two hundred years old and wore funny clothes." She looked up at me again with a puzzled little squint. Tannie related all this to me very matter-of-factly, because she knew I never disbelieved her when she was telling the truth.

I put the kettle on the floor and sat beside her on the step. "What did the lady do?"

"Nothin'. She wouldn't talk to me."

I took her hand and stood up. "Come on back to the fire. Ann and I will go see."

Mom, Dad, Poe, and Linda were playing bridge. Carl was looking out the window again, and Jud was reading Rex Reed's *Conversations in the Raw*. Weatherly sat on the couch looking depressed.

"Mom," I said. "Tannie was exploring."

"What? I thought she was with you. Tannie, you know better than to wander off without telling us."

"Heck, Mom." Tannie sighed, expressing the triviality of her offense. "I was just talking to the ghost."

The reaction from Weatherly was so strong that I turned and looked at him. He was a severely startled man.

Mom smiled. "Sure you were."

"I'll be back in a minute," I said, still watching the professor. "Ann and I are gonna look around."

"Okay. Be careful."

"Sure." I retrieved the lamp from where Tannie left it on the stairs. "Tannie was telling the truth," I said. "She saw somebody."

"Yes, I know." Ann smiled.

I smiled back at her because it was the easiest and most pleasant thing in the world to do. "I keep forgetting. Professor Weatherly is definitely keeping secrets from us."

"I know that too. He wasn't telling the exact truth when he said he lived here as a child."

"Didn't he?"

"That part's true. He did. But he was evading the issue somewhere. Didn't you pick it up?"

"I wasn't thinking about it. I seldom read people without a good reason. It's usually too discomfiting and embarrassing. I just sorta close them out like a background noise you get used to and don't hear unless you listen for it—or unless it's very strong, like when Tannie mentioned the ghost. I picked up an extreme dose of surprise and confusion. I don't think the professor was expecting to find anyone here."

We checked out several upstairs rooms, all bedrooms,

before we found the burned room. One door, which should have led to the tower if my memory of its position was correct, was locked. I raised my eyebrows questioningly at Ann. She shrugged. The burned room had been a bedroom as well. It looked as if no one had touched it since the fire fifty years ago. The furniture and walls were charred in places but only scorched in others, as if the fire had raged fiercely for a few minutes and then been instantly doused.

But there was no old lady with funny clothes.

When we got back downstairs, Tannie was facing the others defiantly, and near tears. She turned and ran to me. "Ben, would you please tell these people what I saw?" she said with a quiver in her voice.

I knelt and took her in my arms. She put her arms around my neck and valiantly kept from crying. "I'm sorry, honey," I said softly. "When we got there she was gone."

"Do you think I'm imagining things too?" The quiver had grown more pronounced at the thought that I, too, might be against her.

"Of course not," I said firmly. "She really did see someone," I said to the others. I stood up, but Tannie kept a grip on my hand.

"How are you so sure?" Judson Bradley Ledbetter asked with a supercilious sneer.

"Has the ghost made an appearance?" Poe asked with genuine interest.

"You'll have to ask Professor Weatherly about that," I said.

The professor frowned at me as if one of his own troops had turned on him. He fidgeted a bit and then sighed. "I can assure you there are no ghosts in this house," he snapped irritably. "However, you are due an explanation, as I see some of you are letting your imaginations run away with you. Before I explain anything, and I still can't tell you everything, I want to show you something." He went to the table where the bridge game had been abandoned.

"Why can't you tell us everything?" Dad asked, becoming a little bit irritable himself.

"You wouldn't believe me, Mr. Henderson." He sighed impatiently. "And there's no point in alarming you unnecessarily."

Poe grunted. "It's statements like that that alarm me unnecessarily."

"Mr. McNeal," Weatherly snapped, "there are no ghosts; you are in no danger. Please stop this wild speculation." Poe hunkered his head protectively between his shoulders and grinned at me. Ann and I cocked an eyebrow at each other. Weatherly was difficult. He was telling the truth, but I had a feeling it was only *technically* the truth. "Now, everyone," he continued and sat at the table, "gather around. Ben, you and two others sit down."

I sat opposite him, eager to cooperate and find out what was going on. Ann stood behind me. Mom and Dad sat in the other chairs. Everyone else gathered around except Carl, who watched from the other side of the room. I had the impression he was staying close to the door, on the verge of bolting. Weatherly gathered up the cards and handed them to Mom. "Now, Mrs. Henderson, please shuffle the cards carefully and deal out four hands."

Mom gave him a quizzical frown but did as he asked. Weatherly picked up his cards and fanned them. The rest of us did the same. I had thirteen clubs neatly arranged in order, with the deuce on the left and the ace on the right.

"Now, Ben," Weatherly said, "tell us who has the winning hand if we were playing bridge."

"Dad," I said.

He nodded with satisfaction. "Correct," he said crisply, and laid his cards face-up on the table. He had thirteen hearts. Mom had thirteen diamonds and Dad had thirteen spades. "Explain how you knew."

"I can't explain," I said with a frown. "It's like . . . like explaining sight or sound or smell to someone lacking them.

Dad knew he had the winning hand, and I . . . felt . . . sensed him knowing it."

"Did you know exactly which cards he had?" Weatherly asked intensely.

"No. But it wasn't hard to figure out when I saw mine."

"Read everyone in the room, Ben," he said like a wire stretched to the breaking point. He never took his eyes off mine. "Your parents."

"Concern. Love."

"Tannie."

"She's still mad."

"Poe."

"Interest. Wonder."

"Linda."

"Love. Incomprehension."

"Mr. Ledbetter."

"Disbelief. Annoyance."

"Mr. Willingham."

"Nervousness. Stoicism."

"Me."

"Determination." I narrowed my eyes a little, and he knew I read more than that, but I didn't say anything else.

"Ann."

I hesitated. How could I put Ann into words? I couldn't, and so I just grinned like a sap. Ann put her arm around my shoulder.

"Ben . . ." Mom said in a tight little voice.

I hadn't really wanted my parents to find out like this, though my father had known subconsciously for quite some time. He'd never said anything; he hadn't wanted to upset Mom and didn't really want to believe it himself. Now they were both confused and frightened. I started to say something, to try to ease their worries, but Ann beat me to it.

"Don't you see, Clare?" she said quietly. "You and Charles think of Ben as an adolescent. So he acts the part to please you. It's difficult for us to be ourselves and not just the reflections of others. I went through the same thing. No one likes an uppity kid." She ran her fingernails through the hair on the back of my neck.

All I could do was grin and turn red. She hit me lightly on the back of the head.

"Ben . . ." Mom said again.

"I know, Mom."

"So, there you are," Weatherly said, getting us back on the path of his purpose, whatever that was. "Ann could have told me the same things. They are both telepathic and empathic, though Ben is the more sensitive."

"Telepathic," Jud snorted, and poured himself another cup of coffee.

"Don't worry, Jud," Ann assured him. "We can't read your thoughts, only your emotions, your state of mind, and the like."

"But I also knew who had the winning hand," Weatherly barreled ahead. "I knew where every card lay, because I controlled the deal. If I hadn't, I wouldn't have known any more than . . . the man in the moon."

"I figured that," I said.

"How did you control the deal?" Dad had accepted everything completely.

"That, too, is difficult to explain." Weatherly sighed. "Ben and Ann are telepathic and empathic. My own ability is telekinesis, though I believe these days they are calling it psychokinesis."

There was a momentary silence. "What's that?" Linda asked, wide-eyed. Poe had his arm around her and she leaned against him. Poe was quiet, absorbing everything.

"The ability to mentally control physical objects," Weatherly explained tersely.

"You mean mind over matter?" Linda breathed.

"Yes," he sighed, "I believe that is the popular term."

Jud was pacing a short path on the faded carpet. "Let's see you make that shoe move," he snorted, and pointed to Poe's still damp sneaker on the hearth.

Weatherly leaned back in the chair and tiredly ran his

hand over his face. He broadcast resignation to the constant interruptions. He nodded and the shoe rose into the air. Mom and Linda gasped. Tannie was watching bug-eyed. Carl Willingham eased a little closer to the door. The shoe made a circle of the room and plopped back on the hearth.

"There's more to it than moving shoes about, Mr. Ledbetter," Weatherly explained impatiently. "Matter can also be controlled on a molecular level. Mrs. Henderson, lift the top card, please, and look at it."

She gave him a curious look and turned the card. It was the three of hearts.

"Turn it face down again." Mom did so. "Now look at it." Mom exposed it once more. The hearts had been replaced by little yellow daisies. "It is now the three of daisies," Weatherly said without looking at it. "I could continue to perform carnival tricks until morning, but there are more important matters. There is something absolutely vital which I must do. I could not do it alone, not without the aid of a telepath. I have been searching for thirty-five years. I had just about given up hope. And then I found Ann. My dear, I must apologize for the way I maneuvered you here."

"Maneuvered?"

"Yes. I'm afraid it's turned into something of an imbroglio, however. I instigated your weekend drive by thinking it at you for the past two weeks. Naturally, you thought it your own idea. I created the rainstorm, the roadblock, and the flooded detour. Of course, I never intended the rest of you people to fall into my little charade. Yes," he sighed, "I seem to have botched it rather badly." He brightened. "But, actually, it has turned out rather well. If things had gone according to plan, I wouldn't have found Ben."

"I don't believe any of this!" Jud flopped onto the couch and stretched his long, fashionably sheathed legs in front of him. He looked away with a sour expression.

"Really, young man," Weatherly said in exasperation, "creating a rainstorm, a couple of wooden barricades, an animated yellow slicker, and a little water over the road differs from controlling a deck of cards only in degree. It's exactly the same principle."

"If you can do all that," Dad said suspiciously, "you could've gotten my car out of the ditch."

"Most assuredly, Mr. Henderson. But, you see—and I must apologize—it was I who put your car *in* the ditch."

"Why?" Mom asked.

"Oh, dear, isn't it obvious?" Weatherly whined. "In order to keep Ann here, I was forced to keep all of you."

"Why did you go through all these elaborate machinations, Professor?" Ann asked seriously. "Why didn't you just ask me to help you?"

"I couldn't take the chance. If you had refused . . . It was imperative that you come. I'm an old man, Ann. This is my last chance. If I'm unsuccessful again"—his shoulders slumped—"then God help us."

Stunned silence spread over the room like a blanket and lay there. Then Ann spoke softly. "What is it you want me to do?"

"Please be patient with me, my dear." He sighed and ran his hand over his face again. His eyes were bleary from nervous strain, and his skin had developed a putty-colored pallor. I still didn't know what he was up to, but he didn't appear to be in condition to subdue an irritated kitten. "There are preparations that must be made before I explain fully. Imagine"—he brightened—"after thirty-five years I find *two* telepaths."

"Just a minute," Dad said with a hardness in his voice I'd seldom heard before. "If Ann wants to help you with whatever you're doing, that's her affair, but Ben is not to be involved."

Weatherly's chin set firmly. He was about to argue, but Jud jumped up to pace again. He rubbed his hands on the fabric molding his hips and said with nervous volume, "I think you're all nuts! You're sitting around talking about telepathy, telekinesis, and created rainstorms and . . . and . . . as if you were talking about . . . about the weather.

All I've seen is a man, whose sanity I am beginning to doubt, do card tricks." He stopped and fixed Weatherly with a pale blue glare.

"Jud, please," Linda whispered in embarrassment.

"Don't forget the shoe," Poe said brightly. Jud transferred the glare to his brother-in-law. Poe grinned and raised his eyebrows.

Jud turned back to the professor. "If you can do all this hocus-pocus, will you kindly turn off the rain, get Mr. Henderson's car out of the ditch, and let us get out of this freak show?" His voice rose a little in volume with each word.

Weatherly matched him decibel for decibel. "I am not a magician, Mr. Ledbetter. I can't snap my fingers and *turn off* the rain. It took two days of careful manipulation to create it in the first place. Besides"—his voice lowered to conciliatory tones—"there is no point in your leaving. You have to spend the night somewhere. It might as well be here. There are very comfortable bedrooms upstairs. If any of you wish to retire, I'll show you the way."

Jud wasn't giving up so easily. "You mean we stay whether we like it or not? My parents are expecting us tonight, and I want to leave!"

"I'm sorry, Mr. Ledbetter. Take my word. It is impossible."

Ann and I looked at each other. We had both caught the same thing. He was telling the truth as he saw it. It *was* impossible for us to leave—and not because of the weather. But neither of us could get the real reason.

"Take it easy, Jud," Poe said sensibly. "We're so late now, a few more hours won't matter."

"Okay, okay." Jud shrugged elaborately and sat at the now empty table. He picked up the cards and shuffled them. "You go right ahead with your spook hunt. I shall sit right here and play solitaire all night. I don't care if twenty ghosts come traipsing through here rattling chains and moaning their heads off. I shall be totally oblivious to them." He dealt out a hand of solitaire and pointedly ignored us.

Everyone looked at him with some amusement for a moment. His shouting match with the professor had done quite a bit to break the tension in the air. Then Mom sort of shook her head and said, "I know one young lady who needs to go to bed."

"Do I have to?" Tannie groaned. "Things are much too interesting to go to bed."

"Yes, you do." Mom laughed.

She took one of the suitcases and led Tannie out. Tannie said good night to everyone, kissed Dad and me, then gave me a defeated look. I winked at her. They left and Tannie came back almost immediately. "Mom forgot the flashlight," she said. Dad was about to hand it to her, when we heard Mom gasp and drop the suitcase. We all scrambled into the hall. Mom was standing at the foot of the stairs with her hand over her mouth, looking up. The suitcase lay on its side at her feet.

"I saw someone standing at the top of the stairs," she said with a controlled voice.

Dad pointed the flashlight at the top of the stairs and turned it on. There was no one there. The grandfather clock suddenly rattled and struck eight o'clock. A startled squeak escaped from Linda. Dad moved the beam lower and caught a man descending toward us.

He was young, about the same age as Poe and Jud, dressed in rough clothes, with no expression on his dark, Slavic face. That's the way he appeared to my eyes. When I looked at him without using my eyes, he was a featureless shimmer. Dad kept the flashlight on him.

"It's Lester Gant," Carl Willingham said from behind us as if he were identifying a rabid dog.

The man reached the bottom of the stairs and stood looking at us, still with no expression. The clock stopped striking. For some reason, we all took a half-step backward.

"You know him?" Weatherly asked, slipping back into
the befuddlement he had only recently escaped. I had the
impression he couldn't take very many more interruptions
or complications.

"Is this the caretaker?" Dad asked.

"What?" Weatherly turned to him with a slight jerk of
his head. "Of course not. That was thirty-five years ago.
Wait, yes, the man's name was Gant. What was it? Horace?
Homer?"

"Lester's father was Harold Gant," Carl supplied. "Is that
it?"

"Possibly." The professor nodded and turned back to the
dark young man. "Mr. Gant, is your father the caretaker I
hired?"

"Old man Gant's been dead over ten years," Carl said.
"Least ways, him and his wife disappeared."

"Ah"—Poe widened his eyes—"more mysteries."

"You don't keep very close track of your caretakers, Professor," Dad grunted.

"What?" His head did another revolution. "Oh, the bank
in Hawley handles all that. I suppose they gave the job to
the boy when the father disappeared. Can't he talk, Mr.
Willingham?"

"He can talk. Heard him myself," Carl stated.

And he did. Four words. I never heard him say anything else. "Missus will be down," he said in flat, colorless
tones.

"Who else is here?" Jud groaned.

Weatherly sighed. "I imagine he means my mother, Mr.
Ledbetter."

"Your mother?" Mom squeaked. "Why didn't you tell
us your mother was living here?"

"I wasn't sure that she was." Weatherly sounded on his
last legs. "I didn't expect she would still be alive."

Gant turned without another word and vanished into the
darkness at the top of the stairs. Weatherly looked as if he
had been kicked in the stomach. He had had one compli-

cation too many. After a moment Dad picked up Mom's suitcase and escorted her upstairs.

"You want to go to bed, hon?" Poe asked his wife. "You must be exhausted."

"If it's all the same to you," Linda laughed nervously, "I'll wait until you go. I couldn't sleep up there by myself."

Poe grinned and put his arm around her. They all drifted back to the parlor, but I gave Ann a signal and went out to the front porch. The rain had stopped. I could see stars in the west and a smudge of light where the moon hid behind clouds. Frogs were screaming in damp ecstasy, and a few bold crickets had emerged from their dry hidey-holes. The air had the fresh, clean smell it gets right after a rain, pointing up the slight mustiness of the house. I took a deep breath and leaned against the railing, looking at the cars on the road at the bottom of the hill.

"Did you see it?" I asked when I felt Ann behind me.

"Yes. I've run across it a few times before. Apparently some people have natural shields." She leaned on the railing beside me.

I turned when I heard the door open, but I knew who it was. Carl Willingham nodded to us and went down the porch steps.

"Where are you going, Mr. Willingham?" Ann asked politely.

He stopped and turned, looking up at us. "Leavin', ma'am. Rain's stopped and I'd rather walk four miles than stay in the same house with Lester Gant. I can take magicians and mindreaders"—he dipped his head—"no offense, and even flying shoes, but he's too much. I'd advise the rest of you to do the same."

"What's the matter with him?" I asked, because he was genuinely frightened.

"Folks say he killed his parents. Never found 'em, no proof he did it, but folks know just the same." He nodded again and started down the hill. We watched him for a moment.

"Folks around here sure say a lot," I observed wryly, and we went back in the house. Weatherly was sitting on the couch deep in gloomy thought. I had the impression of swirling, muddy water. Poe, Linda, Jud, and Dad were starting another card game. "Mr. Willingham just left," I said, certainly not expecting the reaction I got.

Weatherly jumped up and stared at me. "Left? What do you mean?"

"He said he was gonna walk to town," I said, completely mystified.

Weatherly was severely agitated. He moved around as if he couldn't decide which direction was the right one. "He can't leave!" he wailed. "He'll be killed! Stop him! Bring him back by force if you have to! Hurry! Hurry!"

Weatherly's anxiety was so strong and sharp that I ran from the room and out the front door. They all followed me, confused and frightened. Carl was almost to the bottom of the hill. I yelled at him. Dad and Poe were right behind me, not knowing what was going on. The others stayed on the porch.

Carl turned and looked at us curiously. His eyebrows rose in bewilderment at the sight of us bounding down the hill, floundering in the slippery mud, yelling like madmen.

Carl, the only one looking toward the house, was the first to see it. His eyes got big. He took a step backward.

Then I felt it, like static electricity in my head. I skidded to a halt on the muddy ground and fell to my knees with a grunt. I looked back at the house. Weatherly was waving his arms and yelling. The crickets stopped singing.

The house was surrounded by a glow, an iridescent nimbus, like a soap bubble growing larger and larger. Dad and Poe had stopped, looking at the house. Weatherly was screaming, waving us back. My head was singing with the sweet chill of fear, but not my fear. The air crackled with energy. I could feel the hair on my arms standing up. Sparks danced across the hill, flowing down it like a faerie river. I turned to look at Carl.

He stared at the house, backing slowly away. The static electricity in the air made his clothes cling to his skin. Then he whirled and ran. The energy pressure was growing unbearable.

Then there was light, an eye-burning flash, a fierce discharge. All the energy floating free in the air gathered at one point. It circled around like a whirlwind of fireflies, swept by me, contracted, converged at one point.

On Carl.

He screamed. Then he was covered with fire. He screamed and ran and burned. He beat at his clothes with his hands, beat at flames with flames. His glowing feet kicked through the damp grass and left little curls of steam that sizzled and disappeared.

Carl stopped his useless flailing and just ran, his arms stretching before him, seeking. Then he stumbled, staggered a few steps, and fell, still screaming. He kept moving, trying to crawl.

The screaming stopped.

Then the movement.

Carl was nothing but a shapeless lump, burning, sending a shaft of black smoke into the night air. The energy and the pressure was gone. The crickets started up again.

I had thrown up my tattered barriers, trying to shut him out, trying to block his agonies from my mind. Then, I think I felt the muddy ground hit me in the face.

I was moving, floating in warmth. Dad was carrying me as he had when I was three and had fallen asleep. I tightened my grip around his neck. Then he was prying me loose, putting me on the couch.

They were all crowded around, looking at me, except Jud. He was staring out the window, pale and shaken. Tannie, in her pajamas, was round-eyed with wonder. Ann put her hand on my forehead and pushed the hair out of my eyes.

Dad was standing a few feet away watching me. I had never known him to be so angry. "Professor Weatherly," he said in a low voice, "you told me there was no danger. I want you to explain exactly what's going on. No evasions. No promises. We'd like to make a few decisions for ourselves."

"I'm sorry, Mr. Henderson," he said with honest regret. "It's too late for independent decisions. There is only one course open to us."

"Did you hear what I said? *I want an explanation.*"

"Of course, Mr. Henderson." He fluttered like a moth. "Give everyone a chance to calm down and I'll tell you all I know."

"Jud. Come away from the window," Linda said. Her voice was hoarse and trembled a little. Jud turned without comment and sat in a chair.

"So the spirits are malignant after all, Professor," Poe said quietly.

"Be patient a few minutes, please. Let's get Ben back on his feet." He looked down at me with real concern on his face. "Are you feeling better?"

"Yes. I think so." I took Ann's hand in mine and squeezed it. Tannie looked at me with her little face pinched and pale. I grinned and winked at her.

"I absolutely refuse to give you a hug, Benjamin Henderson," she stated uncategorically. "You had me scared to death. I thought I was gonna be a widow."

Everyone laughed—more than it deserved, to be sure, but it broke the tension. Even Jud managed an anemic grin. Tannie sniffled. I sat up and held my arms out to her. She threw herself at me and sobbed on my chest.

"I'm sorry, honey," I said.

"Oh, Tannie!" Mom groaned, thankfully finding something practical on which to focus her attention. "Ben is covered with mud. You're getting it all over you." She extracted Tannie bodily. "Ben, go change your clothes and wash your face."

So I went to the suitcase and got clean blue jeans and a clean shirt. I was a bit wobble-kneed, but I tried not to show it. You can take just so much fussing. I went in a corner behind a chair and changed while they talked.

"Are you ready, Professor?" Dad asked, nearing the end of his patience.

"Yes, Mr. Henderson. Everyone get comfortable. I want to explain as well as I can what happened. Ben. Are you feeling it?"

"Yes."

"Describe it to me."

"There's really nothing to describe. It's just there. It's aware of us. And . . . it's just . . . there."

"That's right," Ann agreed.

"There's no hostility? No anger?" Weatherly asked as if he expected there would be.

"Not now," I answered. "It's frightened. I think it's always frightened. There was anger . . . no not anger . . . panic, when Mr. Willingham tried to leave." I finished changing clothes and joined the group.

I was so busy concentrating on Weatherly, I didn't sense her presence. Neither did Ann. No one knew she was in the room until she spoke in her brassy bellow. "Philip!" she brayed. "What are these people doing in my house?"

Everyone turned quickly. I felt Weatherly's resolve become as fragile as cobwebs. She stood in the doorway, surveying us. She wore a long black dress that reached the floor. It had a high collar that pushed her flesh into wrinkles around her sharp chin. The long-sleeved dress was unadorned but for a large cameo at her throat. Her hands rested on a silver-headed stick and her pewter-colored hair was piled on top of her head. Her skin was almost white and had a peculiar sheen—like a waxworks figure come to life. Lester Gant lurked behind her ramrod-straight figure, as inscrutable as ever.

"I'm waiting for an answer, Philip."

"It's good to see you again, Mother." He sounded like a little boy who had been caught doing something naughty in the bathroom.

"You're a fool, Philip," she stated in her clarion voice. "You've always been a fool."

"Yes, Mother, very good to see you again." He sighed.

She speared him with a look and sat regally in a chair near us. She moved as if her spine were of one piece. Gant remained in the doorway.

"You've come to try again, have you." It was a statement rather than a question. The rest of us sat there with our mouths open.

"Yes," he said. "I was about to explain to these people."

"It will kill you as it did the man just now. I knew you were fool enough to keep trying, but I didn't know you were so obsessed as to endanger others."

"They are not here by design, Mother."

"How long has it been since your last futility, Philip?"

"Thirty-five years."

"So long?" she said a little wistfully.

"Professor," Dad said through clenched teeth, "we're waiting."

"What?" He started as if he had forgotten the rest of us. "Yes. Excuse me, Mother." He turned away from her. "You heard how it began from Mr. Willingham. I was ten years old. It was in my room that fire was seen. I had for some time been aware of my powers, but I thought everyone had them. After almost disastrously finding out that wasn't the case, that I was unique, I kept them secret and practiced. However, as you heard Mr. Willingham say, I didn't do it in time to avoid getting a reputation in the area for being . . . ah . . . peculiar. My powers developed with practice, but I was so immature."

"You were a fool."

"Yes, Mother. It happened the night Mr. Willingham told you about. I unfortunately thought I knew all there was to know. You see, I had just read Wells's *The Time Machine*. I . . . ah . . . I'm afraid I attempted to travel in time." He looked at us with an ironic frown.

"Why?" Dad asked, a bit dumbfounded.

Weatherly shrugged. "I was ten years old and it seemed like an excellent idea."

"What happened?" Poe asked in rapt fascination.

"My powers were quite strong," he continued, "but my control wasn't. I didn't know at the time exactly what I had done, but I believe, now, that in some way I warped space. And something came through. It was ferocious. All fire and energy. It attacked me the same way it did Mr. Willingham. I tried to fight it but was successful only in saving myself. I ran out of the house and didn't return for fifteen years."

"He ran away and left his family to be destroyed."

"There was nothing I could do, Mother."

"Why did nothing happen to you, Mrs. Weatherly?" Dad asked.

Her head swiveled toward him. "I do not know why I was not destroyed, but I was not. It kept me like a souvenir. Like an insect in amber. I often wish I had been . . . destroyed."

Dad inclined his head toward Lester Gant, still standing in the doorway regarding us impassively. "What about him?"

"Mr. Gant is in no danger," she said with a slightly upward twist of the corners of her thin mouth. "Mr. Gant comes and goes as he pleases. It knows he will return. Mr. Gant is a worshiper." I had the impression this was only a casual volley in an old war. Gant looked at her without expression.

"We were awakened by the commotion in Philip's room." Mrs. Weatherly picked up the story. "My husband and daughters reached it first. I saw them destroyed. I hid in the attic. When the neighbors searched the house, they didn't find me, and the thing didn't bother them. By the time I had recovered from my fright, it was too late. I was unable to leave."

"I returned fifteen years later. I was much stronger and completely in control."

"You should have seen the foolish expression on his face when he found me," his mother said with a slight pucker of her thin lips.

"You were here fifteen years?" Mom said in confusion. "How did you live?"

"Insects in amber require nothing," she answered flatly. "I do not eat. I do not sleep. I am not sure that I am even alive."

"The thing I brought here has no physical existence as we know it," the professor explained. "I think it sustains my mother with its own life energy."

"Is it the same for him?" Poe asked, and indicated Lester Gant. I looked at Gant, still standing immobile in the doorway. His eyes were slightly narrowed and focused on Ann. I didn't think much about it at the time.

"Mr. Gant is here for other purposes," Mrs. Weatherly said with that tightening of her mouth that seemed to denote amusement. "Mr. Gant is here voluntarily. Mr. Gant has secret appetites."

Gant gave her a malevolent look and turned on his heel. She watched him leave, her porcelain eyes twinkling. She turned back to us. "Mr. Gant is blasphemed."

"What did you do when you came back?" Dad asked Weatherly, getting back on the subject.

"I'll tell you what the fool did," his mother brayed as Weatherly opened his mouth. "He tried to destroy it. But it had grown stronger also. And he ran again. Then, rather than letting the house fall down as it deserves, he hired Mr. Gant's father to keep it in repair."

"I did it for you, Mother. I couldn't—" She stopped him with a snort.

"What happened to Mr. Gant's parents?" Ann asked.

"Mr. Gant and I talk of many things, but that is not one of them. They moved into the house when he was a baby. It didn't matter to me. I never left my room. When Mr. Gant was about that boy's age"—she pointed a bony finger at me—"the parents weren't here anymore."

"What are you planning to do now, Professor?" Ann asked.

"My mistake was in trying to destroy it." He frowned. "I know now it probably can't be destroyed. But it must be stopped before it moves out of this house. I don't know why it's still here. I must communicate with it, find out what it wants. That's why I brought you, Ann, to communicate with it. You can't imagine the elation I felt when I found you. Thirty-five years . . ." His voice faded.

"How did you spot me anyway?" she asked.

"Tests." He raised his forefinger. "That's why I became a professor of psychology, so I could test students. Tests of all kinds, to thousands of students. Most of them had been somewhat altered to my purposes rather than the original author's, of course."

"What will communication accomplish," I asked, "other than to satisfy your curiosity?"

"Isn't that enough?" His eyes widened. "But I expect to learn much more. Much more."

"If it can't be destroyed," I asked, "what do you plan to do?"

"I must warp space and sent it back where it came from," he said.

His mother looked at him speculatively. "Perhaps you are no longer such a fool." Then she shook her head. "No. You could have done it without involving the girl. You are still a fool." She stood and walked imperially toward the door. She paused and turned, both her hands resting on the silver-headed stick. "Do not let Mr. Gant know what you are doing." Then she went out the door and up the stairs like a wraith to disappear in the darkness.

"Mom," Tannie said droopily, "could I go back to bed, please? I'm sleepy."

Mom put her hand on Tannie's head. "Maybe you'd better sleep down here, dear."

"Why?"

"Isn't she frightened of anything?" Jud groaned.

Tannie looked at him, surprised at his ignorance. "My brother is here."

Jud grimaced and sighed. "I wish I had your confidence, kid. I really do."

"I guess we're as safe in bed as we are here," Poe said sensibly. "I'm ready myself."

I started for the door and Ann met me halfway there. I took her hand. We went back to the porch while the others bustled around preparing for bed. The sky had almost completely cleared. The night was bright out over the Kansas pastureland. I couldn't see Carl's body, if there was anything left to see. We sat on the railing.

"Ben," she said softly, "do you think we ought to be doing this? You know what happened to you when it killed Mr. Willingham."

"I've been working on that," I said, and turned to face her. "Read me."

She concentrated for a moment then looked at me in surprise. "You're completely shielded. I wouldn't even know you were there if I couldn't see you."

"When Mr. Willingham was killed"—the memory made my skin crawl—"I got the full blast. I've always had a shield of sorts. I don't pick up anything unless it's especially strong or I want to. Background babble doesn't get through at all. That's why I didn't spot you."

She nodded. "I wonder how many others there are, how many we've passed on the street and didn't recognize?"

"I've been trying to strengthen my shield," I continued. "It was relatively easy. It just never occurred to me to try. Here, concentrate on me. I'll let it down slowly. See how it works."

I showed her how it worked and she tried it. We practiced it for a while until she was as good at it as I was. She was quiet then, looking at me.

She stood up and stepped in front of me, facing me. She put her hands on either side of my neck. Tannie has nothing on me when it comes to looking wide-eyed.

"Ben . . ." she said solemnly. "I know what you're feeling about what you can do. You've never explored it before, never really tried to extend the limits of your ability. I know you're strong, stronger than I. But . . . be careful. Don't get in over your head with this thing. Don't get overconfident. Just . . . be careful."

I nodded, understanding. We looked at each other, not reading, just being physical. Then I slid my hands up her arms and interlaced my fingers behind her neck. I pulled her head down to mine slowly. She didn't resist. I kissed her very lightly on the lips, still not reading, enjoying the purely physical sensation. She pulled her head back and smiled at me. I stood up and let my arms slip lower down her back. I felt hers do the same thing. I kissed her again, harder. She kissed back.

We were sitting on the steps, not doing anything, not talking, just being together, when I felt it. It was like a hobnail boot in the groin. Fear and pain, but mostly rage and anger. Ann got it too. She jerked and grunted and looked at me with pain. We jumped up and ran inside. I knew who it was. I did a quick survey of the house. Only one was missing.

I stuck my head in the parlor, where the professor sat meditatively before the dying fire. "Where's Jud?"

He jumped at the sound of my voice and looked at me blankly. I repeated the question more insistently. "He's sharing a room with you," he said bewildered. "The second one on the right at the top of the stairs. What's the matter?" He rose and moved toward us.

"He's dead," I said over my shoulder as Ann and I ran up the stairs. We found him in the bathroom, on the floor, facedown. He was wearing only gold jockey shorts. Blood was still seeping along the crevices between the white floor tiles. His blond fairness was now a pallor. Judson Bradley Ledbetter wasn't beautiful anymore. His shaving kit was scattered about as if he'd had it in his hands when attacked. I knelt beside him and turned him over. I shouldn't have.

His chest and abdomen had been thoroughly worked over with a large-bladed knife.

Ann gasped and Weatherly let the air hiss out between his teeth. "Who could have done it?" he whispered.

"Gant."

"Why?"

"We don't know. Perhaps your mother does. She's in the hall."

She was standing there watching us, looking exactly as she had earlier. Poe opened the door across from us and stepped sleepily into the hall wearing pajama bottoms. "What's the commotion?" he asked, rubbing his face. Ann went to him and talked quietly. He looked frightened and hurried into the room we had come out of.

"Mrs. Weatherly," I said. "Jud Ledbetter has been killed." She turned her porcelain eyes on me but said nothing. "We've read everyone in the house except Gant. He's the only one who could've done it. We need to know why."

She narrowed her eyes at me and then turned to her son. "Your foolishness is catching up with you, Philip. Mr. Gant is also a fool. He killed the wrong one."

"What?" Weatherly gasped.

"Don't be an idiot," she snapped. "Mr. Gant is protecting the thing." She turned back to me. "Young man, Mr. Gant will undoubtedly discover his error." She wheeled and walked away into the darkness.

"Ben," Ann hissed. "He meant to kill you."

"I'm trying to remember what we said while he was in the room. He knows that you and someone else are here to help the professor get rid of it, but you were sitting next to Jud when he mentioned it. That means he'll be coming after you next."

"We've got to find him," Weatherly whined. "He could ruin everything."

I gave him a disgusted look, but he didn't really mean it the way it came out. "I'll wake Dad," I said. Poe came back

into the hall looking a little sick. Ann and the professor
went to him.

Mom and Dad were both asleep. Tannie was on a daybed
screwed up like a worm, the way she always slept. I put my
hand on Dad's shoulder and his eyes popped open. He
started to say something, but I put my finger to my lips and
motioned him to come outside. He got out of bed, careful
not to wake Mom, and put on his robe, looking at me
questioningly.

In the hall we explained everything that had happened.
"Do you think Linda and your mother will be safe?" Poe
asked.

"Wake Linda and put her in with Mom. Ann, stay with
them and bolt the door." She nodded.

Poe was worried. "Don't tell Linda what happened to
Jud. Not yet." He went back in his room and closed the
door.

"Professor," I said, "you know the house. Where could
he be hiding?"

He shook his head. "I don't know. Lots of places. I suggest
we start downstairs and work up to the attic. Ben, can you
read him at all?"

"No."

We started in the cellar and searched every hidey-hole.
He wasn't down there and he wasn't on the ground floor
either. Dad had his flashlight, and I had one of the kerosene
lamps so we could split up when necessary to prevent Gant
from doubling back on us. Poe had a poker he took from
the parlor fireplace. He grinned at me nervously and smacked
it a couple of times in his palm.

We went back upstairs. Dad shined the flashlight down
the hall. Gant was at the door of Mom's room crouched
over the doorknob. He had a large butcher knife in his
hand. He looked up at us and ran off in the opposite direction, through a door. When we got to it, it was locked.

"That's the stairway to the attic," Weatherly said.

Dad rattled the door a few times, frowning at it. It had one of those old mortise-type locks that could be locked from either side, but only with a key.

"Wait a moment," Weatherly muttered. The lock rattled and went *snick*. The door swung open about two inches with a lazy creak.

Dad glanced at Weatherly, then opened the door the rest of the way. He pointed the flashlight up the steep, narrow steps, but there was nothing except gloom and cobwebs. Dad took a deep breath and started up very cautiously. Poe was behind him with the poker, then the professor. I brought up the rear with the kerosene lamp.

The stairs entered the attic through a hole in the middle of the floor, a perfect place to get your head knocked off when you poked it up. Dad shined the flashlight around, keeping down as far as he could, ready to duck if Gant was waiting. When he motioned the rest of us up, I realized I'd been holding my breath.

The attic was a jumble of discards and had a fifty-year accumulation of dust. The floor was velvety smooth, disturbed only by Mr. Gant's footprints leading into the pile of rubble, and little stitcherylike marks made by crawling beetles. Dad followed Mr. Gant's footprints with the flashlight beam, but we couldn't see him.

Twenty people could have been hiding in all the clutter. I held the lamp high, trying to see into the darkness. It was practically useless; it lit everything beautifully—for three feet in every direction. And when one of us moved, he cast a shadow the size of Godzilla.

The rafters were draped with dusty cobwebs and spotted with little brown mounds made by mud daubers. The flashlight passed over a wasp nest the size of a dinner plate back in the corner. The yellow jackets stirred sluggishly, lethargic in the cool night air.

Dad kept swinging the flashlight around, covering as much of the attic as he could, but Mr. Gant was as invisible to my eyes as he was to my mind. He could have been hiding in any one of many places.

I was about to suggest we lock the attic securely and leave Mr. Gant to the spiders, when something toppled behind me.

We whirled in that direction. The flashlight caught Mr. Gant charging straight at us with the butcher knife drawn back. The whole thing couldn't have taken more than a couple of seconds, but I suddenly had a sensation of slow motion, of Gant running at me through a narrow aisle between stacks of cardboard boxes, of the knife glinting in the flashlight beam, of his shirt flaring out at each step.

I remember studying his face, remember feeling surprise that it was almost emotionless, surprise that he wasn't slavering like a madman. All of this must have been only in my mind because my muscles didn't correspond. I just stood there like a dummy, watching him.

Then he tripped. His toe caught in a picture frame leaning against the stack of boxes. A startled expression crossed his face as his body got ahead of his feet. Instead of getting me with the knife, he rammed into me bodily.

My arms went up and the lamp slipped smoothly from my fingers. I grunted as the wind was knocked out of me. Then Gant and I landed on the floor in a tangle, but the lamp stayed in my line of vision, arching up slowly, very slowly. The thin glass chimney hit a rafter and shattered, then the base, the wick still burning, smashed against a trunk engulfing one end of the attic in burning kerosene.

Mr. Gant lost no time in getting himself untangled; he had landed on top. I was flat on my back. The next thing I knew he was straddling my stomach with the knife drawn back. I twisted as he brought the knife down, and I heard it thunk into the floor beside my ear.

Then good old Poe swung the poker with both hands as if he were chopping wood. It caught Mr. Gant across the shoulders. He yelled and arched his back, his face twisting with pain. He lurched up, gasping for breath, and staggered into the darkness, the knife still in his hand. He upset several piles of uncertain junk, bringing them down with a clatter. Poe and Dad helped me up and I grinned thanks at Poe.

Mr. Gant was out of sight again, hidden by the darkness and the smoke. We turned to the fire. The whole end of the attic was burning furiously. The heat was rapidly becoming uncomfortable. We edged toward the stairs, but the professor was staring at the flames, deep in concentration. We stopped and watched.

A mist began forming in the attic, like heavy fog rolling in. It even smelled like fog. It grew thicker and thicker, closing in on the fire until, finally, it was completely obscured by the bank of white. The crackle of the flames gradually changed to a damp hissing, and then nothing. I could no longer feel the heat. Little beads of water stood on the hairs on my arms, like a heavy dew. The thick mist swirled away as if in a wind, and the fire was out. The end of the attic was blackened and charred, shiny with moisture. Drops of water fell from the rafters, thumping against the boxes and trunks and other debris. Weatherly sighed deeply.

"You're sure handy to have around, Professor," Poe said with a certain amount of awe.

"Carnival tricks." He perished the thought.

Dad swung the flashlight away from the burned area and started to say something. He stopped with his mouth open, looking at something. We turned. Gant was creeping toward us with the knife in his hand. Mr. Gant may have had his faults, but lack of determination wasn't one of them. He stopped when the light hit him. His eyes glittered like marbles. Weatherly was concentrating again.

I heard a harsh buzzing, and the wasp nest almost directly over Gant's head erupted in a yellow and black storm. I don't know what Weatherly did, but the yellow jackets swarmed all over Gant. He screamed and stumbled back, crashing through a pile of discards, swatting at the stinging insects. He kept yelling and threshing, and I guess Weatherly couldn't go through with it any longer because the wasps left Gant and settled back on the nest.

Then, unbelievably, Gant rose from the junk and started toward us again. His face and hands were solid with welts that grew redder and larger by the second. One eye was almost closed, but he came at us, staggering and stumbling, entangling himself in the clutter. He warded off the collapsing debris with one hand and held the knife in the other.

Professor Weatherly groaned. Then the knife in Gant's hand glowed a cherry red. Gant sucked air through his teeth and dropped it, clutching his hand with the other. The knife clattered to the floor. A curl of smoke rose from it. But before another fire could get started, Weatherly did something to it and it was cold once more.

Dad kept the flashlight on Gant. He backed away, still hunched over his burned hand. We moved toward him. His eye was now completely closed, and the other didn't look too good. He still hadn't given up. He grabbed the base of a piano stool with his good hand and drew back to throw it.

Then he froze. The piano stool slipped from limp fingers and bounced off a three-legged table. Gant sucked in air like a fish. He clutched at his chest. I looked at Weatherly, then back at Gant. He breathed in great, roaring gasps, tearing at his shirt. He dropped to one knee, then doubled up and fell sideways into a rusty bird cage. He didn't move. We went to him. He was unconscious but breathing evenly.

I looked at Weatherly. "You could have killed him."

"Yes."

"What do we do with him now?" Dad asked softly.

The professor didn't answer for a moment, then looked up. "The closet in the upstairs hall has a strong lock on it."

So we wrestled Gant down the steep, narrow stairs and locked him in the empty closet. The lock didn't seem to me any stronger than any of the others, but it worked and wasn't loose. The door opened outward, but there wasn't enough room for Gant to get much of a run at battering it down. If he tried, we would hear him. We propped a chair under the knob just in case and stood there looking at each other.

"Now what?" Poe finally said, plucking stray cobwebs from the hair on his chest.

"Everyone should go back to bed. There's nothing more to be done," the professor said.

Dad brushed dust from his robe. "How long do you plan to wait before you attempt to send your monster back where it came from?"

Weatherly glanced at me, then looked morosely at Dad. "I don't know," he sighed. "Tomorrow, in the daylight, after everyone's rested . . . I don't know." He glanced at me again. "We must make sure everything is right. I doubt if we'll have a second chance." He looked at the floor, then back at Dad. "I'm terribly sorry all of you were involved in this, Mr. Henderson. Mr. McNeal. Terribly sorry." He turned and walked slowly toward the stairs.

"Claire and Linda will be very curious about all this commotion," Dad observed.

"Don't tell Linda until in the morning . . . about Jud," Poe said in a strained voice. "She needs sleep."

"Ann has already satisfied their curiosity," I explained.

We moved Jud's body downstairs to the dining room and covered it with a sheet. None of us could think of anything else to do. Then we went back to bed.

I don't know how long I'd been asleep. I'm not at my most lucid when suddenly awakened. I found myself sitting in the middle of the bed wondering what woke me. Then I knew.

I ran into the hall, barefooted and in my underwear. The closet door was wide open. I never found out how Gant got it open without waking someone. I should have known his determination wouldn't have been dampened by a simple locked door.

I burst into Ann's room without slowing and skidded to a halt. Gant had his arm around her throat so she couldn't cry out. They stood near the foot of the bed. Ann was fighting him, but he was too strong for her. He had gone back to the attic for the knife and held it at her breast. His face and hands looked like raw hamburger. He didn't even look at me, though I imagine he could barely see. His good eye was almost swollen shut. But he was lost in some fantasy of his own, and I thought I could detect an expression of rapture on his swollen face. He wasn't holding Ann as a shield or a hostage, but as a sacrifice.

I stood petrified in the middle of the room as he drew back the knife. My face contorted in rage and hate and I screamed a silent mental scream. I don't know exactly what I did, and I've never tried to repeat it. I drew on something I hope never emerges again.

My mind raged at Gant, blasted him with primal hate. Synapses opened like floodgates. The knife froze in the air. My fingernails dug into my palms. My body trembled uncontrollably. Sweat popped out on my face. My eyes locked on his. The arm around Ann's neck fell away. The knife slipped from his upraised hand. He took a step backward, staring at me uncomprehendingly with his red slit of an eye, his mouth slack. Ann stumbled away from him and got behind me.

I didn't stop because Ann was free. The vision of the knife buried in her breast was too vivid. I could have rationalized it as the only way, but I wasn't thinking at the time, only hating.

Gant backed against the wall, but his legs kept moving, trying to get him farther away. His head jerked back and forth, as if he wanted to loosen something clinging to his face. He put his red, puffy hands over his ears and breathed through his mouth. A low moan began deep in his throat. The moan grew slowly in volume and pitch until it was a shrill keening, ending only when his lungs were empty.

I hammered at the bright mirror surrounding him, beat at it, battered against it until it shattered, and I plunged through into his mind.

I thought I screamed, but Ann said later it was a whimper.

I threw up my shields and fought my way out, ripping and tearing, clawing my way free, slashing through the bright chaos and blinding disorder of Gant's mind. As I broke free, I felt his mind dim and go black.

I felt like jelly and slumped to my knees. I couldn't get my breath. My arms hung limp and immovable. Gant was in a crumpled heap against the wall. Ann was beside me, kneeling beside me, her arms around me, feeling me.

A heartbeat began.

Oh, Ben.

Yes. My God! Do you know what I did?

I felt it. Part of it reflected off his shield.

Are you all right? Did he hurt you?

No. I was only frightened. You came.

We can do it now.

No. Not now. Later.

Yes.

The heartbeat continued.

They're all still asleep.

Yes. I never thought it could be so . . .

I know. I know.

I keep forgetting. Ann . . .

I know. Don't be sad.

We've lost something. But we've gained more, so very much more.

The heartbeat ended.

I put my arm around her. She leaned her head against mine and we went to my room. I closed the door behind me and leaned against it, looking at her. She stepped toward me. I met her halfway. We kissed, melded in mind and body. We undressed and moved to the bed, touching and loving. It wasn't only physical love, but I wasn't reading her. It was no longer necessary.

I was me.

I was Ann.

We were us.

When the sun came up we got out of bed and dressed. I went to my parents' room. Ann went to Poe and Linda's. "Dad. Mom," we said. "Poe. Linda," we said. "Wake up. Get dressed and ready to leave. Pack everything and go out on the porch."

"Ben?" Mom said.

"Ann?" Linda said.

"Everything's okay," we said. "We're ready to help the professor get rid of his monster. Hurry."

Ann and I met in the hall and went downstairs. Professor Weatherly was asleep on the couch, tired and gray, slipping into despair.

"Professor," we said with my voice.

"What?" He sat up suddenly, confused. "Oh. Ben. Is it morning?"

"Yes."

"We're ready," the Ann part of me said.

"What?" He stood up, rubbing his eyes.

"We're ready to help you exorcise your monster."

He looked at us. "Something has happened."

"Yes. Ann and I are telepathically linked. It's permanent."

"Describe it to me."

"I'm not sure I can. I know everything Ben's thinking; I remember; I feel everything he feels."

"But there's more than that," I said. "I'm both of us and we're one of us. We're . . . well, essentially we're one person in two bodies. Yet we still retain our separate egos. Perhaps a better explanation would be we're two people cohabiting two bodies. I don't know how it would be with two men, or two women, but with us, it's . . . it's love."

"Yes," he whispered. "Yes. It would have to be, wouldn't it? Total love or . . . total loathing. There could be no other way."

"There's no way to really know what it's like without

experiencing it," Ann said. "People who know only physical love are missing so much." We grinned. "Though, I guess there is something faintly masturbatory about it."

"This is absolutely marvelous." He beamed like a child on Christmas morning. "Will you allow me to study this further?"

We smiled at him. "Of course, Professor," I said. "As soon as the others are ready to leave, we can contact your monster. Your mother will not leave. Mr. Gant is dead."

"Dead?" He blinked.

"I killed him," I said. I locked my muscles to stop the trembling I could feel about to begin. "I willed him dead and he died," I said numbly.

Ann put her hand on my shoulder. "We're ready," she said. Vocalizing was slow and clumsy, but it was an old habit.

"Wait here," I told him, and went to the entry hall. They came down the stairs with their suitcases and uncertain expressions, Linda crying, but trying to stop. Poe had told her about Jud. I herded them unresisting onto the porch. Mom and Dad turned and looked at me, frightened. I smiled. "Don't worry," I said. Tannie peeked back at me, saucer-eyed and solemn. I winked at her. She grinned and went on out. I closed the door and went back to the parlor.

"Are you ready?"

"Yes." Weatherly nodded.

"I hope what you find out justifies everything, Professor." We concentrated. A brilliant flash. A sheet of energy swirled around us, held away by the professor, and died out. "Take it easy," I said softly, "take it easy. It's almost insane with fright."

We touched that alien mind. Not entered, only touched. We would have been lost if we had entered. Its alienness was indescribable. There was no point of reference to human thought. We stared in awe at its great shining immature mind. Its alienness made details, even large details, impossible to grasp; but basic emotions, which must be common to all intelligent life, were clear to read. It was aware of our minds, but did not fear them. It feared only what was alien to *it*: Weatherly's *physical* assault.

A smile came involuntarily to our lips. "I'll be damned," I said aloud. "Do you know what we've got, Professor? It's a . . . a baby, if that's the right word. Its memory goes back millions, billions of years; so far it can't remember its origin, but it knows it's immature. The reason it's never left this house is that it's basically a frightened child. It wants only to go home. Send it back, Professor, while I try to keep it calm."

Another flash and another swirl of energy. "It's too frightened," I said anxiously. "I'm having trouble. It wants to go home more than anything, but you'll have to force it. It's irrational with fear. It's been here only a moment by its time scale."

Ann left to get the others to the cars, away from the house. I waited until they were at a safe distance.

"Now. Force it, Professor."

Energy whirled around us like a tornado. The walls, the ceilings, the floors, the furniture, all were burning fiercely, except for the bubble in which we stood.

Weatherly opened a path through the inferno, a path from us to the door. "Go with the others, Ben," he said. I started to protest, but he shut me up. "You can do just as much from outside as you can in here. And I can do more if I don't have you to worry about."

He was right. I had no protection from the thing's physical energy, energy which I suspected was manifesting itself physically because it was *here*, not where it came from. I ran through the tunnel he opened and turned at the door. The tunnel closed and I couldn't see him anymore.

I hurried down the hill to the others, still in contact with the professor's monster. The just-risen sun gleamed on the still-damp house, turning the weathered gray to copper, but flames poured from the parlor windows. Smoke billowed from other openings, the gray clouds also gilded by the sun.

Flames suddenly spurted from under the eaves. The fire had gotten upstairs. Energy popped like lightning bolts.

All this I saw with my eyes and heard with my ears. What I saw and heard with my mind was different.

I caught a thought from the professor's mother but shut it out quickly, unable to bear it. The monster threshed in the professor's grip, frightened out of its mind, screaming pitifully.

I watched Professor Weatherly in the parlor but not with my eyes. He stood in a clear island surrounded by raging flames and energy. It began. The inferno cycloned away on one side of him and a tunnel opened, an endless, gleaming tunnel. He stood still, hunched in concentration.

I knew, suddenly, what was about to happen, but the professor was caught completely by surprise. There was nothing I could do to help him. I slammed shields around Ann. She jerked out of her trance and looked wildly about. She screamed at me, "No! Ben! Don't block me out!"

More energy popped. Everyone's clothing clung to their skin. I could feel my hair standing up, charged with static electricity. Helplessly I watched the professor force his monster into the tunnel.

He hadn't moved. He stood before the tunnel, surrounded by an inferno, hunched in concentration. Then, gradually, slowly, his body smudged outward, toward the tunnel. He felt it. He looked up. He strained away from the tunnel, held out his arms, warding it away. The distortion, the stretching outward, continued. His arms were caught in it, extending to half again their former length, blurring toward the tunnel.

Then a particle of his little finger broke away and streamed down the tunnel like a shooting star. More particles broke free. The tunnel was filled with shooting stars, streaking to infinity.

I threw up my shield. Weatherly's terror was too great. But, in that last split-second, I saw a comet roar away down the tunnel, and he was gone. The tunnel was closing.

I was aware of physical sensations only. I stood swaying, trying to keep from toppling over. Ann threw her arms around me. Dad put his hand on the back of my neck, not saying anything. I dropped the shields. Ann and I were one again.

"He did it," I said on an exhaustion high. "It's gone home. He sent it back. But it dragged him back with it. I was with him for a moment."

The energy was gone but the fire wasn't. The old wood of the house burned ferociously. Dad propelled us away, to the bottom of the hill, where the others waited numbly. We stood for a long time, saying nothing, watching the house burn.

Tannie had come to me and stood watching the house with her arm clutching my thigh. I had my arm on her shoulder. "What about you, Ann?" Dad asked.

"With me," I said.

"Yes." She smiled.

Tannie peeked around me, staring at Ann. Ann smiled at her and winked the same way I would. Tannie grinned like a supernova. She launched herself at Ann and hugged her.

The sheriff's car pulled up as we were about to leave. He was a nice person named Robin Walker. We told him a simplified version of what happened, a version he would believe. Ann and I made sure he believed it.

Dad backed the station wagon out of the ditch. I got in the yellow VW with Ann, and we went on to Wichita.

FREE DIRT

CHARLES BEAUMONT

Charles Beaumont is the pseudonym of story and scriptwriter Charles Nutt (1929–1967), who produced a prodigious number of science fiction and horror short stories during his career in addition to scripting such films as *The Seven Faces of Dr. Lao* (1964). A great many of his stories appeared in *F & SF* originally, and from 1955–1956 he collaborated with Chad Oliver to produce the Claude Adams series for *F & SF*. His stories often combined humor with horror, a recipe that left his readers laughing nervously while glancing over their shoulders. "Free Dirt" is one such story. It is the tale of Mr. Aorta, a man who never learned that there's "no such thing as a free lunch."

No fowl had ever looked so posthumous. Its bones lay stacked to one side of the plate like kindling: white, dry, and naked in the soft light of the restaurant. Bones only, with every shard and filament of meat stripped methodically off. Otherwise, the plate was a vast glistening plain.

The other, smaller dishes and bowls were equally virginal. They shone fiercely against one another. And all a pale cream color fixed upon the snowywhite of a tablecloth unstained by gravies and unspotted by coffee and free from the stigmata of bread crumbs, cigarette ash, and fingernail lint.

Only the dead fowl's bones and the stippled traceries of hardened red gelatin clinging timidly to the bottom of a dessert cup gave evidence that these ruins had once been a magnificent six-course dinner.

Mr. Aorta, not a small man, permitted a mild belch, folded the newspaper he had found on the chair, inspected his vest for food leavings, and then made his way briskly to the cashier.

The old woman glanced at his check.

"Yes, sir," she said.

"All righty," Mr. Aorta said, and removed from his hip pocket a large black wallet. He opened it casually, whistling "The Seven Joys of Mary" through the space provided by his two front teeth.

The melody stopped abruptly. Mr. Aorta looked concerned. He peered into his wallet, then began removing things; presently its entire contents was spread out.

He frowned.

"What seems to be the difficulty, sir?"

"Oh, no difficulty," the fat man said, "exactly." Though the wallet was manifestly empty, he flapped its sides apart, held it upside down, and continued to shake it, suggesting the picture of a hydrophobic bat suddenly seized in midair.

Mr. Aorta smiled a weak, harassed smile and proceeded to empty all of his fourteen separate pockets. In time the counter was piled high with miscellany.

"Well!" he said impatiently. "What nonsense! What bother! Do you know what's happened? My wife's gone off and forgotten to leave me any change! Heigh-ho, well, ah— my name is James Brockelhurst: I'm with the Pliofilm Corporation: I generally don't eat out, and—here, no, I insist. This is embarrassing for you as well as for myself. I *insist* upon leaving my card. If you will retain it, I shall return tomorrow evening at this time and reimburse you."

Mr. Aorta shoved the pasteboard into the cashier's hands, shook his head, shoveled the residue back into his pockets, and, plucking a toothpick from a box, left the restaurant.

He was quite pleased with himself—an invariable reaction to the acquisition of something for nothing in return. It had all gone smoothly, and what a delightful meal!

He strolled in the direction of the streetcar stop, casting occasional licentious glances at undressed mannequins in department store windows.

The prolonged fumbling for his car token worked as efficiently as ever. (Get in the middle of the crowd, look bewildered, inconspicuous, search your pockets earnestly, the while edging from the vision of the conductor—then, take a far seat and read a newspaper.) In four years' traveling time, Mr. Aorta computed he had saved a total of $211.20.

The electric's ancient list did not jar his warm feeling of serenity. He studied the amusements briefly, then went to work on the current puzzle, whose prize ran into the thousands. Thousands of dollars, actually for nothing. Something for nothing. Mr. Aorta loved puzzles.

But the fine print made reading impossible.

Mr. Aorta glanced at the elderly woman standing near his seat; then, because the woman's eyes were full of tired pleading and insinuation, he refocused out the wire cross-hatch windows.

What he saw caused his heart to throb. The section of town was one he passed every day, so it was a wonder he'd not noticed it before—though generally there was little prov-

ocation to sight-see on what was irreverently called Death
Row—a dreary round of mortuaries, columbariums, cre-
matories, and the like, all crowded into a five-block area.

He yanked the stop signal, hurried to the rear of the
streetcar, and depressed the exit plate. In a few moments
he had walked to what he'd seen.

It was a sign, artlessly lettered though spelled correctly
enough. It was not new, for the white paint had swollen
and cracked and the rusted nails had dripped trails of dirty
orange over the face of it.

The sign read:

> FREE DIRT
> APPLY WITHIN
> LILYVALE CEMETERY

and was posted upon the moldering green of a woodboard
wall.

Now Mr. Aorta felt a familiar sensation come over him.
It happened whenever he encountered the word "free"—a
magic word that did strange and wonderful things to his
metabolism.

Free. What is the meaning, the *essence* of free? Why,
something for nothing. And, as has been pointed out, to
get something for nothing was Mr. Aorta's chiefest pleasure
in this mortal life.

The fact that it was dirt which was being offered *free* did
not oppress him. He seldom gave more than fleeting thought
to these things; for, he reasoned, nothing is without its use.

The other, subtler circumstances surrounding the sign
scarcely occurred to him: why the dirt was being offered,
where free dirt in a cemetery would logically come from,
et cetera. In this connection he considered only the probable
richness of the soil.

Mr. Aorta's solitary hesitation encircled such problems
as: Was this offer an honest one, without strings whereby
he would have to buy something? Was there a limit on how

much he could take home? If not, what would be the best method of transporting it?

Petty problems: all solvable.

Mr. Aorta did something inwardly that resembled a smile, looked about, and finally located the entrance to the Lilyvale Cemetery.

These desolate grounds, which had accommodated in turn a twine factory, an upholstering firm, and an outlet for ladies' shoes, now lay swathed in a miasmic vapor—accreditable, in the absence of nearby bogs, to a profusion of windward smokestacks. The blistered hummocks, peaked with crosses, slabs, and stones, loomed gray and sad in the gloaming: withal, a place purely delightful to describe, and a pity it cannot be—for how it looked there that evening had little to do with the fat man and what was eventually to become of him.

Important only that it was a place full of dead people on their backs underground, moldering and moldered.

Mr. Aorta hurried because he despised to waste, along with everything else, time. It was not long before he had encountered the proper party and had this conversation:

"I understand you're offering free dirt."

"Yes."

"How much may one have?"

"Much as you want."

"On what days?"

"Any days—and there'll always be some fresh."

Mr. Aorta sighed in the manner of one who has just acquired a lifetime inheritance or a measured checking account. He then made an appointment for the following Saturday and went home to ruminate agreeable ruminations.

At a quarter past nine that night he hit upon an excellent use to which the dirt might be put.

His backyard, an ocher waste, lay chunked and dry, a

barren stretch repulsive to all but the grossest weeds. A tree had once flourished there, in better days, a haven for suburbanite birds; but then the birds disappeared for no good reason except that this is when Mr. Aorta moved into the house, and the tree became an ugly naked thing.

No children played in this yard.

Mr. Aorta was intrigued. Who could say, perhaps something might be made to grow! He had long ago written an enterprising firm for free samples of seeds and received enough to feed an army. But the first experiments had shriveled into hard useless pips, and seized by lassitude, Mr. Aorta had shelved the project. Now . . .

A neighbor named Joseph William Santucci permitted himself to be intimidated. He lent his old Reo truck, and after a few hours the first load of dirt had arrived and been shoveled into a tidy mound. It looked beautiful to Mr. Aorta, whose passion overcompensated for his weariness with the task. The second load followed, and the third, and the fourth, and it was dark as a coalbin out when the very last was dumped.

Mr. Aorta returned the truck and fell into an exhausted, though not unpleasant, sleep.

The next day was heralded by the distant clangor of church bells and the *chink-chink* of Mr. Aorta's spade, leveling the displaced graveyard soil, distributing it and grinding it in with the crusty earth. It had a continental look, this new dirt: swarthy, it seemed, black and saturnine—not at all dry, though the sun was already quite hot.

Soon the greater portion of the yard was covered, and Mr. Aorta returned to his sitting room.

He turned on the radio in time to identify a popular song, marked his discovery on a postcard, and mailed this away, confident that he would receive either a toaster or a set of nylon hose for his trouble.

Then he wrapped four bundles containing, respectively, a can of vitamin capsules, half of them gone; a half-tin of coffee; a half-full bottle of spot remover; and a box of soap flakes with most of the soap flakes missing. These he mailed, each with a note curtly expressing his total dissatisfaction, to the companies that had offered them to him on a money-back guarantee.

Now it was dinnertime, and Mr. Aorta beamed in anticipation. He sat down to a meal of sundry delicacies such as anchovies, sardines, mushrooms, caviar, olives, and pearl onions. It was not, however, that he enjoyed this type of food for any esthetic reasons, only that it had all come in packages small enough to be slipped into one's pocket without attracting the attention of busy grocers.

Mr. Aorta cleaned his plates so thoroughly, no cat would care to lick them; the empty tins also looked new and bright: even their lids gleamed iridescently.

Mr. Aorta glanced at his checkbook balance, grinned indecently, and went to look out the back window. (He was not married, so he felt no urge to lie down after dinner.)

The moon was cold upon the yard. Its rays passed over the high fence Mr. Aorta had constructed from free rocks and splashed moodily onto the now-black earth.

Mr. Aorta thought a bit, put away his checkbook, and got out the boxes containing the garden seeds.

They were good as new.

Joseph William Santucci's truck was in use every Saturday thereafter for five weeks. This good man watched curiously as his neighbor returned each time with more dirt and yet more, and he made several remarks to his wife about the oddness of it all, but she could not bear even to talk about Mr. Aorta.

"He's robbed us blind!" she said. "Look! He wears your old clothes, he uses my sugar and spices, and borrows everything else he can think of! Borrows, did I say? I mean steals. For years! I have not seen the man pay for a thing yet! Where does he work, he makes so little money?"

Neither Mr. nor Mrs. Santucci knew that Mr. Aorta's daily labors involved sitting on the sidewalk downtown, with dark glasses on and a battered tin cup in front of him. They'd both passed him several times, though, and given him pennies, both unable to penetrate the clever disguise. It was all kept, the disguise, in a free locker at the railroad terminal.

"Here he comes again, that loony!" Mrs. Santucci wailed.

Soon it was time to plant the seeds, and Mr. Aorta went about this with ponderous precision, after having consulted numerous books at the library. Neat rows of summer squash were sown in the richly dark soil; and peas, corn, beans, onions, beets, rhubarb, asparagus, watercress, and much more, actually. When the rows were filled and Mr. Aorta was stuck with extra packs, he smiled and dispersed strawberry seeds and watermelon seeds and seeds without clear description. Shortly the paper packages were all empty.

A few days passed and it was getting time to go to the cemetery again for a fresh load, when Mr. Aorta noticed an odd thing.

The dark ground had begun to yield to tiny eruptions. Closer inspection revealed that things had begun to grow in the soil.

Now, Mr. Aorta knew very little about gardening, when you got right down to it. He thought it strange, of course, but he was not alarmed. He saw things growing; that was the important point. Things that would become food.

Praising his weltanschauung, he hurried to Lilyvale, and there received a singular disappointment: Not many people had died lately. There was scant dirt to be had, hardly one truckful.

Ah, well, he thought, things are bound to pick up over the holidays; and he took home what there was.

Its addition marked the improvement of the garden's growth. Shoots and buds came higher, and the expanse was far less bleak.

He could not contain himself until the next Saturday, for obviously this dirt was acting as some sort of fertilizer on his plants—the free food called out for more.

But the next Saturday came a cropper. Not even a shovel's load. And the garden was beginning to desiccate. . . .

Mr. Aorta's startling decision came as a result of trying all kinds of new dirt and fertilizers of every imaginable description. Nothing worked. His garden, which had promised a full bounty of edibles, had sunk to new lows: It was almost back to its original state. And this Mr. Aorta could not abide, for he had put in considerable labor on the project and this labor must not be wasted. It had deeply affected his other enterprises.

So, with the caution born of desperation, he entered the quiet gray place with the tombstones one night, located freshly dug but unoccupied graves, and added to their six-foot depth yet another foot. It was not noticeable to anyone who was not looking for such a discrepancy.

No need to mention the many trips involved: It is enough to say that in time Mr. Santucci's truck, parked a block away, was a quarter filled.

The following morning saw a rebirth in the garden.

And so it went. When dirt was to be had, Mr. Aorta was obliged; when it was not, well, it wasn't missed. And the garden kept growing and growing, until—

As if overnight, everything opened up! Where so short a time past had been a parched little prairie was now a multifloral, multivegetable paradise. Corn bulged yellow from its spiny green husks; peas were brilliant green in their half-split pods, and all the other wonderful foodstuffs glowed full rich with life and showcase vigor. Rows and rows of them.

Mr. Aorta was almost felled by enthusiasm.

A liver for the moment and an idiot in the art of canning, he knew what he had to do.

It took a while to systematically gather up the morsels; but with patience, he at last had the garden stripped clean of all but weeds and leaves and other unedibles.

He cleaned. He peeled. He stringed. He cooked. He boiled. He took all the good free food and piled it geometrically on tables and chairs and continued with this until it was all ready to be eaten.

Then he began. Starting with the asparagus—he had decided to do it in alphabetical order—he ate and ate clear through beets and celery and parsley and rhubarb, paused there for a drink of water, and went on eating, being careful not to waste a jot, until he came to watercress. By this time his stomach was twisting painfully, but it was a sweet pain, so he took a deep breath and, by chewing slowly, did away with the final vestigial bit of food.

The plates sparkled white, like a series of bloated snow-flakes. It was all gone.

Mr. Aorta felt an almost sexual satisfaction, by which is meant he had had enough for now. He couldn't even belch.

Happy thoughts assailed his mind, as follows: His two greatest passions had been fulfilled: life's meaning acted out symbolically like a condensed Everyman. These two things only are what this man thought of.

He chanced to look out the window.

What he saw was a speck of bright in the middle of blackness. Small, somewhere at the end of the garden—faint yet distinct.

With the effort of a brontosaurus emerging from a tar pit Mr. Aorta rose from his chair, walked to the door, and went out into his emasculated garden. He lumbered past dangling grotesqueries formed by shucks and husks and vines.

The speck seemed to have disappeared, and he looked carefully in all directions, slitting his eyes, trying to get accustomed to the moonlight.

Then he saw it. A white-fronded thing, a plant, perhaps only a flower; but there, certainly, and all that was left.

Mr. Aorta was surprised to see that it was located at the bottom of a shallow declivity very near the dead tree. He couldn't remember how a hole could have got dug in his garden, but there were always neighborhood kids and their pranks. A lucky thing he'd grabbed the food when he did!

Mr. Aorta leaned over the edge of the small pit and

reached down his hand toward the shining plant. It resisted his touch somehow. He leaned farther over and yet a little farther, and still he couldn't lay fingers on the thing.

Mr. Aorta was not an agile man. However, with the intensity of a painter trying to cover one last tiny spot awkwardly placed, he leaned just a mite farther and *plosh!* he'd toppled over the edge and landed with a peculiarly subaqueous thud. A ridiculous damned bother—now he'd have to make a fool of himself clambering out again. But, the plant . . . He searched the floor of the pit, and searched it, and no plant could be found. Then he looked up and was appalled by two things: Number one, the pit had been deeper than he'd thought; Number two, the plant was waving in the wind above him, on the rim he had so recently occupied.

The pains in Mr. Aorta's stomach got progressively worse. Movement increased the pains. He began to feel an overwhelming pressure in his ribs.

It was at the moment of his discovery that the top of the hole was up beyond his reach that he saw the white plant in full moonglow. It looked rather like a hand, a big human hand, waxy and stiff and attached to the earth. The wind hit it, and it moved slightly, causing a rain of dirt pellets to fall upon Mr. Aorta's face.

He thought a moment, judged the whole situation, and began to climb. But the pains were too much and he fell, writhing a bit.

The wind came again and more dirt was scattered down into the hole: Soon the strange plant was being pushed to and fro against the soil, and the dirt fell more and more heavily. More and more. More heavily and more heavily.

Mr. Aorta, who had never up to this point found occasion to scream, screamed. It was quite successful, despite the fact that no one heard it.

Mr. and Mrs. Joseph William Santucci found Mr. Aorta. He was lying on the floor in front of several tables. On the tables were many plates. The plates on the tables were clean and shining.

His stomach was distended past burst belt buckle, popped buttons, and forced zipper. It was not unlike the image of a great white whale rising from placid forlorn waters.

"Ate hisself to death," Mrs. Santucci said in the manner of the concluding line of a complex joke.

Mr. Santucci reached down and plucked a tiny ball of soil from the fat man's dead lips. He studied it. And an idea came to him. . . .

He tried to get rid of the idea, but when the doctors found Mr. Aorta's stomach to contain many pounds of dirt—and nothing else—Mr. Santucci slept badly for almost a week.

They carried Mr. Aorta's body through the weedy but otherwise empty and desolate backyard, past the mournful dead tree and the rock fence.

And then they laid him to rest in a place with a moldering green woodboard wall: The wall had a little sign nailed to it, artlessly lettered though spelled correctly enough.

And the wind blew absolutely Free.

RISING WATERS

PATRICIA FERRARA

"Rising Waters" was Patricia Ferrara's first fantasy publication, in the July 1987 issue of *F & SF,* and rarely do we encounter such polish and elegance in a first story. Ms. Ferrara was born in Attleboro, Massachusetts, within spitting distance of H. P. Lovecraft's grave. After taking a doctoral degree in literature at Yale, she moved to Atlanta, where she now teaches English and film at Georgia State University. "Rising Waters" is a ghostly tale about strange doings on a southern river. It is also the reason, Ms. Ferrara informed us, that she swims only in very small pools which have lifeguards on duty.

A nd eventually what had been the flood plain of the river became part of the river itself, as age changed the Ohana from a thin, angry sluice into a flat ribbon that rippled in the sunlight, still as a lake. But Rory had not yet been born when his grandparents had deserted their house by the old riverbank and moved far up into the gentle hills to a broad swell of land safe from the runoff of a hundred snowy winters. To him, the river existed with the same reliable constancy as the school bus. Every morning in the summer he woke up to the river; and every night he slept beside it, thinking it of only average interest.

Mostly he wondered how he could get a ride into town to play the video games at the supermarket. Space Invaders had been his favorite, and he was startled when, in rapid succession, a Pac-Man game displaced it, and then a Millipede game. The constant change was irritating, because his quarter bought more time on a familiar game. His wrist had never gotten the trick of slipping the gobbling button around the corners, and then the bouncy spiders had proved more than he could handle. The two quarters Grandma allotted per trip bought maybe five minutes of Millipede. Grandma took him to the supermarket only once a week to help with the groceries, unless she forgot something; and since she never forgot anything, he never got any better at the games. Once they had to go back because the milk was sour, and he had to stand with her at the manager's high window while she talked bitterly about out-of-state milk and a sweet-tempered cow that had been dead and gone for fifty years. She'd held on to his arm tightly, grasping at something other than her grandson. Afterward she wouldn't let him play even one game, although he'd come all that way with her. She wanted to go straight home, and she drove there silently, her lips forming a mushy rosebud as she pouted and trembled.

Then the great boiling heat of August came, and the water of the river retreated from its banks, leaving several feet of unpleasantly sharp stones embedded in dank clay between the clipped grass and the flood. Then he was glad to be near the river. It was something to do to go down to the riverbank with his lunch in a box and spend the day cooling off in the water and getting hot in the sun. The process tired him out pretty much if he stayed until dinnertime, and the sweltering heat kept it from being boring.

He was lying on the bank one day in August, with a whiff of evening breeze reminding him that it was almost time to go in for dinner. And while he was lying there, thinking about nothing in particular, a peculiar noise drew his attention to the river. The river had never made a noise like that before. He looked west, his hands cupped over his eyes against the sun, and saw that a dark triangular streak lay motionless far out on the waves, jutting hard-edged above the line of the water, but blurry where it merged into the shining ripples. He stood up to get a closer look, but it remained a sharp outline, its details lost in the backlight of the round red sun directly behind it. He stared at it until the setting sun made his eyes water and slit closed; in the meantime, he lost track of the vitally important timing that would land him at the dinner table just as the food came onto it. His grandma was angry with him when he finally came home, and he ate his dinner lukewarm and alone.

The thing was gone when he came back the next day. Yet it had been so odd, not like a log, but geometric, like something someone had made. He let it pass until, a few days later, he flopped down on his towel, fairly winded from a swim, and breathed in great whooshes of air for a few minutes before turning over. As he sighed and vainly rolled west against the glare of the sun, the dark streak reemerged so suddenly that he jumped. The sun was just past meridian, and he could see the object clearly. It was not a triangle at all, but a quadrangle that sort of tilted in the water, and out of it thrust another flat geometric form at an angle to the first. He brooded on the puzzle for a bit until he noticed two pillars or posts propping up the second plane from beneath. The object was a roof, then, sloping down to the

overhang of a porch. He debated the probability of this guess
being true. He had seen pictures of houses in floods, but
the river was bone-dry. He looked down to check his facts.
The water stood limpid and still, and three feet back from
its banks. And the roof wasn't moving, not even rocking on
the water. After a bit of brooding he concluded that if it
couldn't have floated down the river, then the river must
have uncovered it. The physics of the matter troubled him,
but he dismissed the improbabilities. After all, the thing
was there.

He watched it from the bank for a while longer, wondering what house it was, when he remembered Grandma's
often-repeated story of the old house, and how they had
had to desert it after the last flood had wrecked it, when the
federal government had made one last payment and refused
to insure the place again. No one had ever heard such a
thing, Grandma said. That was always the last line of her
house chant. He had heard it so often, and he had paid so
little attention that the upshot was he defined insurance
vaguely as something no one had ever heard of. But the
appearance of the house in the river made the story interesting, and he pieced odd bits of the tale together from
memory and rolled it over in his mind while he looked.
This might be the house. He wondered whether he should
tell Grandma. But that would mean having to leave it behind while he ran up the hill, and the last time he left the
thing alone, it had gone under.

After a while he struck on the idea that he might swim
out to it. It was a long way out, over half a mile maybe,
but the porch roof was flat enough to serve as a pier. He
could rest once he was out there, and with a safe haven
halfway in the round trip, it was no farther than he had
swum before. And so he plunged in.

The water seemed cooler than it should have been this
time of day; after he'd gotten over the shock of the first swim
of the morning, the river should feel like bathwater. But
this was an adventure, and adventures always made things

seem different. He pushed on through the clear water, stopping now and again to look up and correct his course. The house seemed to get no nearer, not for a long time, and he did not look back to see that nonetheless the shore was getting smaller behind him.

He was far out when his efforts were finally repaid by a better look at the house. As he paused and trod water, he could see the weathered shingles making a shaggy web of the roof, and only a great ragged gap in the grid remained inpenetrably black in the distance. This encouragement had to last him a good while longer, for his neck was aching too much for him to keep on looking as he swam. His breathing was getting uncoordinated, too, and occasionally he choked and snorted out an inadvertent gulp of water. But there was nothing to do; he had to keep on paddling to the resting place on top of the porch. When the water suddenly turned tan and thick with churned-up mud from the river bottom, he stopped and looked up again for the first time in a long time. The house rose up less than twenty feet from where he swam. It seemed to stand higher out of the water now, and he could see the top of a third pillar holding up the porch roof, and the pediment over a doorway that gaped empty beneath.

He swam through the dirty water to grasp the post closest to him, but it was slick with moss, and his hands slipped. His heart thumped fearfully in his ears. He might be too tired to climb up. His enervated fingers scratched at the rotting wood, but it flaked and splintered in his hands. He pushed his feet up around the pillar, and shimmied and hopped and scrambled until his belly creased up over the edge of the roof. And there he lay for a moment, exhausted, until a creak and a slight tilt indicated the house was listing, and he pushed himself frantically, spread-eagle, out onto the smooth grid of shingles. The creaking stopped, and he tried to rest. But his heart pounded and his nerves sang, and he could not rest.

He was not familiar with the stink of things long buried coming into the air again. It was not a comfortable smell, and as soon as he could catch his breath, he lifted his head up away from the reeking shingles, slick with mud and fungus. His body was covered with patches of the stuff in front. He tried wiping the smears off his face, away from his nose. But he only complicated the stink with a perpetual itch of red clay that clung to him from the water, and the stink and the itch together exasperated him. If he scratched or wriggled, the house creaked and moved; and when he scraped a foot on the roof to ease the itch, down he stepped, dangling into the attic. He pulled his leg back with the frantic delicacy necessary on thin ice, flattening his body out belly-up on the slimy shingles. The warmth of the sun encouraged the foul odor of the house to spread itself around and made black spots flicker in front of his eyes. He closed the lids over his eyes tightly, but the sun shone through each individual cell, and he risked lifting up a forearm over the sockets. This brought the itch to his eyes, but he kept the cool forearm aloft anyway until the red fire died down behind his eyelids and he could breathe regularly.

When he cautiously removed the arm and blinked, he saw that the sun had gone far west of the meridian. He raised himself up slowly, and eased away from the hole he'd made in the roof. He'd have to start swimming back pretty soon. It was getting late. But the tan pool spread out widely, and he felt a certain revulsion toward jumping through its opaque surface.

His cautious movements again irritated the delicate balance of the house, and he lay back down quickly to soothe it. From inside came a slight scuffling sound and then a thump that made the thin membrane of the roof quiver. The noise was startling, for Rory had assumed the house had been washed clean by the current of the river. But, of course, something could have drifted in through an empty windowframe and rattled around like a fly trying to find its way back out through a screen. The house kept shifting restively despite his stillness as he thought, and he crept carefully over to the end opposite the tilt to appease it.

This maneuver left him only inches from the original hole in the roof, and he could hear quite clearly the rattle and bump as the contents of the house wove from wall to wall. But there was no splashing noise involved, and that was odd. He looked down into the hole, something of his original curiosity rekindling. A sort of drier smell came up, equally as foul as the wet smell outside. He leaned in farther, and still nothing was visible, for little light came in through the two holes in the roof. It looked like some sort of attic or loft.

But he had leaned over too far, and with a faint whoosh the rotten shingles collapsed feebly inward and dropped him gently on the floor. He grabbed immediately upward at the sky-hanging light above him. But after his first lunges failed, he realized that his leaps brought on a chorus of angry squeaks from the house, and he stopped dead until they subsided. It was cold in there, even if he stood in the patches of light, and his teeth chattered as he stood rigidly still from his ankles to his earlobes, and his toes did a little terrified dance on the dry floor. It was dangerous inside, however low the river might be. Something rolled at him from a dark corner, and he jumped, heedless of his movement's effect on the creaking house. As the thing flashed into the sunlight, he recognized it rolling green and white in front of him, and he picked it up. It was a can of peas. It was a new can of peas, with the label dry, the tin ends still shiny. A green giant grinned at him above a heap of perfect green dots. The can was a good bit dented, and the rims were mucky from rolling on soft, rotten wood, but it was only an ordinary can of peas.

His teeth had stopped chattering, although shudders kept seizing his shoulders. He held the can of peas in his hand tightly, for he needed to grip on to something as he struggled to formulate options. The house was teetering constantly now whether he moved or not. He decided that it would be best to go to the lowest part of the sloped roof and poke through the brittle shingles with his hands; and then he would clamber onto the roof and jump off as soon as ever he could, and swim toward shore. His shoulders still ached from the swim out, but it didn't matter; he would make it back. He could float if he had to for a while, and then swim some more. But he had to get started right away. And so he slid his right foot forward like a skater across the floor toward the end of the roof. The floor leaned to follow. Then his left foot slid forward, and a slow, mushy sound squished behind him. He looked back.

There was something else in the corner where the peas came from. The sun threw one great, slanting shaft of light through the biggest hole in the roof, and he could just see a kind of gray mass standing out from the dark wall behind him. But he had no time to explore. He turned to his task again, sliding his feet forward. The gray thing scraped on the planking as the floor tipped under him. The house had bent forward far enough so that he could see the clay water through the gap in the shingles now. He leaned his body toward the opening, keeping his feet still, and one hand clutched at a rafter while the other batted the can of peas at bits of shingles and river ooze. After he'd cleared a hole big enough to jump through, his fingers curled around the rafter gently, and he pulled. It held firm, strong enough to bear his weight. He readied himself to jump. But as he closed his eyes, a vision seized him: he jumped up beautifully, up, out into the water, and the house tumbled in the air and dived after him, turning upside down over him like an empty basket. He forced his mind away from this, opened his eyes, and tossed the can of peas into the river, then clutched at the rafter with both hands. He tried to push the thoughts away, and jerked himself forward to jump; then he pulled back again from the vision of the capsized house, and his little dance of indecision shook the house more, making the gray mass behind him rock and tumble down and then up the floor, down and then up again until the lumpen mass flipped cozily around his legs and came to rest. He froze his fingers onto the rafter and pointed his tightly shut eyes straight up to the sky. His ears rang a bit, and he could hear himself panting. The tangle around his legs was heavy. He tried to move his left leg. It was stuck. He would have to look down to see how to free himself.

The sunlight hit the mass full on as he swiveled one eye down and sideways. A few details confirmed that the thing was human. He swallowed once and said, "He-hello?" There was no answer. He had expected none. He shifted his right foot gently and pushed. The body wobbled, but his left foot was still trapped. He kicked hard, and an arm rolled free from his foot, and for one strangled moment he saw the face before it shot him screaming up through the roof hole.

After the first fit of screams he descended into a whimper. He wanted to jump into the clear water and swim, but the clay pool stretched out for yards in front of him, and the body beneath still entangled him, pulling his legs under the water in his thoughts. He crawled away from the hole to the far end of the porch, away from the sound of her tumbling in the attic.

The face stood between him and his own eyelids if he shut his eyes, between him and the sun and the water if he dared open them. It was a woman's face, smashed in by great round black marks that made swollen crescents all over it. And he laughed hysterically, mixed up a little with wailing, to think she'd got her head smashed in with a can of peas.

He'd have to yell for help; there was nothing else to do, and he bellowed as loud as he could. But his voice was small and cramped with fear, and the yells didn't carry. The shore was very far away, and he could see that his grandparents' house was beginning to be covered with the shadows of the aspen trees in front. He looked up sharply. The sun had slid almost to the horizon while he was inside the attic. It was still bright on the river, but dark would come quickly once the sun was down; the river would soon be a great mirrored sheen by the darkened shore, and then the river itself would grow dark. His grandma must be looking for him. It was past dinnertime, and she knew he was down by the river. His towel would still be there on the bank. He waved his arms, hoping that she could see him backlit by the sun; he cried out a few times more. He couldn't see anyone, just the faint glow of the white house, and the vivid yellow-green of the trees and grass where the sun hit, and the shadows growing more purple behind them.

But there were police. They had motorboats; even in the dark he would be able to hear them, see their lights. Yet the shifting house might not wait. It creaked constantly now, no matter what. He tried to think of swimming again; but he couldn't, he just couldn't. He might swim round and round in circles in the dark, unable to see the shore, with the body drifting after him, waiting to ensnare his legs with its dead arms.

Soon the sun was a thin red rim glowing behind the hills, and the river was opaque and shining. He looked around for the last time, he knew, for a long time. And in the distance he saw something: a boat perhaps, for it was moving. He yelled at it, his voice hoarse from the water and the stink. It was coming swiftly, purposefully downriver toward the house, more swiftly than the current would carry it. He yelled again and waved his arms. There was more than one. Five or six specks emerged; they were boats, surely. He stopped yelling for a moment, thinking he would hear a reply; but there was no response, not even a cry muffled by the wind, nor any sound of motors or paddles lapping in the water. The boats came silently toward him, closer and closer, and his voice died in his throat. They carried no flashlights. And as they grew larger, a faint glimmer of light showed that the shallow boats streaked forward in their own widening pool of clay-colored water, and the breeze brought him the penetrating sour smell of something long buried as the house gently shifted, and knelt into the water like a trained horse bowing to its rider.

THE NIGHT OF THE TIGER

STEPHEN KING

A native of Maine, Stephen King is currently the world's best-selling author, and could be thought of as the heavyweight champion of the modern horror story. He skillfully spars with conventional horror motifs and figures and also explores more science-fictional topics such as telekinesis and telepathy. His stories, novels, and movies are gripping, mordant masterpieces with very real, very believable characters. In many of his tales—including "The Night of the Tiger"—Stephen King realistically portrays "down-home" folks suddenly confronted with situations that turn and twist to show their darker sides. "The Night of the Tiger" tells of such a dark time; it is a haunting tale of what happened at Farnum and Williams' All-American 3-Ring Circus and Side Show one stormy night.

I first saw Mr. Legere when the circus swung through Steubenville, but I'd been with the show for only two weeks; he might have been making his irregular visits indefinitely. No one much wanted to talk about Mr. Legere, not even that last night when it seemed that the world was coming to an end—the night that Mr. Indrasil disappeared.

But if I'm going to tell it to you from the beginning, I should start by saying that I'm Eddie Johnston, and I was born and raised in Sauk City. Went to school there, had my first girl there, and worked in Mr. Lillie's five-and-dime there for a while after I graduated from high school. That was a few years back . . . more than I like to count, sometimes. Not that Sauk City's such a bad place; hot, lazy summer nights sitting on the front porch is all right for some folks, but it just seemed to *itch* me, like sitting in the same chair too long. So I quit the five-and-dime and joined Farnum & Williams' All-American 3-Ring Circus and Side Show. I did it in a moment of giddiness when the calliope music kind of fogged my judgment, I guess.

So I became a roustabout, helping put up tents and take them down, spreading sawdust, cleaning cages, and sometimes selling cotton candy when the regular salesman had to go away and bark for Chips Baily, who had malaria and sometimes had to go someplace far away and holler. Mostly things that kids do for free passes—things I used to do when I was a kid. But times change. They don't seem to come around like they used to.

We swung through Illinois and Indiana that hot summer, and the crowds were good and everyone was happy. Everyone except Mr. Indrasil. Mr. Indrasil was never happy. He was the lion tamer, and he looked like old pictures I've seen of Rudolph Valentino. He was tall, with handsome, arrogant features and a shock of wild black hair. And strange, mad eyes—the maddest eyes I've ever seen. He was silent most of the time; two syllables from Mr. Indrasil was a sermon. All the circus people kept a mental as well as a physical distance, because his rages were legend. There was a whispered story about coffee spilled on his hands after a particularly difficult performance and a murder that was almost done to a young roustabout before Mr. Indrasil could be hauled off him. I don't know about that. I do know that I grew to fear him worse than I had cold-eyed Mr. Edmont, my high school principal, Mr. Lillie, or even my father, who was capable of cold dressing-downs that would leave the recipient quivering with shame and dismay.

When I cleaned the big cats' cages, they were always spotless. The memory of the few times I had the vituperative wrath of Mr. Indrasil called down on me still has the power to turn my knees watery in retrospect.

Mostly it was his eyes—large and dark and totally blank. The eyes, and the feeling that a man capable of controlling seven watchful cats in a small cage must be part savage himself.

And the only two things he was afraid of were Mr. Legere and the circus's one tiger, a huge beast called Green Terror.

As I said, I first saw Mr. Legere in Steubenville, and he was staring into Green Terror's cage as if the tiger knew all the secrets of life and death.

He was lean, dark, quiet. His deep, recessed eyes held an expression of pain and brooding violence in their green-flecked depths, and his hands were always crossed behind his back as he stared moodily in at the tiger.

Green Terror was a beast to be stared at. He was a huge, beautiful specimen with a flawless striped coat, emerald eyes, and heavy fangs like ivory spikes. His roars usually filled the circus grounds—fierce, angry, and utterly savage. He seemed to scream defiance and frustration at the whole world.

Chips Baily, who had been with Farnum & Williams since Lord knew when, told me that Mr. Indrasil used to use Green Terror in his act, until one night when the tiger leapt suddenly from its perch and almost ripped his head from his shoulders before he could get out of the cage. I noticed that Mr. Indrasil always wore his hair long down the back of his neck.

I can still remember the tableau that day in Steubenville. It was hot, sweatingly hot, and we had a shirt-sleeve crowd. That was why Mr. Legere and Mr. Indrasil stood out. Mr. Legere, standing silently by the tiger cage, was fully dressed in a suit and vest, his face unmarked by perspiration. And Mr. Indrasil, clad in one of his beautiful silk shirts and white whipcord breeches, was staring at them both, his face dead-white, his eyes bulging in lunatic anger, hate, and fear. He was carrying a currycomb and brush, and his hands were trembling as they clenched on them spasmodically.

Suddenly he saw me, and his anger found vent. "You!" He shouted. "Johnston!"

"Yes, sir?" I felt a crawling in the pit of my stomach. I knew I was about to have the Wrath of Indrasil vented on me, and the thought turned me weak with fear. I like to think I'm as brave as the next, and if it had been anyone else, I think I would have been fully determined to stand up for myself. But it wasn't anyone else. It was Mr. Indrasil, and his eyes were mad.

"These cages, Johnston. Are they supposed to be clean?" He pointed a finger, and I followed it. I saw four errant wisps of straw and an incriminating puddle of hose water in the far corner of one.

"Y-yes, sir," I said, and what was intended to be firmness became palsied bravado.

Silence, like the electric pause before a downpour. People were beginning to look, and I was dimly aware that Mr. Legere was staring at us with his bottomless eyes.

"Yes, sir?" Mr. Indrasil thundered suddenly. "Yes, sir? Yes, sir? Don't insult my intelligence, boy! Don't you think I can see? *Smell?* Did you use the disinfectant?"

"I used disinfectant yest—"

"Don't answer me back!" He screeched, and then the

sudden drop in his voice made my skin crawl. "Don't you *dare* answer me back." Everyone was staring now. I wanted to retch, to die. "Now you get the hell into that toolshed, and you get that disinfectant and swab out those cages," he whispered, measuring every word. One hand suddenly shot out, grasping my shoulder. "And don't you ever, ever speak back to me again."

I don't know where the words came from, but they were suddenly there, spilling off my lips. "I didn't speak back to you, Mr. Indrasil, and I don't like you saying I did. I—I resent it. Now let me go."

His face went suddenly red, then white, then almost saffron with rage. His eyes were blazing doorways to hell.

Right then I thought I was going to die.

He made an inarticulate gagging sound, and the grip on my shoulder became excruciating. His right hand went up . . . up . . . up, and then descended with unbelievable speed.

If that hand had connected with my face, it would have knocked me senseless at best. At worst, it would have broken my neck.

It did not connect.

Another hand materialized magically out of space, right in front of me. The two straining limbs came together with a flat smacking sound. It was Mr. Legere.

"Leave the boy alone," he said emotionlessly.

Mr. Indrasil stared at him for a long second, and I think there was nothing so unpleasant in the whole business as watching the fear of Mr. Legere and the mad lust to hurt (or to kill!) mix in those terrible eyes.

Then he turned and stalked away.

I turned to look at Mr. Legere. "Thank you," I said.

"Don't thank me." And it wasn't a "don't thank *me*," but a *"don't* thank me." Not a gesture of modesty, but a literal command. In a sudden flash of intuition—empathy, if you will—I understood exactly what he meant by that comment. I was a pawn in what must have been a long combat between the two of them. I had been captured by Mr. Legere rather than Mr. Indrasil. He had stopped the lion tamer not because he felt for me, but because it gained him an advantage, however slight, in their private war.

"What's your name?" I asked, not at all offended by what I had inferred. He had, after all, been honest with me.

"Legere," he said briefly. He turned to go.

"Are you with a circus?" I asked, not wanting to let him go so easily. "You seemed to know—him."

A faint smile touched his thin lips, and warmth kindled in his eyes for a moment. "No. You might call me a policeman." And before I could reply, he had disappeared into the surging throng passing by.

The next day we picked up stakes and moved on.

I saw Mr. Legere again in Danville and, two weeks later, in Chicago. In the time between I tried to avoid Mr. Indrasil as much as possible and kept the cat cages spotlessly clean. On the day before we pulled out for St. Louis, I asked Chips Baily and Sally O'Hara, the redheaded wire walker, if Mr. Legere and Mr. Indrasil knew each other. I was pretty sure they did, because Mr. Legere was hardly following the circus to eat our fabulous lime ice.

Sally and Chips looked at each other over their coffee cups. "No one knows much about what's between those two," she said. "But it's been going on for a long time—maybe twenty years. Ever since Mr. Indrasil came over from Ringling Brothers, and maybe before that."

Chips nodded. "This Legere guy picks up the circus almost every year when we swing through the Midwest and stays with us until we catch the train for Florida in Little Rock. Makes old Leopard Man touchy as one of his cats."

"He told me he was a policeman," I said. "What do you suppose he looks for around here? You don't suppose Mr. Indrasil—?"

Chips and Sally looked at each other strangely, and both just about broke their backs getting up. "Got to see those weights and counterweights get stored right," Sally said, and Chips muttered something not too convincing about checking on the rear axle of his U-Haul.

And that's about the way any conversation concerning Mr. Indrasil or Mr. Legere usually broke up—hurriedly, with many hard-forced excuses.

We said farewell to Illinois and comfort at the same time. A killing hot spell came on, seemingly at the very instant we crossed the border, and it stayed with us for the next month and a half, as we moved slowly across Missouri and into Kansas. Everyone grew short of temper, including the animals. And that, of course, included the cats, which were Mr. Indrasil's responsibility. He rode the roustabouts unmercifully, and myself in particular. I grinned and tried to bear it, even though I had my own case of prickly heat. You just don't argue with a crazy man, and I'd pretty well decided that was what Mr. Indrasil was.

No one was getting any sleep, and that is the curse of all circus performers. Loss of sleep slows up reflexes, and slow reflexes make for danger. In Independence, Sally O'Hara fell seventy-five feet into the nylon netting and fractured her shoulder. Andrea Solienni, our bareback rider, fell off one of her horses during rehearsal and was knocked unconscious by a flying hoof. Chips Baily suffered silently with the fever that was always with him, his face a waxen mask, with cold perspiration clustered at each temple.

And in many ways, Mr. Indrasil had the roughest row to hoe of all. The cats were nervous and short-tempered, and every time he stepped into the Demon Cat Cage, as it was billed, he took his life in his hands. He was feeding the lions inordinate amounts of raw meat right before he went on, something that lion tamers rarely do, contrary to popular belief. His face grew drawn and haggard, and his eyes were wild.

Mr. Legere was almost always there, by Green Terror's cage, watching him. And that, of course, added to Mr.

Indrasil's load. The circus began eyeing the silk-shirted figure nervously as he passed, and I knew they were all thinking the same thing I was: *He's going to crack wide open, and when he does—*

When he did, God alone knew what would happen.

The hot spell went on, and temperatures were climbing well into the nineties every day. It seemed as if the rain gods were mocking us. Every town we left would receive the showers of blessing. Every town we entered was hot, parched, sizzling.

And one night, on the road between Kansas City and Green Bluff, I saw something that upset me more than anything else.

It was hot—abominably hot. It was no good even trying to sleep. I rolled about on my cot like a man in a fever delirium, chasing the sandman but never quite catching him. Finally I got up, pulled on my pants, and went outside.

We had pulled off into a small field and drawn into a circle. Myself and two other roustabouts had unloaded the cats so they could catch whatever breeze there might be. The cages were there now, painted dull silver by the swollen Kansas moon, and a tall figure in white whipcord breeches was standing by the biggest of them. Mr. Indrasil.

He was baiting Green Terror with a long, pointed pike. The big cat was padding silently around the cage, trying to avoid the sharp tip. And the frightening thing was, when the staff did punch into the tiger's flesh, it did not roar in pain and anger as it should have. It maintained an ominous silence, more terrifying to the person who knows cats than the loudest of roars.

It had gotten to Mr. Indrasil too. "Quiet bastard, aren't you?" He grunted. Powerful arms flexed, and the iron shaft slid forward. Green Terror flinched, and his eyes rolled horribly. But he did not make a sound. "Yowl!" Mr. Indrasil hissed. "Go ahead and yowl, you monster! *Yowl!*" And he drove his spear deep into the tiger's flank.

Then I saw something odd. It seemed that a shadow moved in the darkness under one of the far wagons, and the moonlight seemed to glint on staring eyes—green eyes.

A cool wind passed silently through the clearing, lifting dust and rumpling my hair.

Mr. Indrasil looked up, and there was a queer listening expression on his face. Suddenly he dropped the bar, turned, and strode back to his trailer.

I stared again at the far wagon, but the shadow was gone. Green Tiger stood motionlessly at the bars of his cage, staring at Mr. Indrasil's trailer. And the thought came to me that it hated Mr. Indrasil not because he was cruel or vicious, for the tiger respects these qualities in its own animalistic way, but rather because he was a deviate from even the tiger's savage norm. He was a rogue. That's the only way I can put it. Mr. Indrasil was not only a human tiger, but a rogue tiger as well.

The thought jelled inside me, disquieting and a little scary. I went back inside, but still I could not sleep.

The heat went on.

Every day we fried, every night we tossed and turned, sweating and sleepless. Everyone was painted red with sunburn, and there were fistfights over trifling affairs. Everyone was reaching the point of explosion.

Mr. Legere remained with us, a silent watcher, emotionless on the surface, but, I sensed, with deep-running currents of—what? Hate? Fear? Vengeance? I could not place it. But he was potentially dangerous, I was sure of that. Perhaps more so than Mr. Indrasil was, if anyone ever lit his particular fuse.

He was at the circus at every performance, always dressed in his nattily creased brown suit, despite the killing temperatures. He stood silently by Green Terror's cage, seeming to commune deeply with the tiger, who was always quiet when he was around.

From Kansas to Oklahoma, with no letup in the temperature. A day without a heat prostration case was a rare day indeed. Crowds were beginning to drop off; who wanted to sit under a stifling canvas tent when there was an air-conditioned movie just around the block?

We were all as jumpy as cats, to coin a particularly applicable phrase. And as we set down stakes in Wildwood Green, Oklahoma, I think we all knew a climax of some sort was close at hand. And most of us knew it would involve Mr. Indrasil. A bizarre occurrence had taken place just prior to our first Wildwood performance. Mr. Indrasil had been in the Demon Cat Cage, putting the ill-tempered lions through their paces. One of them missed its balance on its pedestal, tottered, and almost regained it. Then, at that precise moment, Green Terror let out a terrible ear-splitting roar.

The lion fell, landed heavily, and suddenly launched itself with rifle-bullet accuracy at Mr. Indrasil. With a frightened curse he heaved his chair at the cat's feet, tangling up the driving legs. He darted out just as the lion smashed against the bars.

As he shakily collected himself preparatory to reentering the cage, Green Terror let out another roar—but this one monstrously like a huge, disdainful chuckle.

Mr. Indrasil stared at the beast, white-faced, then turned and walked away. He did not come out of his trailer all afternoon.

That afternoon wore on interminably. But as the temperature climbed, we all began looking hopefully toward the west, where huge banks of thunderclouds were forming.

"Rain, maybe," I told Chips, stopping by his barking platform in front of the sideshow.

But he didn't respond to my hopeful grin. "Don't like it," he said. "No wind. Too hot. Hail or tornadoes." His face grew grim. "It ain't no picnic, ridin' out a tornado with a pack of crazy-wild animals all over the place, Eddie. I've thanked God more'n once when we've gone through the tornado belt that we don't have no elephants.

"Yeah," he added gloomily, "you better hope them clouds stay right on the horizon."

But they didn't. They moved slowly toward us, cyclopean pillars in the sky, purple at the bases and awesome blue-black through the cumulonimbus. All air movement ceased, and the heat lay on us like a woolen winding-shroud. Every now and again thunder would clear its throat farther west.

About four, Mr. Farnum himself, ringmaster and half owner of the circus, appeared and told us there would be no evening performance; just batten down and find a convenient hole to crawl into in case of trouble. There had been corkscrew funnels spotted in several places between Wildwood and Oklahoma City, some within forty miles of us.

There was only a small crowd when the announcement came, apathetically wandering through the sideshow exhibits or ogling the animals. But Mr. Legere had not been present all day; the only person at Green Terror's cage was a sweaty high school boy with a clutch of books. When Mr. Farnum announced the U.S. Weather Bureau tornado warning that had been issued, he hurried quickly away.

I and the other two roustabouts spent the rest of the afternoon working our tails off, securing tents, loading animals back into their wagons, and making generally sure that everything was nailed down.

Finally only the cat cages were left, and there was a special arrangement for those. Each cage had a special mesh "breezeway" accordioned up against it, which, when extended completely, connected with the Demon Cat Cage. When the smaller cages had to be moved, the felines could be herded into the big cage while they were loaded up. The big cage itself rolled on gigantic casters and could be muscled around to a position where each cat could be let back into its original cage. It sounds complicated, and it was, but it was just the only way.

We did the lions first, then Ebony Velvet, the docile black panther that had set the circus back almost one season's receipts. It was a tricky business coaxing them up and then back through the breezeways, but all of us preferred it to calling Mr. Indrasil to help.

By the time we were ready for Green Terror, twilight had come—a queer, yellow twilight that hung humidly around us. The sky above had taken on a flat, shiny aspect that I had never seen and which I didn't like in the least.

"Better hurry," Mr. Farnum said as we laboriously trundled the Demon Cat Cage back to where we could hook it to the back of Green Terror's show cage. "Barometer's falling off fast." He shook his head worriedly. "Looks bad, boys. Bad." He hurried on, still shaking his head.

We got Green Terror's breezeway hooked up and opened the back of his cage. "In you go," I said encouragingly.

Green Terror looked at me menacingly and didn't move.

Thunder rumbled again, louder, closer, sharper. The sky had gone jaundice, the ugliest color I have ever seen. Wind-devils began to pick jerkily at our clothes and whirl away the flattened candy wrappers and cotton-candy cones that littered the area.

"Come on, come on," I urged, and poked him easily with the blunt-tipped rods we were given to herd them with.

Green Terror roared ear-splittingly, and one paw lashed out with blinding speed. The hardwood pole was jerked from my hands and splintered as if it had been a greenwood twig. The tiger was on his feet now, and there was murder in his eyes.

"Look," I said shakily. "One of you will have to go get Mr. Indrasil, that's all. We can't wait around."

As if to punctuate my words, thunder cracked louder, the clapping of mammoth hands.

Kelly Nixon and Mike McGregor flipped for it; I was excluded because of my previous run-in with Mr. Indrasil. Kelly drew the task, threw us a wordless glance that said he would prefer facing the storm, and then started off.

He was gone almost ten minutes. The wind was picking up velocity now, and twilight was darkening into a weird six o'clock night. I was scared, and am not afraid to admit it. That rushing, featureless sky, the deserted circus grounds, the sharp, tugging wind-vortices—all that makes a memory that will stay with me always, undimmed.

And Green Terror would not budge into his breezeway.

Kelly Nixon came rushing back, his eyes wide. "I pounded on his door for 'most five minutes!" He gasped. "Couldn't raise him!"

We looked at each other, at a loss. Green Terror was a big investment for the circus. He couldn't just be left in the open. I turned bewilderedly, looking for Chips, Mr. Farnum, or anybody who could tell me what to do. But everyone was gone. The tiger was our responsibility. I considered trying to load the cage bodily into the trailer, but *I* wasn't going to get my fingers in that cage.

"Well, we've just got to go and get him," I said. "The three of us. Come on." And we ran toward Mr. Indrasil's trailer through the gloom of coming night.

We pounded on his door until he must have thought all the demons of hell were after him. Thankfully, it finally jerked open. Mr. Indrasil swayed and stared down at us, his mad eyes rimmed and oversheened with drink. He smelled like a distillery.

"Damn you, leave me alone," he snarled.

"Mr. Indrasil—" I had to shout over the rising whine of the wind. It was like no storm I had ever heard of or read about, out there. It was like the end of the world.

"You," he gritted softly. He reached down and gathered my shirt up in a knot. "I'm going to teach you a lesson you'll never forget." He glared at Kelly and Mike, cowering back in the moving storm shadows. "Get out!"

They ran. I didn't blame them; I've told you—Mr. Indrasil was crazy. And not just ordinary crazy—he was like a crazy animal, like one of his own cats gone bad.

"All right," he muttered, staring down at me, his eyes like hurricane lamps. "No juju to protect you now. No grisgris." His lips twitched in a wild, horrible smile. "He isn't here now, is he? We're two of a kind, him and me. Maybe the only two left. My nemesis—and I'm his." He was rambling, and I didn't try to stop him. At least his mind was off me.

"Turned that cat against me, back in 'fifty-eight. Always had the power more'n me. Fool could make a million— the two of us could make a million if he wasn't so damned high and mighty . . . what's that?"

It was Green Terror, and he had begun to roar ear-splittingly.

"Haven't you got that damned tiger in?" he screamed, almost falsetto. He shook me like a rag doll.

"He won't go!" I found myself yelling back. "You've got to—"

But he flung me away. I stumbled over the fold-up steps in front of his trailer and crashed into a bone-shaking heap at the bottom. With something between a sob and a curse, Mr. Indrasil strode past me, face mottled with anger and fear.

I got up, drawn after him as if hypnotized. Some intuitive part of me realized I was about to see the last act played out.

Once clear of the shelter of Mr. Indrasil's trailer, the power of the wind was appalling. It screamed like a runaway freight train. I was an ant, a speck, an unprotected molecule before that thundering cosmic force.

And Mr. Legere was standing by Green Terror's cage.

It was like a tableau from Dante. The near-empty cage clearing inside the circle of trailers; the two men, facing each other silently, their clothes and hair rippled by the shrieking gale; the boiling sky above; the twisting wheatfields in the background, like damned souls bending to the whip of Lucifer.

"It's time, Jason," Mr. Legere said, his words flayed across the clearing by the wind.

Mr. Indrasil's wildly whipping hair lifted around the livid

scar across the back of his neck. His fists clenched, but he said nothing. I could almost feel him gathering his will, his life force, his id. It gathered around him like an unholy nimbus.

And then I saw with sudden horror that Mr. Legere was unhooking Green Terror's breezeway—and the back of the cage was open!

I cried out, but the wind ripped my words away.

The great tiger leapt out and almost flowed past Mr. Legere. Mr. Indrasil swayed, but did not run. He bent his head and stared down at the tiger.

And Green Terror stopped.

He swung his huge head back to Mr. Legere, almost turned, and then slowly turned back to Mr. Indrasil again. There was a terrifyingly palpable sensation of directed force in the air, a mesh of conflicting wills centered around the tiger. And the wills were evenly matched.

I think, in the end, it was Green Terror's own will—his hate of Mr. Indrasil—that tipped the scales.

The cat began to advance, his eyes hellish, flaring beacons. And something strange began to happen to Mr. Indrasil. He seemed to be folding in on himself, shriveling, accordioning. The silk shirt lost shape, the dark, whipping hair became a hideous toadstool around his collar.

Mr. Legere called something across to him, and, simultaneously, Green Terror leapt.

I never saw the outcome. The next moment I was slammed flat on my back, and the breath seemed to be sucked from my body. I caught one crazily tilted glimpse of a huge, towering cyclone funnel, and then the darkness descended.

When I awoke, I was in my cot just aft of the grainery bins in the all-purpose storage trailer we carried. My body felt as if it had been beaten with padded Indian clubs.

Chips Baily appeared, his face lined and pale. He saw my eyes were open and grinned relievedly. "Didn't know as you were ever gonna wake up. How you feel?"

"Dislocated," I said. "What happened? How'd I get here?"

"We found you piled up against Mr. Indrasil's trailer. The tornado almost carried you away for a souvenir, m'boy."

At the mention of Mr. Indrasil, all the ghastly memories came flooding back. "Where is Mr. Indrasil? And Mr. Legere?"

His eyes went murky, and he started to make some kind of an evasive answer.

"Straight talk," I said, struggling up on one elbow. "I have to know, Chips. I *have* to."

Something in my face must have decided him. "Okay. But this isn't exactly what we told the cops—in fact we hardly told the cops any of it. No sense havin' people think we're crazy. Anyhow, Indrasil's gone. I didn't even know that Legere guy was around."

"And Green Tiger?"

Chips's eyes were unreadable again. "He and the other tiger fought to death."

"*Other* tiger? There's no other—"

"Yeah, but they found two of 'em, lying in each other's blood. Hell of a mess. Ripped each other's throats out."

"What—where—"

"Who knows? We just told the cops we had two tigers. Simpler that way." And before I could say another word, he was gone.

And that's the end of my story—except for two little items. The words Mr. Legere shouted just before the tornado hit: "*When a man and an animal live in the same shell, Indrasil, the instincts determine the mold!*"

The other thing is what keeps me awake nights. Chips told me later, offering it only for what it might be worth. What he told me was that the strange tiger had a long scar on the back of its neck.

POOR LITTLE WARRIOR!

BRIAN W. ALDISS

Britisher Brian Aldiss is a novelist, editor, poet, and critic whose work has received wide acclaim. His role in the field of science fiction has been one of pathfinder; in his early works he routinely broke with the conventions of sf and tried new approaches to traditional sf ideas, emphasizing imagery and style over "hardware," and writing with unbeatable zest. Although "Poor Little Warrior!" is primarily a science fiction tale, its culmination will shudder the shoes off you. In this story Claude Ford travels to the past to hunt *big* big game . . . only to find that it isn't as easy as he had thought.

Claude Ford knew exactly how it was to hunt a brontosaurus. You crawled heedlessly through the mud among the willows, through the little primitive flowers with petals as green and brown as a football field, through the beauty-lotion mud. You peered out at the creature sprawling among the reeds, its body as graceful as a sock full of sand. There it lay, letting the gravity cuddle it nappy-damp to the marsh, running its big rabbit-hole nostrils a foot above the grass in a sweeping semicircle, in a snoring search for more sausagy reeds. It was beautiful: here horror had reached its limits, come full circle and finally disappeared up its own sphincter. Its eyes gleamed with the liveliness of a week-dead corpse's big toe, and its compost breath and the fur in its crude aural cavities were particularly to be recommended to anyone who might otherwise have felt inclined to speak lovingly of the work of Mother Nature.

But as you, little mammal with opposed digit and .65 self-loading, semi-automatic, dual-barreled, digitally computed, telescopically sighted, rustless, high-powered rifle gripped in your otherwise defenseless paws, slide along under the bygone willows, what primarily attracts you is the thunder lizard's hide. It gives off a smell as deeply resonant as the bass note of a piano. It makes the elephant's epidermis look like a sheet of crinkled lavatory paper. It is gray as the Viking seas, daft-deep as cathedral foundations. What contact possible to bone could allay the fever of that flesh? Over it scamper—you can see them from here!—the little brown lice that live in those gray walls and canyons, gay as ghosts, cruel as crabs. If one of them jumped on you, it would very likely break your back. And when one of those parasites stops to cock its leg against one of the bronto's vertebrae, you can see it carries in its turn its own crop of easy livers, each as big as a lobster, for you're near now, oh, so near that you can hear the monster's primitive heart organ knocking, as the ventricle keeps miraculous time with the auricle.

Time for listening to the oracle is past: you're beyond the stage for omens, you're now headed in for the kill, yours or his; superstition has had its little day for today, from now on only this windy nerve of yours, this shaky conglomeration of muscle entangled untraceably beneath the sweat-shiny carapace of skin, this bloody little urge to slay the dragon, is going to answer all your orisons.

You could shoot now. Just wait till that tiny steam-shovel head pauses once again to gulp down a quarryload of bulrushes, and with one inexpressibly vulgar bang you can show the whole indifferent Jurassic world that it's standing looking down the business end of evolution's sex shooter. You know why you pause, even as you pretend not to know why you pause; that old worm conscience, long as a baseball pitch, long-lived as a tortoise, is at work; through every sense it slides, more monstrous than the serpent. Through the passions: saying here is a sitting duck, O Englishman! Through the intelligence: whispering that boredom, the kite-hawk who never feeds, will settle again when the task is done. Through the nerves: sneering that when the adrenaline currents cease to flow the vomiting begins. Through the maestro behind the retina: plausibly forcing the beauty of the view upon you.

Spare us that poor old slipper-slopper of a word, *beauty*; holy mom, is this a travelogue, nor are we out of it? "*Perched now on this titanic creature's back, we see a round dozen —and, folks, let me stress that round—of gaudily plumaged birds, exhibiting between them all the color you might expect to find on lovely, fabled Copacabaña Beach. They're so round because they feed from the droppings that fall from the rich man's table. Watch this lovely shot now! See the bronto's tail lift. . . . Oh, lovely, yep, a couple of hayricks-full at least emerging from his nether end. That sure was a beauty, folks, delivered straight from consumer to consumer. The birds are fighting over it now. Hey, you, there's enough to go round, and anyhow, you're round enough already. . . . And nothing to do now but hop back up onto the old rump steak and wait for the next round. And now as the sun sinks in the Jurassic West, we say 'Farewell on that diet' . . ."*

No, you're procrastinating, and that's a life work. Shoot the beast and put it out of your agony. Taking your courage in your hands, you raise it to shoulder level and squint down its sights. There is a terrible report; you are half stunned. Shakily, you look about you. The monster still munches, relieved to have broken enough wind to unbecalm the Ancient Mariner.

Angered (or is it some subtler emotion?), you now burst from the bushes and confront it, and this exposed condition is typical of the straits into which your consideration for yourself and others continually pitches you. Consideration? Or again something subtler? Why should you be confused just because you come from a confused civilization? But that's a point to deal with later, if there is a later, as these two hog-wallow eyes pupiling you all over from spitting distance tend to dispute. Let it not be by jaws alone, O monster, but also by huge hooves and, if convenient to yourself, by mountainous rollings upon me! Let death be a saga, sagacious, Beowulfate.

Quarter of a mile distant is the sound of a dozen hippos springing boisterously in gymslips from the ancestral mud, and next second a walloping great tail as long as Sunday and as thick as Saturday night comes slicing over your head. You duck as duck you must, but the beast missed you anyway because it so happens that its coordination is no better than yours would be if you had to wave the Woolworth Building at a tarsier. This done, it seems to feel it has done its duty by itself. It forgets you. You just wish you could forget yourself as easily; that was, after all, the reason you had to come the long way here. *Get Away from It All,* said the time travel brochure, which meant for you getting away from Claude Ford, a husbandman as futile as his name with a terrible wife called Maude. Maude and Claude Ford. Who could not adjust to themselves, to each other, or to the world they were born in. It was the best reason in the as-it-is-at-present-constituted world for coming back here to shoot giant saurians—if you were fool enough to think that one hundred and fifty million years either way made an ounce of difference to the muddle of thoughts in a man's cerebral vortex.

You try to stop your silly, slobbering thoughts, but they have never really stopped since the coca-collaborating days of your growing up; God, if adolescence did not exist, it would be unnecessary to invent it! Slightly, it steadies you to look again on the enormous bulk of this tyrant vegetarian into whose presence you charged with such a mixed death-life wish, charged with all the emotion the human orga(ni)sm is capable of. This time the bogeyman is real, Claude, just as you wanted it to be, and this time you really have to face up to it before it turns and faces you again. And so again you lift Ole Equalizer, waiting till you can spot the vulnerable spot.

The bright birds sway, the lice scamper like dogs, the marsh groans, as bronto sways over and sends his little cranium snaking down under the bile-bright water in a forage for roughage. You watch this; you have never been so jittery before in all your jittered life, and you are counting on this catharsis wringing the last drop of acid fear out of your system forever. OK, you keep saying to yourself insanely over and over, your million-dollar twenty-second-century education going for nothing, OK, OK. And as you say it for the umpteenth time, the crazy head comes back out of the water like a renegade express and gazes in your direction.

Grazes in your direction. For as the champing jaw with its big blunt molars like concrete posts works up and down, you see the swamp water course out over rimless lips, lipless rims, splashing your feet and sousing the ground. Reed and root, stalk and stem, leaf and loam, all are intermittently visible in that masticating maw and, struggling, straggling, or tossed among them, minnows, tiny crustaceans, frogs— all destined in that awful, jaw-full movement to turn into bowel movement. And as the glump-glump-glumping takes place, above it the slime-resistant eyes again survey you.

These beasts live up to two hundred years, says the time travel brochure, and this beast has obviously tried to live up to that, for its gaze is centuries old, full of decades upon decades of wallowing in its heavyweight thoughtlessness until it has grown wise on twitterpatedness. For you it is like looking into a disturbing misty pool; it gives you a psychic shock, you fire off both barrels at your own reflection. Bang-bang, the dum-dums, big as paw-paws, go.

With no indecision, those century-old lights, dim and sacred, go out. These cloisters are closed till Judgment Day. Your reflection is torn and bloodied from them forever. Over their ravaged panes nictitating membranes slide slowly upward, like dirty sheets covering a cadaver. The jaw continues to munch slowly, as slowly the head sinks down. Slowly, a squeeze of cold reptile blood toothpastes down the wrinkled flank of one cheek. Everything is slow, a creepy Secondary Era slowness like the drip of water, and you know that if you had been in charge of creation, you would have found some medium less heartbreaking than Time to stage it all in.

Never mind! Quaff down your beakers, lords, Claude Ford has slain a harmless creature. Long live Claude the Clawed!

You watch breathless as the head touches the ground, the long laugh of neck touches the ground, the jaws close for good. You watch and wait for something else to happen, but nothing ever does. Nothing ever would. You could stand here watching for an hundred and fifty million years, Lord Claude, and nothing would ever happen here again. Gradually your bronto's mighty carcass, picked loving clean by predators, would sink into the slime, carried by its own weight deeper; then the waters would rise, and old Conqueror Sea come in with the leisurely air of a card-sharp dealing the boys a bad hand. Silt and sediment would filter down over the mighty grave, a slow rain with centuries to rain in. Old bronto's bed might be raised up and then down again perhaps half a dozen times, gently enough not to disturb him, although by now the sedimentary rocks would be forming thick around him. Finally, when he was wrapped in a tomb finer than any Indian rajah ever boasted, the powers of the Earth would raise him high on their shoulders until, sleeping still, bronto would lie in a brow of the Rockies high above the waters of the Pacific. But little any of that would count with you, Claude the Sword; once the midget maggot of life is dead in the creature's skull, the rest is no concern of yours.

You have no emotion now. You are just faintly put out. You expected dramatic thrashing of the ground, or bellowing; on the other hand, you are glad the thing did not appear to suffer. You are like all cruel men, sentimental; you are like all sentimental men, squeamish. You tuck the gun under your arm and walk round the dinosaur to view your victory.

You prowl past the ungainly hooves, round the septic white of the cliff of belly, beyond the glistening and how-thought-provoking cavern of the cloaca, finally posing beneath the switch-back sweep of tail-to-rump. Now your disappointment is as crisp and obvious as a visiting card: the giant is not half as big as you thought it was. It is not one half as large, for example, as the image of you and Maude is in your mind. Poor little warrior, science will never invent anything to assist the titanic death you want in the contraterrene caverns of your fee-fi-fo fumblingly fearful id!

Nothing is left to you now but to slink back to your timemobile with a belly full of anticlimax. See, the bright dung-consuming birds have already cottoned on to the true state of affairs; one by one they gather up their hunched wings and fly disconsolately off across the swamp to other hosts. They know when a good thing turns bad, and do not wait for the vultures to drive them off; all hope abandon, ye who entrail here. You also turn away.

You turn, but you pause. Nothing is left but to go back, no, but A.D. 2181 is not just the home date; it is Maude. It is Claude. It is the whole awful, hopeless, endless business of trying to adjust to an overcomplex environment, of trying to turn yourself into a cog. Your escape from it into *the Grand Simplicities of the Jurassic*, to quote the brochure again, was only a partial escape, now over.

So you pause, and as you pause something lands socko on your back, pitching your face forward into tasty mud. You struggle and scream as lobster claws tear at your neck and throat. You try to pick up the rifle but cannot, so in agony you roll over, and next second the crab-thing is greedying it on your chest. You wrench at its shell, but it giggles and pecks your fingers off. You forgot when you killed the bronto that its parasites would leave it, and that to a little shrimp like you they would be a deal more dangerous than their host.

You do your best, kicking for at least three minutes. By the end of that time there is a whole pack of the creatures on you. Already they are picking your carcass loving clean. You're going to like it up there on top of the Rockies; you won't feel a thing.

NINA

ROBERT BLOCH

Although he has been writing since 1934, the name of Robert Bloch instantly conjures up images of that modern masterpiece of horror, *Psycho* (1959), from which Alfred Hitchcock made the classic film. Bloch is a witty and polished writer, and one easily able to manipulate his readers' nerve-endings to heights of terror. Horror stories often employ the device of introducing things or people who are not actually what they appear to be. In "Nina," Robert Bloch takes this idea, transplants it to the steamy jungle of South America, and proceeds to scare us to death with what is and what is not.

After the lovemaking Nolan needed another drink.

He fumbled for the bottle beside the bed, gripping it with a sweaty hand. His entire body was wet and clammy, and his fingers shook as they unscrewed the cap. For a moment Nolan wondered if he was coming down with another bout of fever. Then, as the harsh heat of the sun scalded his stomach, he realized the truth.

Nina had done this to him.

Nolan turned and glanced at the girl who lay beside him. She stared up through the shadows with slitted eyes unblinking above high cheekbones, her thin brown body relaxed and immobile. Hard to believe that only moments ago this same body had been a writhing, wriggling coil of insatiable appetite, gripping and enfolding him until he was drained and spent.

He held the bottle out to her. "Have a drink?"

She shook her head, eyes hooded and expressionless, and then Nolan remembered that she didn't speak English. He raised the bottle and drank again, cursing himself for his mistake.

It had been a mistake, he realized that now, but Darlene would never understand. Sitting there safe and snug in the apartment in Trenton, she couldn't begin to know what he'd gone through for her sake—hers and little Robbie's. Robert Emmett Nolan II, nine weeks old now, his son, whom he'd never seen. That's why he'd taken the job, signed on with the company for a year. The money was good, enough to keep Darlene in comfort and tide them over after he got back. She couldn't have come with him, not while she was carrying the kid, so he came alone, figuring no sweat.

No sweat. That was a laugh. All he'd done since he got here was sweat. Patrolling the plantation at sunup, loading cargo all day for the boats that went downriver, squinting over paperwork while night closed down on the bungalow to imprison him behind a wall of jungle darkness. And at night the noises came—the hum of insect hordes, the bellow of caimans, the snorting snuffle of peccary, the ceaseless chatter of monkeys intermingled with the screeching of a million mindless birds.

So he'd started to drink. First the good bourbon from the company's stock, then the halfway-decent trade gin, and now the cheap rum.

As Nolan set the empty bottle down he heard the noise he'd come to dread worst of all—the endless echo of drums from the huts huddled beside the riverbank below. Miserable wretches were at it again. No wonder he had to drive them daily to fulfil the company's quota. The wonder was that they did anything at all after spending every night wailing to those damned drums.

Of course it was Moises who did the actual driving; Nolan couldn't even chew them out properly because they were too damned dumb to understand plain English.

Like Nina, here.

Again Nolan looked down at the girl who lay curled beside him on the bed, silent and sated. She wasn't sweating; her skin was curiously cool to the touch, and in her eyes was a mystery.

It was the mystery that Nolan had sensed the first time he saw her staring at him across the village compound three days ago. At first he thought she was one of the company people—somebody's wife, daughter, sister. That afternoon, when he returned to the bungalow, he caught her staring at him again at the edge of the clearing. So he asked Moises who she was, and Moises didn't know. Apparently she'd just arrived a day or two before, paddling a crude catamaran downriver from somewhere out of the denser jungle stretching a thousand miles beyond. She had no English, and according to Moises, she didn't speak Spanish or Portuguese either. Not that she'd made any attempts to communicate; she kept to herself, sleeping in the catamaran moored beside the bank across the river and not even venturing into the company store by day to purchase food.

"*Indio*," Moises said, pronouncing the word with all the

contempt of one in whose veins ran a ten percent admixture of the proud blood of the *conquistadores*. "Who are we to know the way of savages?" He shrugged.

Nolan had shrugged, too, and dismissed her from his mind. But that night as he lay on his bed, listening to the pounding of the drums, he thought of her again and felt a stirring in his loins.

She came to him then, almost as though the stirring had been a silent summons, came like a brown shadow gliding out of the night. Soundlessly she entered, and swiftly she shed her single garment as she moved across the room to stand staring down at him on the bed. Then, as she sank upon his nakedness and encircled his thighs, the stirring in his loins became a throbbing and the pounding in his head drowned out the drums.

In the morning she was gone, but on the following night she returned. It was then that he'd called her Nina—it wasn't her name, but he felt a need to somehow identify this wide-mouthed, pink-tongued stranger who slaked herself upon him, slaked his own urgency again and again as her hissing breath rasped in his ears.

Once more she vanished while he slept, and he hadn't seen her all day. But at times he'd been conscious of her secret stare, a coldness falling upon him like an unglimpsed shadow, and he'd known that tonight she'd come again.

Now, as the drums sounded in the distance, Nina slept. Unmindful of the din, heedless of his presence, her eyes hooded and she lay somnolent in animal repletion.

Nolan shuddered. That's what she was; an animal. In repose, the lithe brown body was grotesquely elongated, the wide mouth accentuating the ugliness of her face. How could he have coupled with this creature? Nolan grimaced in self-disgust as he turned away.

Well, no matter—it was ended now, over once and for all. Today the message had arrived from Belem: Darlene and Robbie were on the ship, ready for the flight to Manaos. Tomorrow morning he'd start downriver to meet them, escort them here. He'd had his qualms about their coming; they'd have to face three months in this hellhole before the year was up, but Darlene had insisted.

And she was right. Nolan knew it now. At least they'd be together and that would help see him through. He wouldn't need the bottle anymore, and he wouldn't need Nina.

Nolan lay back and waited for sleep to come, shutting out the sound of the drums, the sight of the shadowy shape beside him. Only a few hours until morning, he told himself. And in the morning the nightmare would be over.

The trip to Manaos was an ordeal, but it ended in Darlene's arms. She was blonder and more beautiful than he'd remembered, more loving and tender than he'd ever known her to be, and in the union that was their reunion Nolan found fulfillment. Of course there was none of the avid hunger of Nina's coiling caresses, none of the mindless thrashing to final frenzy. But it didn't matter; the two of them were together at last. The two of them, and Robbie.

Robbie was a revelation.

Nolan hadn't anticipated the intensity of his own reaction. But now, after the long trip back in the wheezing launch, he stood beside the crib in the spare bedroom and gazed down at his son with an overwhelming surge of pride.

"Isn't he adorable?" Darlene said. "He looks just like you."

"You're prejudiced." Nolan grinned, but he was flattered. And when the tiny pink starshell of a hand reached forth to meet his fingers, he tingled at the touch.

Then Darlene gasped.

Nolan glanced up quickly. "What's the matter?" he said.

"Nothing." Darlene was staring past him. "I thought I saw someone outside the window."

Nolan followed her gaze. "No one out there." He moved to the window, peered at the clearing beyond. "Not a soul."

Darlene passed a hand before her eyes. "I guess I'm just overtired," she said. "The long trip—"

Nolan put his arm around her. "Why don't you go lie down? Mama Dolores can look after Robbie."

Darlene hesitated. "Are you sure she knows what to do?"

"Look who's talking!" Nolan laughed. "They don't call her Mama for nothing—she's had ten kids of her own. She's in the kitchen right now, fixing Robbie's formula. I'll go get her."

So Darlene went down the hall to their bedroom for a siesta, and Mama Dolores took over Robbie's schedule while Nolan made his daily rounds in the fields.

The heat was stifling, worse than anything he could remember. Even Moises was gasping for air as he gunned the jeep over the rutted roadway, peering into the shimmering haze.

Nolan wiped his forehead. Maybe he'd been too hasty, bringing Darlene and the baby here. But a man was entitled to see his own son, and in a few months they'd be out of this miserable sweatbox forever. No sense getting uptight; everything was going to be all right.

But at dusk, when he returned to the bungalow, Mama Dolores greeted him at the door with a troubled face.

"What is it?" Nolan said. "Something wrong with Robbie?"

Mama shook her head. "He sleeps like an angel," she murmured. "But the *señora*—"

In their room Darlene lay shivering on the bed, eyes closed. Her head moved ceaselessly on the pillows even when Nolan pressed his palm against her brow.

"Fever." Nolan gestured to Mama Dolores, and the old woman held Darlene still while he forced the thermometer between her lips.

The red column inched upward. "One hundred and four." Nolan straightened quickly. "Go fetch Moises. Tell him I want the launch ready, *pronto*. We'll have to get her to the doctor at Manaos."

Darlene's eyes fluttered open; she'd heard.

"No, you can't! The baby—"

"Do not trouble yourself. I will look after the little one."
Mama's voice was soothing. "Now you must rest."

"No, please . . ."

Darlene's voice trailed off into an incoherent babbling,
and she sank back. Nolan kept his hand on her forehead;
the heat was like an oven. "Now just relax, darling. It's all
right. I'm going with you."

And he did.

If the first trip had been an ordeal, this one was an agony:
a frantic thrust through the sultry night on the steaming river,
Moises sweating over the throttle as Nolan held Darlene's
shuddering shoulders against the straw mattress in the stern
of the vibrating launch. They made Manaos by dawn and
roused Dr. Robales from slumber at his house near the plaza.

Then came the examination, the removal to the hospital,
the tests, and the verdict. A simple matter, Dr. Robales
said, and no need for alarm. With proper treatment and
rest she would recover. A week here in the hospital—

"A week?" Nolan's voice rose. "I've got to get back for
the loading. I can't stay here that long!"

"There is no need for you to stay, *señor*. She shall have
my personal attention, I assure you."

It was small comfort, but Nolan had no choice. And he
was too tired to protest, too tired to worry. Once aboard the
launch and heading back, he stretched out on the straw
mattress in a sleep that was like death itself.

Nolan awakened to the sound of drums. He jerked upright
with a startled cry, then realized that night had come and
they were once again at anchor beside the dock. Moises
grinned at him in weary triumph.

"Almost we do not make it," he said. "The motor is bad.
No matter, it is good to be home again."

Nolan nodded, flexing his cramped limbs. He stepped
out onto the dock, then hurried up the path across the
clearing. The darkness boomed.

Home? This corner of hell, where the drums dinned and
the shadows leapt and capered before flickering fires?

All but one, that is. For as Nolan moved forward, another shadow glided out from the deeper darkness beside the bungalow.

It was Nina.

Nolan blinked as he recognized her standing there and staring up at him. There was no mistaking the look on her face or its urgency, but he had no time to waste in words. Brushing past her, he hastened to the doorway and she melted back into the night.

Mama Dolores was waiting for him inside, nodding her greeting.

"Robbie—is he all right?"

"*Sí, señor*. I take good care. *Por favor*, I sleep in his room."

"Good." Nolan turned and started for the hall, then hesitated as Mama Dolores frowned. "What is it?" he said.

The old woman hesitated. "You will not be offended if I speak?"

"Of course not."

Mama's voice sank to a murmur. "It concerns the one outside."

"Nina?"

"That is not her name, but no matter." Mama shook her head. "For two days she has waited there. I see you with her now when you return. And I see you with her before—"

"That's none of your business!" Nolan reddened. "Besides, it's all over now."

"Does she believe that?" Mama's gaze was grave. "You must tell her to go."

"I've tried. But the girl comes from the mountains; she doesn't speak English—"

"I know." Mama nodded. "She is one of the snake people."

Nolan stared at her. "They worship snakes up there?"

"No, not worship."

"Then what do you mean?"

"These people—they *are* snakes."

Nolan scowled. "What is this?"

"The truth, *señor*. This one you call Nina—this girl—is not a girl. She is of the ancient race from the high peaks, where the great serpents dwell. Your workers here, even Moises, know only the jungle, but I come from the great valley beneath the mountains, and as a child I learned to fear those who lurk above. We do not go there, but sometimes the snake people come to us. In the spring, when they awaken, they shed their skins, and for a time they are fresh and clean before the scales grow again. It is then that they come to mate with men."

She went on like that, whispering about creatures half serpent and half human, with bodies cold to the touch, limbs that could writhe in boneless contortion to squeeze the breath from a man and crush him like the coils of a giant constrictor. She spoke of forked tongues, of voices hissing forth from mouths yawning incredibly wide on movable jawbones. And she might have gone on, but Nolan stopped her now; his head was throbbing with weariness.

"That's enough," he said. "I thank you for your concern."

"But you do not believe me."

"I didn't say that." Tired as he was, Nolan still remembered the basic rule—never contradict these people or make fun of their superstitions. And he couldn't afford to alienate Mama now. "I shall take precautions," he told her gravely. "Right now I've got to rest. And I want to see Robbie."

Mama Dolores put her hand to her mouth. "I forget—the little one, he is alone—"

She turned and padded hastily down the hallway, Nolan behind her. Together they entered the nursery.

"Ah!" Mama exhaled a sigh of relief. "The *pobrecito* sleeps."

Robbie lay in his crib, a shaft of moonlight from the window bathing his tiny face. From his rosebud mouth issued a gentle snore.

Nolan smiled at the sound, then nodded at Mama. "I'm going to turn in now. You take good care of him."

"I will not leave." Mama settled herself in a rocker beside the crib. As Nolan turned to go, she called after him softly. "Remember what I have told you, *señor*. If she comes again—"

Nolan moved down the hall to his bedroom at the far end. He hadn't trusted himself to answer her. After all, she meant well; it was just that he was too damned tired to put up with any more nonsense from the old woman.

In his bedroom something rustled.

Nolan flinched, then halted as the shadow-shape glided forth from the darkened corner beside the open window.

Nina stood before him and she was stark naked. Stark naked, her arms opening in invitation.

He retreated a step. "No," he said.

She came forward, smiling.

"Go away—get out of here."

He gestured her back. Nina's smile faded and she made a sound in her throat, a little gasp of entreaty. Her hands reached out—

"Dammit, leave me alone!"

Nolan struck her on the cheek. It wasn't more than a slap, and she couldn't have been hurt. But suddenly Nina's face contorted as she launched herself at him, her fingers splayed and aiming at his eyes. This time he hit her hard —hard enough to send her reeling back.

"Out!" he said. He forced her to the open window, raising his hand threateningly as she spewed and spit her rage, then snatched her garment and clambered over the sill into the darkness beyond.

Nolan stood by the window watching as Nina moved away across the clearing. For a moment she turned in a path of moonlight and looked back at him—only a moment, but long enough for Nolan to see the livid fury blazing in her eyes.

Then she was gone, gliding off into the night, where the drums thudded in distant darkness.

She was gone, but the hate remained. Nolan felt its force

as he stretched out upon the bed. Ought to undress, but he was too tired. The throbbing in his head was worse, pulsing to the beat of the drums. And the hate was in his head too. God, that ugly face! Like the thing in mythology—what was it?—the Medusa. One look turned men to stone. Her locks of hair were live serpents.

But that was legend, like Mama Dolores's stories about the snake people. Strange—did every race have its belief in such creatures? Could there be some grotesque, distorted element of truth behind all these old wives' tales?

He didn't want to think about it now; he didn't want to think of anything. Not Nina, not Darlene, not even Robbie. Darlene would be all right, Robbie was fine, and Nina was gone. That left him, alone here with the drums. Damned pounding. Had to stop, had to stop so he could sleep—

It was the silence that awakened him. He sat up with a start, realizing he must have slept for hours, because the shadows outside the window were dappled with the grayish pink of dawn.

Nolan rose, stretching, then stepped out into the hall. The shadows were darker here and everything was still.

He went down the hallway to the other bedroom. The door was ajar and he moved past it, calling softly. "Mama Dolores—"

Nolan's tongue froze to the roof of his mouth. Time itself was frozen as he stared down at the crushed and pulpy thing sprawled shapelessly beside the rocker, its sightless eyes bulging from the swollen purple face.

No use calling her name again; she'd never hear it. And Robbie—

Nolan turned in the frozen silence, his eyes searching the shadows at the far side of the room.

The crib was empty.

Then he found his voice and cried out, cried out again as he saw the open window and the gray vacancy of the clearing beyond.

Suddenly he was at the window, climbing out and dropping to the matted sward below. He ran across the clearing, through the trees, and into the open space before the riverbank.

Moises was in the launch, working on the engine. He looked up as Nolan ran toward him, shouting.

"What are you doing here?"

"There is the problem of the motor. It requires attention. I come early, before the heat of the day—"

"Did you see her?"

"Who, *señor?*"

"The girl—Nina—"

"Ah, yes. The *Indio.*" Moises nodded. "She is gone, in her catamaran, up the river. Two, maybe three hours ago, just as I arrive."

"Why didn't you stop her?"

"For what reason?"

Nolan gestured quickly. "Get that engine started—we're going after her."

Moises frowned. "As I told you, there is the matter of the repairs. Perhaps this afternoon—"

"We'll never catch her then!" Nolan gripped Moises's shoulder. "Don't you understand? She's taken Robbie!"

"Calm yourself, *señor.* With my own eyes I saw her go to the boat and she was alone, I swear it. She does not have the little one."

Nolan thought of the hatred in Nina's eyes, and he shuddered. "Then what did she do with him?"

Moises shook his head. "This I do not know. But I am sure she has no need of another infant."

"What are you talking about?"

"I notice her condition when she walked to the boat." Moises shrugged, but even before the words came, Nolan knew.

"Why do you look at me like that, *señor?* Is it not natural for a woman to bulge when she carries a baby in her belly?"

WEREWIND

J. MICHAEL REAVES

California is a place of dichotomies. On the one hand is the glamour and glitter of the movie industry, the sun and fun and lure of the beaches; on the other there is the blood darkness of Charlie Manson, the Zebra murders, the ominous undercurrent of strange cults and ideas. In "Werewind," J. Michael Reaves captures both faces of California, and in so doing crafts a suspenseful thriller about an out-of-work actor, a series of bizarre Hollywood murders, and a persistent Santa Ana windstorm that mysteriously coincides with the killings.

"**W**arning everyone to stay off the streets if possible, particularly in the coastal and canyon areas. The winds have been clocked at forty-five miles an hour, and the Tujunga and Beverly Glen fires are still out of control. Travelers' advisories are posted for all freeways, Angeles Crest and the Grapevine. I repeat, please do not drive unless absolutely necessary.

"In other news, the Hollywood Scalper's fifth victim has been identified as Karen Lacey, a twenty-two-year-old actress. The pattern of mutilation murders connected with show business thus continues. . . ."

Simon Drake turned the car radio's volume down when he heard a sudden grating sound in the old Chrysler's engine. Holding his breath, he turned off Hollywood Boulevard onto a side street, and a moment later the engine quit, and the car coasted to a stop near an empty parking lot.

"Oh, *Christ!*" Simon twisted the key several times, but the only result was the ominous grinding noise. He slumped back against the hot plastic seat cover and watched the palm trees near Sunset slowly shredding in the wind. "That's it," he muttered. "I've lost the part." He grimaced in disgust, then winced as his chapped lips cracked.

He was thirty-three years old and had ninety-one dollars in the bank. His rent was overdue, and his boss at the Cahuenga Liquor Store had told him not to bother coming back when he had left for his latest interview. And now he was going to miss that interview, and probably a role he wanted more than anything, because of engine trouble.

Simon slammed his hands against the steering wheel. Sweat blurred his vision. The car's interior was stifling; he had the windows up despite the ninety-degree weather. It was impossible to drive otherwise during a Santa Ana windstorm; the hot dry gusts struck like solid blows. Simon looked about. There was no one on this street and only a few people crossing the intersection at Hollywood Boulevard. The wind kept most people indoors. A newspaper was slashed in half by his car's aerial. The wind howled. It hadn't stopped in six days; it wasn't going to stop now just because he had to walk to a phone.

He sighed and opened the door, pushing with all of his hundred and fifty pounds against the wind. His eyes began to water behind his sunglasses. The gusts tore at the permanent his agent had suggested. The air smelled of smoke; sepia clouds from the canyon fires covered most of the sky. The baleful sunlight was appropriate lighting for his life, Simon thought as he walked toward the boulevard, leaning into the wind. He looked at his watch and realized he could not reach Marathon Studios on time now.

He stifled a yawn as he walked; he had gotten little sleep the night before, due to a neighbor's Doberman. The dog had barked all night at the wind. He watched the cars creeping cautiously along. A Dodge van cut in front of a Mercedes, and the little old lady driving the latter hit the horn and shouted a curse. Simon, watching her, stepped on a wad of chewing gum and kicked his foot free with the same curse. The wind fanned anger like it fanned the canyon fires. Even so, Simon felt that he had much to be angry about. He had come to L.A. from New York five years before, a graduate of a good acting school, with several commercials and plays to his credit. His fascination was horror movies; his ambition, to be the next Boris Karloff. But so far he had barely been able to stay alive with a few bit parts on Saturday morning TV shows and a role in a low-budget vampire spoof. He had expected it to be hard. He had expected to struggle. But for five years?

Near a hot dog stand he saw a pay phone. As he reached for it, a spark he could see in the sunlight arced from his finger to the metal casing, painfully. He was too tired even to curse. He put his last dime in and dialed.

The greasy smell from the hot dog stand reminded him that he had had no breakfast or lunch. For the last month he had been living mostly on money from his part-time job, which was not nearly enough for the rent plus photographs and résumé copies. So he had not bought groceries for two weeks.

During those same two weeks, however, Simon's agent had convinced Martin Knox, who was producing a horror picture, to consider Simon for the lead. Knox had been dubious, but after several tests Simon was still in the running. Or had been . . . Martin Knox's temper was legendary in the industry, and he did not like to be kept waiting.

Simon wanted the part, and not only for economic reasons. He was sure that he could do things with the character that would win an Oscar, the first for a horror picture lead since Fredric March in the 1931 *Dr. Jekyll and Mr. Hyde*. He watched the tourists and locals as he waited for the studio switchboard to put him through. The Hollywood freaks would not be out in force until after dark, but some had already braved the heat and the wind. Krishna folk with tambourines and Jesus freaks with tracts eyed each other warily. Aging hippies, long hair beginning to gray, shuffled by. And, of course, there were the few too strange for any description. The Hollywood Scalper, Simon was sure, would look tame in a lineup with some of these. He saw Trapper Jake approaching: an old man, but still tall and burly, with long braided hair, a Bowie knife and pouch, and hand-stitched buckskin clothes. Despite appearances, he was an amiable sort; once, while Simon and a date had waited in a movie line, he had regaled them with a story of being raised by bears in Yosemite. Simon turned and huddled against the phone stall. He wanted no tales from Trapper Jake today.

Martin Knox answered the phone. "Hello, Simon." His voice was barely audible over the wind. "Why aren't you here?" He sounded annoyed.

"Car trouble, Mr. Knox. I was hoping we could reschedule—?"

"I see." Silence for a moment. Simon could picture Knox vividly, sitting owllike behind his desk, eyes hooded. "Well,

I'm afraid it won't be necessary, Simon. I think we'll be going with another actor. Your tests make you look too short for the part."

Simon tightened his fingers around the receiver. "I'm five-eleven," he said.

"You're also late." The phone clicked, and a dial tone began.

Simon hung up carefully, not allowing himself to slam the receiver onto the hook, not allowing himself any feelings at all. Not thinking about how much he had wanted this part, about what he could have done with it. So you want to be in pictures, he said to himself.

He dug into his pocket and came up with a lone nickel. He stared at it, realizing that he couldn't even call a tow truck. He closed his hand over the nickel suddenly, digging fingernails into his palm.

A gust of wind hit the phone stall hard enough to shake the phone; it gurgled and dropped his dime into the return bin. Simon fished it out and looked at it, stifling a sudden strong urge to laugh. Christ, he thought. My SAG dues are coming up too.

He called a tow truck, then stood staring across Hollywood Boulevard, wishing he knew someone he could call and talk to. In five years he had made few friends here. Usually he was too busy to feel the lack of companionship; hustling parts and working took up all of his time. But occasionally the loneliness would hit him hard.

The heat waves from the street, when not scattered by the wind, gave the scene a wavering, dreamlike appearance. Sometimes it seemed to him as if all Los Angeles was a mirage, populated by ghosts. The very ground was insubstantial, prone to earthquakes, and the city's main product was fantasy. Simon stood there, overwhelmed by loneliness and a sense of unreality. Then a sudden loud noise—an empty soft-drink can, propelled by the wind—made him jump nervously backward. He collided with someone and felt himself seized in a powerful grip and spun roughly about. "You watch who the *hell* you're knocking around!" a voice shouted, and he was pushed violently into the hot dog stand; the sharp edge of the counter dug into his back. Half stunned by surprise and pain, Simon saw that it was amiable Trapper Jake who had pushed him. The giant old man, resembling in beard and buckskin the bear he claimed had raised him, came toward Simon. His face was choleric with rage and both fists were raised. Passersby stopped to watch with interest.

Simon ran past the phone stall toward the edge of the building. Jake changed course to intercept him, but at that moment a particularly strong burst of wind upset an overflowing wire trash bin, scattering garbage across the star-inlaid sidewalk. Jake slipped on a paper plate greased with chili and sprawled headlong through the trash, to the vast amusement of the stand's patrons. Simon did not wait to see what would happen next; he turned the corner and ran. The wind seemed almost to help him, lifting him in great lunar leaps down the deserted side street. He ran, full of panic, elbows pumping, lungs sucking in the crackling air. The fear combined with his hunger to exhaust him quickly. He reached the empty parking lot by his car, stumbled across the low chain at its edge, and collapsed. The hot blacktop, dusted with light ash from the fires, scorched his cheek and arms. With a groan of pain he rolled into the shade of a nearby brick building.

He lay there for a few minutes, sobbing with pain and anger. He pounded both scraped hands painfully against the rough asphalt. There had to be an end to this run of bad luck—he would make an end to it, somehow! Someway, he promised himself, aware of the last-reel triteness of it and not caring, he would make of this moment a turning point. He wanted to act, and to eat three times a day; he wanted his name, eventually, on a sidewalk star. And he wanted that role more than he wanted breath in his lungs. He wanted it, and he intended to have it.

The wind was still blowing; harder now, it seemed. Simon

looked about him. There was no one in the lot's kiosk. Against the adjoining wall was a large trash bin; a department store mannikin with a broken head grinned, one-eyed, at him. The sun, like a spotlight with a red gel, cast crimson light over the scene. Simon felt again a dreamlike quality suffusing everything. He could hear the wind, but it seemed somehow distant. The feeling was that of loneliness and waiting.

The wind howled.

A dust devil blew into the parking lot, a skittering whirl of hot dry air, picking up litter and dust and the fine white ash from the fires and spinning it all about. But instead of coming apart after a moment, it kept spinning, faster and faster. It began to shrink. The debris that had defined it before was flung from it. There was only dust and ash now, and then not even that; just a silvery spinning of air, growing denser.

It was assuming a human shape.

The wind was still blowing, but it did not disturb the whirling shape. There was a breathless tension to the air around Simon. The shape coalesced, solidified. . . .

It became a woman.

She seemed younger than Simon, with silver hair and pale skin. She was naked. Though she looked solid, she seemed also insubstantial, as though she would blur or become transparent if viewed from another angle. Her face was beautiful, but somehow he could not make out her features clearly. Her eyes were wide and blank, like unminted silver coins.

She smiled at him. The smile would have been touching had it not been for the blank eyes; they made it hideous. It was a smile full of yearning, full of gratitude, of waiting at last fulfilled. She took two steps toward Simon. He drew back against the wall, making a high, thin sound in his throat. She hesitated—and then a gust seized her, spun her around like a ballerina, faster and faster, until her hair was a thinning silver stain in the air, and the lines of her body ran like pale paint.

Then she was gone, and Simon was alone in the lot, save for the cry of the wind.

It had been a hallucination, of course. That was the only possible explanation. Considering the stress he had been under, it was a wonder he had not seen the beast from 20,000 fathoms in that parking lot. So Simon told himself, starting as he stumbled out of the lot and continuing for the rest of the day. By evening he had almost convinced himself of it.

Hallucination or not, he had made a promise to himself, there in the parking lot. He did not intend to let the part in Knox's picture escape him. He had been invited to a party the following evening, and he knew that Martin Knox would be there. Perhaps Simon could persuade him to reconsider.

He arrived late at the small house deep in the maze of Laurel Canyon. He had almost changed his mind about coming; the thought of confronting Knox did unpleasant things to his stomach. But he had to make the effort. Also, he did not receive invitations to many parties.

Jon Shea, the host, handed him a drink at the door. He was also an actor, tall and well-built—he and Simon were members of the same gym. "How've you been, Simon?" Jon asked. "You're looking a bit wasted."

"Haven't been getting much sleep," Simon said. "Neighbor's dog keeps me up all night." He always felt slightly uncomfortable around Jon—any criticism, no matter how minor, from him always produced in Simon a need to explain and justify. Jon Shea was only a year older than Simon, but he had done much better as an immigrant New York actor: three movies and currently featured player in a TV series. Simon resented him for it, and disliked himself for feeling that way.

"This damn wind keeps me awake," Jon said. "My grandma says—she's from the old country, you know"—Simon recalled that Jon's name had been longer and full of consonants before his agency suggested a change—"anyway, she says a wind like this is a devil wind, an evil spirit—hey, are you okay?"

Simon had stopped in the hallway and leaned against the redwood wall. "Fine. Drink's a little strong . . . what did your grandmother say about the wind?"

"Oh, she's got a lot of old stories like that." He looked past Simon into the living room, where people circulated. "Gotta go play host. Lots of ladies around. Find yourself one." Then he was gone, before Simon could stop him.

Simon walked slowly through the small, cozy house, edging his way around groups of people, still feeling the coldness that had gripped his gut when Jon had mentioned his grandmother's theory about the wind. He thought about the apparition in the parking lot. Coincidence, he said to himself, sounding the word out syllable by syllable, chanting it as he might a mantra. Coincidence. A comforting word to know.

Disco accompanied his nervous heartbeat. The windows rattling in the wind sounded occasionally above the music. Simon rubbed the cool glass he held against one check as he paused in the doorway of the game room. An overhead light and ceiling fan hung over the pool table, where Knox was sinking the last ball. Several onlookers applauded as the cushion shot hit the pocket. The only one not watching was a woman with short dark hair, playing a Pachenko machine in a far corner.

Knox raised his glass to the applause and started out of the room. A large man in a dark suit followed him. Simon took a deep breath and stepped forward as Knox was about to pass him. "Mr. Knox," he said, smiling. That was as far as he got before a large hand encircled his arm, fingers meeting thumb easily. Simon looked up at the man accompanying Knox. He was very large; his face was battered and slightly bored. A pair of black horn-rimmed glasses looked startlingly incongruous on him.

"It's all right, Daniel," Knox said. Simon's arm was released. He recalled that many people in the industry had hired bodyguards in the past week, since the scalper killings began. "Thank you," Simon said to Knox, somehow keeping the smile in place. "I just wanted to talk to you a bit more about the lead in your picture."

Knox's face was expressionless. "What exactly did you want to say?"

Simon dropped the smile for a serious look. The thought crossed his mind that he was acting harder now than he ever had in his life. "Frankly, I hope to talk you into reconsidering. I feel I'm right for the part."

Knox's face was as motionless as a freeze frame. "I'm afraid it's too late for that. Terrence Froseth is set for the part. I've already talked with his agent—"

Simon did not know who Terrence Froseth was, and did not care. Realizing that pressing the issue was bad form, he nevertheless plunged ahead. "It's never too late," he said intensely. "After all, Gable wasn't the first choice for *Gone With the Wind*. Karloff wasn't the first choice for the monster in *Frankenstein*."

"You put yourself in good company," Knox said dryly. "I must say your persistence is admirable, though you need to learn some manners . . . if Froseth cannot take the part for any reason, perhaps we shall talk further. That's all I'll say on the matter." He walked down the hallway. Daniel looked coolly at Simon and followed.

Someone in the room turned on a small television set, and a news anchorman's voice filled the air. "As of this evening the latest fire in Topanga is under control. To repeat, the wind has increased slightly since yesterday, and driving is still hazardous.

"Police have not released the identity of the latest victim of the Hollywood Scalper, but they do confirm that he was a film director. This is the sixth scalper victim in as many days. . . ."

The conversation had stopped, and the room's occupants were gathered intently around the set as Simon walked down the hall. He stood before a window and watched the trees, ghastly in orange and green lawn lights, thrashing in the wind. It had been blowing for a solid week. It suddenly occurred to him that the Hollywood Scalper's spree had started the day after the Santa Anas had begun to blow. The wind makes people crazy, he thought, remembering Trapper Jake.

The Hollywood Scalper was yet another item of worry: a psychotic who killed only show business people, knifing them and then cutting a small scalplock from them, which he presumably kept. But all the victims to date had been people more advanced in their careers than Simon was. Surely he was beneath the scalper's notice.

He was still staring out the window, when there suddenly appeared before him a pale, transparent face floating in the night. He turned with a gasp—someone was standing behind him. Simon sighed in relief. For an instant, the shape of her face and the effect of the reflection had made him think—

The dark-haired woman from the game room stepped back a pace. "I didn't mean to startle you."

Simon smiled. "No problem. I—thought you were someone else."

She smiled as well. "My name's Molly Harren—and you're Simon Drake. I saw you in that movie—"

"Oh, God, no," he said, hiding his head in mock despair. "Don't tell me you saw *Disco Dracula!*"

"You were good," she said, laughing, as did he. "The movie was abysmal, of course, but you were good." Simon grinned at her. Her black hair framed a fascinating face, with large, dark liquid eyes. Though she was laughing at the moment, he could see that her normal expression was studious, almost intense. She wore a sleeveless evening dress, and it showed her to be in very good shape—not merely sleek and well-fed like most of the people there, but lean, with graceful curves of musculature. She obviously kept herself in shape with more than the obligatory morning jog. And her name sounded familiar. . . . "Are you an actress?"

"No. A writer."

It hit him then, and his jaw dropped. "You wrote *Black-out!*"

She nodded. "But that wasn't my title. I called it *The Dark Side of Town.*"

He had been about to compliment her on the screenplay—it had been one of his favorite recent suspense films, about a psychotic terrorizing a town during a power failure. Instead, he said, "That's a much better title."

She nodded, pursing her lips in disgust. "The studios are all into one-word titles now. 'Easier audience understanding.' They're talking a sequel, and of course they want to call it *Blackout II.* So imaginative." Then she shook her head and smiled. "Sorry. I—well, I overheard your conversation with Knox. I just wanted you to know that I understand how you feel. It isn't easy dealing with them sometimes."

Conversation came easily after that. They discussed her screenplay and his career, and the common interest they shared in horror and suspense films. Simon forgot about the disappointment of losing the Marathon part, at least momentarily. It had been quite some time since he had met a woman he could talk with so easily, one with whom he shared so many interests. He was aware once again of how lonely he had been, because now, for a time, he was not.

It was almost two A.M. when they noticed people leaving. "I'd better be going," Molly said. "It was very nice meeting you, Simon."

They were sitting on a rattan couch under a framed one-sheet poster of one of Jon Shea's three movies. Simon glanced at it as they stood and only realized later that he did not feel the usual pang of jealousy. He considered and discarded several clever come-on lines, and instead said simply, "I'd like to follow you home, Molly."

She smiled slightly, almost wistfully. "I think I'd like you to—but not tonight, I'm afraid. Why don't we get together for lunch—say, Wednesday?"

Wednesday was fine with him. He offered to walk her to her car. When they stepped outside, the wind struck at them savagely. Simon leaned into it, his shirt collar whipping at his neck as he watched her drive away in a pale Fiat. The wind was strong enough to buffet the small car over the white line several times—he hoped she reached home safely.

His own car was still in the shop, and so he walked home, down Laurel Canyon to Hollywood, up Highland to Franklin. It was a long, nervous walk. Black and white patrol cars, spectral under the mercury lamps, cruised the streets. He was two blocks from his apartment when one stopped him and, after checking his ID, gave him a ride the rest of the way. It was after three when he wearily climbed the steps to his second-story apartment in the hills above Cahuenga. The building was one of the older Spanish-style constructions, with pantiles and archways and a small open court filled with cactus and jacaranda. Simon could smell the heavy scent of the flowers, now strong, now faint, as the wind gusted. He could hear the power lines above the building humming, and he could also hear the Doberman in the yard next door barking. He saw it, a black shape restlessly prowling the driveway beyond the Cyclone fence. It would be another sleepless night.

The street's acoustics made the wind sound sometimes like wolves howling, sometimes like babies screaming. Something flickered in the corner of Simon's vision as he stepped onto his porch; he heard a sharp *crack!* like a whip. He turned quickly and saw that a TV antenna line had come loose and was flapping against a wall across the street. All the way home he had felt like a character in a Val Lewton film, sure that someone or something had been following him, constantly looking behind him at the skirling leaves and clattering debris that the wind hurled about. He stared down at the deserted street, leached of color by the moon. The wind now sounded like the wailing of lost souls. He could not have felt more alone if he were the last man on Earth; he wished desperately that Molly had said yes.

Despite the night sounds, he managed to fall asleep, but not for long. He dreamed that someone was sinking in a black lake, calling to him, stretching long white arms out to him. He awoke with a start, still hearing his name being called.

The water bed rocked him gently as he rubbed his eyes. His body and shorts were damp with sweat. He looked at the luminous face of his watch: four-thirty. The wind still blew outside, but the dog had stopped barking. He felt more tired than ever. Understandable, with nightmares of someone drowning and calling his name. . . .

He heard the call again.

Simon lay quite still. Over the ceaseless rise and fall of the wind he had heard his name—a long, wailing cry, faint, breathless, like the cry of a woman drowning. He lay and listened with his entire body. And it came again: *Simonnn* . . . drawn out and whispered, almost as though the wind itself had cried to him.

It *was* the wind! He heard it again, the rising whistle outside shaping itself into his name. He stared at the ceiling, not daring to turn his head, afraid to look at the silvered square of the window, knowing he would have to when the call came again.

Simonnn. . . .

He turned his head toward the window.

Limned in the moonlight, hair like streamers of fog, she stared at him with eyes cold as stars.

Simon rolled over and out of the bed with a cry and ran down the hall. The light of the full moon, coming through the living room window, spotlighted a large poster of Lon Chaney, Jr., as the wolf man. It seemed to be coming out of the poster toward him, jaws opening wide; Simon gasped, turned, and stumbled into a hanging planter. The leaves scratched his face like spiders' legs. He clawed open the front door, lunging outside into the hot, moving air, not thinking, simply running. He looked down from the porch at the street—shadows crawled in the wind. Then something—a blown leaf, his hair, or *her hand*—brushed his cheek. With a shriek he leapt down the tiled steps, tripped and fell, scrambled to his feet, turned—

She stood before him.

She was not more than three feet away. As before, she appeared corporeal and yet ghostly. Her hair floated behind her like a gossamer web. Her eyes were still silver wells, looking at him but not seeing him. Her expression was that of ineffable loneliness and longing.

She reached for him.

Simonnn. . . .

He did not see her lips move; the wind seemed to whisper his name. Frozen with fear, he saw the approaching hands very clearly: they were as pale and smooth as blown snow, no trace of fingerprints or veining. Her lips parted in a smiling rictus, and behind them was only darkness. . . .

Simon shut his eyes and flung himself backward, hands flailing the air before him. He felt one pass through coldness, and then he had turned and was plunging through a flower bed, not feeling the cactus rake his bare legs, fingers hooking into the links of the Cyclone fence, the wind tearing, shrieking at him. He pulled himself up and over the fence, fell against cool concrete and heard a low growl nearby. He realized then where he had fled.

The Doberman leapt, a shadow with gleaming teeth. Simon lurched to his feet and ran, knowing it was useless. Then, above the wind's howling, he heard a crackling sound. He ran against a wall, knocking the breath from his lungs and falling. He turned over and saw that one of the high-tension lines from the power pole overhead had come loose. Like a sparkling whip it fell, lashing the charging dog squarely across the back. The dog's growl changed to an agonized yelp—the force of the shock hurled it across the driveway to land, quivering, against the fence. The broken power line danced and scattered sparks across the concrete.

Simon looked about him quickly, but there was no sign

of her anywhere. The only sounds were the wind and the hissing of the power line. Oddly enough, all the noise had not aroused the neighbors. He looked at the dog—it had stopped quivering.

The wind brought the smell of burned flesh to him, and he turned away to be sick.

Hey, Simon," Jon Shea said. "You're just in time to applaud. I'm going for two-seventy-five today."

Simon had just entered the workout area of the Golden West Health Spa. The large room, walled with mirrors, was filled with men working body-building equipment. An AM rock station played over the members' grunts and groans. Jon lay prone on a bench press, seized the bar, and raised it over his chest, straining as he lifted a stack of weights six times. He rose slowly, skin shining with sweat, and looked at Simon. "You don't look good. Maybe you shouldn't work out."

"I—didn't get much sleep last night," Simon replied. He was pale, and he leaned against a rack of barbells. His legs still smarted from the cactus and the fall onto the driveway. "I just came in to ask you a question," he continued.

"Sure. Shoot."

Simon stared through the floor-to-ceiling window at the jogging track outside. No one was jogging, despite the rarity of a smog-free day. The wind vibrated the glass before him and he stepped back hastily.

"Your grandmother called this a demon wind, you said. What did she mean?"

Jon blinked in surprise. "Oh, it's just legends, you know. They had stories about werewinds, that were supposed to take human shape—you better sit down, you look awful."

Simon did so. "Go on, please," he said faintly.

Jon scratched his head. "I don't remember that much about it . . . they're not evil so much as just lonely, sort of lost souls, I guess. You know how the wind is always described as sounding lonely? Well, the werewind is drawn

to lonely people." He peered closely at Simon, who was
staring out the window at the wind-shook spires of the Chinese
Theatre. "Why the interest?"

"Oh . . . I had an idea it might make a good horror
movie."

Jon snorted. "Everybody's a writer. But I think you're too
late on that one. Molly Harren asked me about it days ago."

Simon asked, "How do you stop a werewind?"

"That's what Molly asked. I'll tell you what I told her—
look in the library. I don't remember. It's all bullshit anyway."

"Yeah," Simon said, standing. "Right." He opened the
door to leave, but at that moment the music piped into the
spa stopped, and a voice said: "This is a news bulletin from
KCCO. Yet another Hollywood Scalper victim has been
found, this one in West Los Angeles. The body has been
identified as that of Terrence Froseth, a young actor. This
is the seventh scalper victim in seven days . . ."

Simon saw Jon go pale beneath his tan. Across the floor
another actor released his grip on a pulley and a stack of
weights crashed down.

Simon leaned against the door, feeling quite weak. He
felt a number of other emotions as well: horror and sympathy
were among them. But the dominant feeling was a hideous
sense of relief. And unbidden into his mind came a thought
that disgusted him: I'm back in the running again.

Outside, the wind howled.

Simon left the gym and took a bus down to Mannie's
Auto Repair on Melrose. He gave Mannie a check, wondering vaguely how he would cover it, then drove downtown
to the main branch of the Los Angeles Library. There he
spent several hours under the high, carved ceilings leafing
through books of legends and superstitions.

He found several spells to make the wind blow, and a few
references to various kinds of wind demons and manifesta-
tions both malign and benign. At last he discovered a passing

reference to the legend of the werewind. According to the paragraph, the werewind could be bound by tying knots in a length of hair. The stronger the wind, the more knots were required, and it would not abate until the last knot had been tied. The passage cited an in-depth work on the subject in *The Omnibus of the Occult*, but when he looked for that book, he found that it had already been checked out.

Simon stood before the card catalogue files and pressed the heels of his hands against his eyes until green patterns spun in the darkness. He was not quite sure what to do next. He told himself that he should be out job-hunting, or looking through the trades and nagging his agent. But he did not move. He stood quietly, wishing he could stop the thoughts that whirled like dust devils through his head.

Such an apparition simply could not be—at least not as he stood there with the sun streaming through the latticed windows. And so, Simon thought, I am probably having a nervous breakdown. He clasped his hands together to stop their trembling. Was any career worth this? But on the other hand, what else could he do? At thirty-three, with only odd jobs behind him, how could he hope to make a decent living even if he was interested in anything other than acting? He had been through worse times. He had lived in a Greenwich Village loft without heat during the winter while auditioning for plays. Things had gotten better since then. They would get better still, he told himself. Persistence, determination; those were the keys, even more than talent. Knox had indicated that he would reconsider if Froseth could not take the part. And Froseth certainly could not take the part now. He was dead.

And did the Hollywood Scalper or someone like him lie in wait for the next lead as well? Who knew—who could decipher the motivations of a sociopath? The wind seemed to encourage such psychotics—he had heard that there had already been one copycat killing similar to the scalper's work. If Simon came into the limelight, might he not be the next victim?

He shook his head. He could not let fear rule him. Acting was his life—it had to be worth risking his life for. He wanted the lead in that picture more than he had ever wanted any role. He would wait a day or so, out of respect to the dead, and then call Knox again.

The library would be closing soon; he turned toward the exit. It was rush hour now. Usually he tried to avoid the bumper-to-bumper crawl of freeway traffic, but he knew that today he would feel safer driving in that sluggish flow, surrounded by cars and people. In the wind.

"We repeat, Los Angeles police have taken into custody twenty-seven-year-old Greg Corey. He is charged with the Hollywood Scalper murders that have terrorized Los Angeles for the past eight days. . . ."

Simon heard the news while driving down La Cienega toward a health food restaurant where he was to meet Molly for lunch. He almost cheered out loud. Things at last seemed to be looking up! According to the report, it was a virtual certainty that the suspect was the scalper—he had been caught in an attack on a producer and had admitted to the other slayings. Thank God, Simon thought. At least I don't have to worry about that anymore.

He found Molly sitting at a corner table, all but hidden by a large potted fern. The corner was dark save for a candle's glow; after the merciless sunlight, Simon could see little except dazzle. "I hope you don't mind," she said. "I like seclusion when I eat." She looked different; he realized her hair was longer. She was wearing a fall.

They ordered. "Did you hear the news?" he asked. "The Hollywood Scalper's been caught."

She nodded and smiled. "But not before your competition was removed."

Simon blinked, somewhat nonplused and secretly uncomfortable because of his similar thoughts. "Well, of course, I don't look at it that way—"

"I understand," she said. "It is a terrible thing, but you

mustn't let that stop you from taking advantage of it." She frowned at his expression. "Does that sound ruthless? I guess I am rather ruthless—you have to be in this town if you care about your art at all. If you have to work with people who think that having money gives them the right to dictate creativity."

Simon felt vaguely uncomfortable at her intensity. "Well, I haven't been in a position to argue with them too much. And I'm under no delusions about the artistic quality of my work so far."

"Everyone has to start somewhere. You were good in that cheap film; you don't have to worry. But the frustration applies more to me than to you, because I'm a writer. The film *starts* with me. No matter how good the actor, the director, the effects, without a good script the film is nothing. And so when a good script is written and they ruin it, it's a crime. More—it's a sin. You see?"

He saw that this was obviously her holy crusade, and so he merely nodded, though privately he felt that an actor's interpretation of a script was just as important as the script. Their lunch arrived and they spoke of other things. "I've raised the money to produce my latest script," she said. "That way, no idiot can ruin my work—if it fails it will be my fault. But this damned Santa Ana weather is delaying production. I'm losing money each day the wind blows. Not to mention nearly losing my house in Topanga to the fire."

Simon agreed with considerable feeling that the wind must stop soon. The subject changed, and he told her how much he wanted the lead in Knox's picture.

Molly nodded. "Martin Knox is one of the few good producers. Be careful of him, though; he has a temper, and money to back it up."

Simon looked stubborn. "I *know* I'm right for that part."

"Then you will probably get it, now that Froseth is dead. The show must go on—people have to have their fix of cinematic fantasy." She sounded slightly bitter. "The hell of it is, movies and TV are what's real to the rest of the world. Not us—not the ones responsible. We're just ghosts."

Her use of the word startled him. They split the check and left the cool interior for the wind and the sun.

The wind struck them both with a hard, dry gust as they descended the brick steps to the parking lot—Molly missed her footing and almost fell. Simon grabbed her arm, steadying her. "Thanks!" she shouted over the howling. "I really think this goddamn wind is out to get me."

Again her innocent words jarred him; he looked quickly, fearfully, around the parking lot, but there was no sign of the werewind. They walked over to her car and hesitated in the inevitable awkward moment of good-bye. Simon realized that he was very much afraid of her leaving him today—afraid to be alone again. "Molly," he said, "I'd like to invite you back to my place. I—it's not a come-on, really." The truth surprised him. He was not thinking of sex at all. He simply wanted to be with her; almost as big a fear as the werewind was the fear of his loneliness.

She looked away from him at the distant Hollywood Hills, clear and sharp in the dry air. The wind tore at her long dark fall; he wondered fleetingly why she wore it on such a day. At last she said, "I'm tempted." She chuckled as though surprised at herself. "You don't know what it takes to admit even that much; we Hollywood ghosts shy away from emotional commitments." She looked at him, then took his face in her hands and kissed him lightly on the mouth. The wind staggered them, almost ruined the moment. "I appreciate the offer very much, but . . . no. I have work that must be done."

"I understand, but—" The wind pushed them against the car. "Goddammit!" Simon shouted, losing his temper and striking futilely at the air.

"Relax. You can't stop it that way," she said. "You've more important things to think about, like talking to Martin Knox. Let me know how that turns out, okay?"

He nodded. Then she was in the car and backing out of

the lot. He saw a smile thrown his way, and then she was gone. The sound of the engine was quickly lost in the wind's roar.

Too late, he thought of asking her what she knew about the werewind. Jon had told him she was possibly thinking about a script based on it. Simon shuddered. He would not want to be in it.

The streets were almost deserted. The news station said that the wind in the canyons at times reached near-hurricane force. Simon drove carefully. On his way back to his apartment he saw one lone pedestrian—a tall woman with silver hair, standing on a corner of Santa Monica Boulevard. His heartbeat shook him for an instant before he realized that it was one of the few hookers still braving the wind. She looked at him with flat curiosity. He drove on.

At home the mail contained a notice from his answering service that he was being dropped for nonpayment. Simon hurled the notice at the wall. The fact that it was too light to strike with any degree of force and instead only drifted to the floor increased his anger. He seized the telephone, tempted to throw it; instead, he sat down and pressed the number of Marathon Studios. He had intended to wait a day or so, but he had been waiting too long, he told himself.

There was a long wait after he gave the secretary his name, during which time Simon breathed deeply to relax. I will not sound eager or get angry, he told himself. I will offer my condolences and then ask about the part. After all, as Molly had said, the show must go on.

"Yes, Simon."

"I just wanted to say I was sorry to hear about Froseth, Mr. Knox."

"Yes, it is a tragedy." Knox's voice was emotionless.

"A pity they couldn't have caught the scalper before this." Simon hesitated; Knox said nothing. "Have you given any thought to a replacement? I know this is rather quick, but . . ."

He trailed off. Knox said, "I'm sorry, Simon, but after further thought, I still don't think you'd be right for the part."

Simon heard someone say, "Am I still too short, Mr. Knox? I could wear stacked heels, you know."

"It's not exactly—"

"Or am I 'too' something else?" Simon realized that he was saying these words to Knox; he listened, faintly embarrassed, as if he were a bystander eavesdropping on a quarrel. "Am I too tall now? Too fat maybe? Too thin?"

"We have your résumé on file," Knox said distantly. "Good-bye, Simon."

Simon sat listening numbly to the dial tone. It's over, he thought. I've done it now.

He hung up and stared out the window at the waving trees. He listened to the wind—the omnipresent, maddening wind. That was the cause of it all, he thought. He had been doing okay until the wind had started, so long ago. The future had not looked particularly bright, but he had been able to handle the pressure. Now he had ruined everything because of that damned wind. . . .

The dial tone gave way to a siren; he depressed the cradle button, then began to punch his agent's number. He stopped before hitting the last digit. What would he say? Well, Sid, I went a little crazy, started yelling at Martin Knox, so I'll be about as welcome at Marathon now as the scalper would be at Disneyland. He hung up again, then looked at the clock. It was after six—Knox would have left the studio by now. If I could talk to him again, Simon thought, face-to-face. Apologize. Explain about the wind, how it had sawed away at his nerves . . . it was understandable, surely. . . .

It took several phone calls to learn Knox's home address; he finally got it from Jon Shea. Simon told Jon part of what had happened, and Jon tried to counsel a different course: "Let it lie for a while, Simon. Give him a call in a few days; maybe the wind'll die down by then, everybody'll be back to normal. We've all been under stress—he understands that. But don't push it now. He's got a temper too. . . ."

He did not listen. That evening he drove west on Sunset, toward the ocean. As usual, there were few cars out; even on the Strip the lanes were clear. The wind hammered at the Chrysler. As the evening grew darker, Simon had to restrain himself from driving faster. Near Beverly Glen the boulevard was blocked off—he had to detour around UCLA. Ashes from the canyon fire fell like dirty snowflakes; at one point he had to turn on his wipers.

It was almost dark when he reached Knox's house in Pacific Palisades. The day's end washed the ocean in neon-red and orange. Knox's house was on a cliff overlooking the Pacific Coast Highway. Simon parked at one end of the long, curved driveway, next to a lawn mower and a trash can full of shrubbery clippings left by a gardener.

He had given no thought to what he would say—he had not thought at all during the long drive. He pressed the doorbell and stood before the massive carved door. It opened; Martin Knox stared at him in disbelief.

"What the hell do you want?"

"To apologize," Simon said.

"This is absurd." Knox began to close the door.

"Wait, please," Simon said; then, as the door continued to close, he suddenly shouted "I said *wait*!" and grabbed it. The burst of anger had struck like a wind gust and vanished as quickly, but it had done its harm—it had aroused Knox's temper. "That does it," the producer said in a low voice. He turned and shouted, "Daniel!"

Simon stepped off the porch into the wind. "Mr. Knox, I came only to apologize . . . it's the wind, don't you see? It's making everyone crazy. . . ."

Knox opened the door again, and Daniel stood beside him. "Throw him off the property," Knox said. "Don't be too gentle."

Simon backed up as Daniel came toward him. The wind whirled about them. Daniel approached quickly, looking bored. Simon turned and ran toward his car, fumbling his keys from his pocket. He had parked near the edge of the bluff. He stabbed the keys at the door lock; living in Hollywood had habituated him to locking the car. Daniel came around the front of the car and reached for him.

As he did, a blast of wind knocked Simon off balance; he fell backward, away from the huge bodyguard. The same gust knocked the gardener's can over. The wind seized the leaves and grass trimmings and spun them in a green flurry across the lawn. As Daniel bent to seize Simon's shirt, the cloud of leaves and grass struck them like confetti, swirling around them, blinding them. Daniel waved his arms, staggered to one side—and slipped, falling over the bluff.

Simon screamed. He crawled to the edge, looking down. It was not a sheer drop to the highway below, but it was close enough. He saw Daniel's motionless dark form sprawled on the steep slope.

He stood carefully, holding on to the car. He looked back toward the house and saw Knox standing in the doorway, staring at him. He knew it appeared as if he had pushed Daniel over the cliff. Knox slammed the door. He's calling the police, Simon thought.

But another thought came to him, far more terrifying than that. There was a pattern to these events: when the wind struck, *she* appeared.

The Chrysler spun out of the driveway and down the winding road toward Sunset. Simon had no idea where he was going. He merely wanted to get away, to escape what he knew would surely come to him—the soulless, smiling werewind. He breathed raggedly, looking about frantically for any sign of her. There was none. He began to wonder where he could go.

Not back to his apartment, surely. He needed someone he could trust, someone he could tell what had happened. Molly. It had to be Molly.

She had said she lived in Topanga, in an A-frame on Grandview Drive. He did not have her number with him, did not know if she was home, but he started north on the Pacific Coast Highway nonetheless. She *had* to be home!

Soon he was driving recklessly up the winding road between sheer cliffs, toward Fernwood. Black skeletal trees, remnants of the recent fire, surrounded him. The wind between the close canyon walls was like a shotgun blast. He found the street and the house, high on a hillside. Parked in the gravel driveway was her Fiat.

As he stepped out of his car, the wind knocked him off balance again; he sprawled in an untended bed of ivy beside the ramshackle porch. Scrambling to his feet, teeth clenched against screaming, he pounded on the door. Beyond the flimsy shelter of porch and bushes it seemed that demons shrieked and tore at the earth.

The yellow porch light went on above him and he saw her silhouette behind the door window. After a moment, the door opened a crack.

"Simon?" She sounded tired and confused. "What is it? What are you doing here?"

"Let me in, please, Molly," he pleaded. "Please. I'm in trouble."

"I can't, Simon." Half of her face was visible against the crack, sallow in the porch light. "I'm working on something very important—"

"*Please!*" The wind screamed about him, tugging at his hair like fingers, *her* fingers. . . .

Molly looked torn with indecision. At last she said, "All right, if you're in trouble. But it can be only a moment. Then you'll have to go." She opened the door and Simon entered quickly.

They stood in a small living room. A picture window in the far wall looked out on the lights of Topanga. Simon noticed distractedly that the place was a mess—dead plants in pots, clothing strewn everywhere, books and records stacked haphazardly on old, worn furniture. Far in the back of his mind he was surprised and slightly disappointed—he had thought she would be neater.

A television was on in one corner, inaudible due to the wind outside.

Molly faced him, wearing jeans and a dark T-shirt. He noticed she was not wearing her fall this time. "Well?" she said. "What's wrong?"

"I don't know where to start," he said wearily. Even inside, the wind forced him to speak loudly. The whole house shook with its force. The lights dimmed, then returned. Molly looked at them in concern.

"Simon, I don't want to turn you out if you're in trouble, but you have to hurry! The wind is getting worse!"

"I know!" he said. "Jon Shea was right! It's a werewind —I've seen it!"

Her eyes went wide and her face paled. She seized his arms in a surprisingly strong grip. "*What?*"

"We've got to try the hair," he said, aware that he was babbling and not caring. "The spell, tying knots in the hair—"

"*How did you know about that?*" She was shaking him, her gaze burning with sudden rage. For an instant Simon was more afraid of her than of the werewind.

And then a blast of air hit the house and the picture window exploded into the room. Simon saw it but had no time to dodge. He felt flying splinters of glass sting his cheeks, miraculously missing his eyes. And he saw the rage in Molly's face turn to shock as a score of cuts and lacerations stitched the length of her back. She sagged into his arms and he felt blood running over his hands. He looked at her back, pulled strips of her shirt, cut by the glass, away from the wounds. None appeared to be serious. He looked about for something to serve as bandages—

—and saw who stood in the shattered window, framed by the night and the jagged glass.

Simon backed up, letting Molly fall to her knees. The gales still boomed and battered outside, but did not enter the house. The werewind approached him as he retreated in terror. Behind him a narrow flight of stairs led up to darkness; Simon turned and fled up them. They opened onto a narrow loft lit by a single dim bulb. A door at the far end led out onto a porch. On the walls hung several varying lengths of dark, knotted rope; on the table was an open book. The title at the top of the page was *The Omnibus of the Occult*. Also on the table was another length of rope—then he realized it was hair, Molly's dark fall, with knots tied in half its length.

Simonnn. . . .

Simon grabbed the fall, hands sweaty with terror. Simultaneously the wind struck the house again, shaking it to its foundations with a sound like thunder as she appeared at the head of the stairs, facing him.

Sobbing, Simon tied another knot in the fall. Her mouth opened in a silent scream, revealing darkness; arms extended, she came toward him. Simon backed up, whimpering, somehow managing to fumble yet another knot together. Then he turned and flung himself against the porch door as she came around the table.

He stumbled out onto the porch, into the wind.

It struck him like a giant fist, hurling him, half stunned, against the railing. It tore at the length of hair in his hand, but somehow he managed to retain it. She followed him onto the porch, unaffected by the wind. Simon hooked one arm around the railing as the wind buffeted him, and she came closer, closer. . . .

Hanging there over darkness, half paralyzed with fear, he managed to twist the final knot in the length of hair as the werewind touched him with her cold hands.

The howling rose to a scream. A final blast struck him, almost hurling him from the porch—and seized her as well, tearing at her, streaming her away like mist. Simon thought he heard a single, long-drawn-out cry. . . .

And the wind stopped.

Suddenly there was silence, louder than the wind, and stillness. Simon sagged to his knees, hearing his blood pounding. Hardly daring to believe it, he pulled himself to his feet. The air was motionless. For the first time in over a week the wind had stopped.

He began to laugh as he looked out at the night and the still trees. He did not laugh long—his throat was too dry. Welcome tears moistened his eyes and cheeks. It was over. He had won! He and Molly were safe!

Then he turned toward the house with a gasp. "Jesus. Molly!" he shouted, running back into the loft. He staggered down the stairs into the living room.

She was not there.

The TV set droned quietly in the corner, broadcasting the news.

"I repeat, the winds seem to have stopped everywhere.

"Recapping our top story, police have admitted that Greg Corey, arrested earlier today, is not the Hollywood Scalper. New evidence shows him to be a copycat killer who imitated the scalper's crimes. The real scalper is still at large. . . ."

"Molly?"

He looked closely for the first time at the fall he still held. It was not a fall. He could see very clearly the knot of flesh on one end of it, dark with dried blood. He remembered the other knotted lengths he had thought were ropes, hanging on the loft wall. He knew now that they were not ropes.

It occurred to him then that the werewind had never harmed him, had in fact saved him from Trapper Jake and the Doberman and Daniel.

Simon heard a noise behind him and turned.

Light glinted on a knife blade.

"I'm sorry, Simon," Molly said. "I did like you. . . ."

DRESS OF WHITE SILK

RICHARD MATHESON

In the early years of *F & SF,* editors Anthony Boucher and J. Francis McComas accepted a story, "Born of Man and Woman," (1950) from one Richard Matheson. "As we read the manuscript," they wrote, "we assumed that it was by some well-established professional, indulging in an off-trail literary exercise under a pseudonym. We hastily accepted that story and asked Mr. Matheson for some personal information . . . to learn to our happy astonishment that this was the first story he had ever sold!" Richard Matheson has since gone on to become the professional Messrs. McComas and Boucher assumed him to be in 1950, writing numerous stories and novels and working extensively in films and television, most recently with Steven Spielberg. "Dress of White Silk," first published in *F & SF* in October 1951, is typical of his style. It is a terrifying, moving, and beautifully written story of a mere . . . child.

Quiet is here and all in me.

Granma locked me in my room and wont let me out. Because its happened she says. I guess I was bad. Only it was the dress. Mommas dress I mean. She is gone away forever. Granma says your momma is in heaven. I don't know how. Can she go in heaven if shes dead?

Now I hear granma. She is in mommas room. She is putting mommas dress down the box. Why does she always? And locks it too. I wish she didnt. Its a pretty dress and smells sweet so. And warm. I love to touch it against my cheek. But I cant never again. I guess that is why granma is mad at me.

But I amnt sure. All day it was only like everyday. Mary Jane came over to my house. She lives across the street. Every day she comes to my house and play. Today she was.

I have seven dolls and a fire truck. Today granma said play with your dolls and it. Dont you go inside your mommas room now she said. She always says it. She just means not mess up I think. Because she says it all the time. Dont go in your mommas room. Like that.

But its nice in mommas room. When it rains I go there. Or when granma is doing her nap I do. I dont make noise. I just sit on the bed and touch the white cover. Like when I was only small. The room smells like sweet.

I make believe momma is dressing and I am allowed in. I smell her white silk dress. Her going out for night dress. She called it that I dont remember when.

I hear it moving if I listen hard. I make believe to see her sitting at the dressing table. Like touching on perfume or something I mean. And see her dark eyes. I can remember.

Its so nice if it rains and I see eyes on the window. The rain sounds like a big giant outside. He says shushshush so everyone will be quiet. I like to make believe that in mommas room.

What I like almost best is sit at mommas dressing table. It is like pink and big and smells sweet too. The seat in front has a pillow sewed in it. There are bottles and bottles with bumps and have colored perfume in them. And you can see almost your whole self in the mirror.

When I sit there I make believe to be momma. I say be quiet mother I am going out and you cannot stop me. Its something I say I dont know why like hear it in me. And oh stop your sobbing mother they will not catch me I have my magic dress.

When I pretend I brush my hair long. But I only use my own brush from my room. I didnt never use mommas brush. I dont think granma is mad at me for that because I never use mommas brush. I wouldnt never.

Sometimes I did open the box up. Because I know where granma puts the key. I saw her once when she wouldnt know I saw her. She puts the key on the hook in mommas closet. Behind the door I mean.

I could open the box lots of times. Thats because I like to look at mommas dress. I like best to look at it. It is so pretty and feels soft and like silky. I could touch it for a million years.

I kneel on the rug with roses on it. I hold the dress in my arms and like breathe from it. I touch it against my cheek. I wish I could take it to sleep with me and hold it. I like to. Now I cant. Because granma says. And she says I should burn it up but I loved her so. And she cries about the dress.

I wasnt never bad with it. I put it back neat like it was never touched. Granma never knew. I laughed that she never knew before. But she knows now I did it I guess. And shell punish me. What did it hurt her? Wasnt it my mommas dress?

What I like the real best in mommas room is look at the picture of momma. It has a gold thing around it. Frame is what granma says. It is on the wall on top of the bureau.

Momma is pretty. Your momma was pretty granma says. Why does she? I see momma there smiling on me and she *is* pretty. For always.

Her hair is black. Like mine. Her eyes are even pretty like black. Her mouth is red so red. I like the dress and its the white one. It is all down on her shoulders. Her skin is white almost white like the dress. And so too are her hands. She is so pretty. I love her even if she is gone away forever I love her so much.

I guess I think thats what made me bad. I mean to Mary Jane.

Mary Jane came from lunch like she does. Granma went to do her nap. She said dont forget now no going in your mommas room. I told her no granma. And I was saying the truth but then Mary Jane and I was playing fire truck. Mary Jane said I bet you havent no mother I bet you made up it all she said.

I got mad at her. I have a momma I know. She made me mad at her to say I made up it all. She said Im a liar. I mean about the bed and the dressing table and the picture and the dress even and everything.

I said well Ill show you smarty.

I looked into granmas room. She was doing her nap still. I went down and said to Mary Jane to come on because granma wont know.

She wasnt so smart after then. She giggled like she does. Even she made a scaredy noise when she hit into the table in the hall upstairs. I said youre a scaredy cat to her. She said back well *my* house isnt so dark like this. Like that was so much.

We went in mommas room. It was more dark than you could see. So I took back the curtains. Just a little so Mary Jane could see. I said this is my mommas room I suppose I made up it all.

She was by the door and she wasnt smart then either. She didnt say any word. She looked around the room. She jumped when I got her arm. Well come on I said.

I sat on the bed and said this is my mommas bed see how soft it is. She didnt say nothing. Scaredy cat I said. Am not she said like she does.

I said to sit down how can you tell if its soft if you dont sit down. She sat down by me. I said feel how soft it is. Smell how like sweet it is.

I closed my eyes but funny it wasnt like always. Because Mary Jane was there. I told her to stop feeling the cover. You said to she said. Well stop it I said.

See I said and I pulled her up. Thats the dressing table. I took her and brought her there. She said let go. It was so quiet and like always. I started to feel bad. Because Mary Jane was there. Because it was in my mommas room and momma wouldnt like Mary Jane there.

But I had to show her the things because. I showed her the mirror. We looked at each other in it. She looked white. Mary Jane is a scaredy cat I said. Am not am not she said anyway nobodys house is so quiet and dark inside. Anyway she said it smells.

I got mad at her. No it doesnt smell I said. Does so she said you said it did. I got madder too. It smells like sugar she said. It smells like sick people in your mommas room.

Dont say my mommas room is like sick people I said to her.

Well you didnt show me no dress and youre lying she said there isnt no dress. I felt all warm inside so I pulled her hair. Ill show you I said and dont never say Im a liar again.

She said Im going home and tell my mother on you. You are not I said youre going to see my mommas dress and youll better not call me a liar.

I made her stand still and I got the key off the hook. I kneeled down. I opened the box with the key.

Mary Jane said pew that smells like garbage.

I put my nails in her and she pulled away and got mad. Dont you pinch me she said and she was all red. Im telling my mother on you she said. And anyway its not a white dress its dirty and ugly she said.

Its not dirty I said. I said it so loud I wonder why granma didnt hear. I pulled out the dress from the box. I held it up to show her how its white. It fell open like the rain whispering and the bottom touched the rug.

It is too white I said all white and clean and silky.

No she said she was so mad and red it has a hole in it. I got more madder. If my momma was here shed show you I said. You got no momma she said all ugly. I hate her.

I have. I said it way loud. I pointed my finger to mommas picture. Well who can see in this stupid dark room she said. I pushed her hard and she hit against the bureau. See then I said mean look at the picture. Thats my momma and shes the most beautiful lady in the whole world.

Shes ugly she has funny hands Mary Jane said. She hasnt I said shes the most beautiful lady in the world!

Not not she said *she has buck teeth.*

I dont remember then. I think like the dress moved in my arms. Mary Jane screamed. I dont remember what. It got dark and the curtains were closed I think. I couldnt see anyway. I couldnt hear nothing except buck teethfunny hands buck teeth funny hands even when no one was saying it.

There was something else because I think I heard some one call *dont let her say that!* I couldnt hold to the dress. And I had it on me I cant remember. Because I was like grown up strong. But I was a little girl still I think. I mean outside.

I think I was terrible bad then.

Granma took me away from there I guess. I dont know. She was screaming god help us its happened its happened. Over and over. I dont know why. She pulled me all the way here to my room and locked me in. She wont let me out. Well Im not so scared. Who cares if she locks me in a million billion years? She doesnt have to even give me supper. Im not hungry anyway.

Im full.

GLADYS'S GREGORY

JOHN ANTHONY WEST

"Gladys's Gregory" is a tale that could perhaps be categorized more as black humor or satire than as traditional horror—yet the events it depicts are more than gruesome (it's one of our favorite stories). First published in *F & SF* in February 1963, it has been anthologized many times—perhaps because its topic is always current and one that concerns us all— yet, because of its merit, we have included it again in this volume. In "Gladys's Gregory," John Anthony West shows us an entire community that is preoccupied with weight, and each member of the community has in fact—one might say—a "steak" in the outcome.

L adies, members of the club, I am honored to be here today, to tell you about this year's contest in our community, and this year's contest winner, Gladys's Gregory. And I want to thank you all for your interest and for your kind attention.

I begin with statistics from the medical record. Gladys's Gregory upon his arrival at our community.

HEIGHT:	6′5½″
WEIGHT:	242
CHEST:	49″
WAIST:	36″
NECK:	18½″

I anticipate your admiration, ladies. Therefore, let me present the dark side of the coin immediately. Gregory, upon arriving, was 28 years old, yet his weight had scarcely changed since his college days when he was an all-American football player. He had been married three *full* years. Club members! Please jump to no hasty conclusions. Hear me out before you heap blame on Gladys. Bear in mind that here, true, we have Gregory; 242 pounds of raw material. But this figure had not changed for *eight* years.

Unfortunately, I admit, the women of our community did not view the situation objectively either. "Gladys's fault," they shouted, and indignation ran rampant.

We thought of Beth Shaefer, who had brought her Milton from a gangling 164 to 313 pounds in less than three years; Sally O'Leary with three strikes against her at the onset, her Jamie an ex-jockey, fighting gamely nevertheless and bringing him out finally at 245; Joan Granz, who nursed her Marvin to 437 and a second prize despite his dangerous cardiac condition. Certainly, all of you can appreciate our feelings.

Now, Gladys's Gregory was a football coach, and one day, driving past the stadium, the first clue to a nasty situation revealed itself. Gladys's Gregory was participating in the *actual* physical exercise.

I saw him hurl himself repeatedly at a stuffed dummy; saw him lead five minutes of strenuous calisthenics, then, undaunted, lead his team in a race around the track. The bitterest among Gladys's enemies would be forced to admit that perhaps it wasn't her fault entirely. To this day I see the flesh-building calories dripping from his pores in perspiration.

The next morning I paid a call on Gladys. She was a sweet young thing, far from the malicious vixen rumor had painted her. I recounted the stadium scene, and poor Gladys knew it all too well. She had even stranger tales to tell. He mowed the lawn with a *hand* mower, played handball off season, ran the two miles from the school to his home in a track suit. The girl was desolate.

We discussed his diet, and I was shocked beyond words. Red meat! She fed him red meat, and fish, and eggs, and green vegetables. . . .

"Eclairs!" I shouted at her. "Potatoes! Chocolate layer cake! Beer! Butter!"

But no. Gregory hated these things. Wouldn't touch them.

"He doesn't love you," I said.

"But he does," Gladys moaned, her voice cracking, "in his own way he does."

I suggested the strategy that was so often effective when contests had not yet gained their present popularity and opposition was stronger.

As we all know, we have more sexual stamina than our mates. A wife, subtly camouflaging her motives under the attractive cover of passion, can reduce a husband to a state of sexual fatigue in a matter of weeks. And a sexually sated husband is ripe for intelligent handling. Evening after evening he sits quietly. Eating. He marshals his energies for the night ahead and gradually he puts on weight. At a certain point his obesity interferes with his virility, and at this point the intelligent wife begins to demand less. The husband, by this time swathed in comfortable flesh, is only too happy to be let alone. Now the wife decreases her demands to nothing, and the husband, carrying no burden of calorie-consuming anxiety, prepares for the contest.

With Gladys's Gregory, this method proved futile. After a month's trial Gladys was but a shadow of her former self, while Gregory was seen everywhere, with his squad, mowing the lawn, his unsightly muscles bulging, a smug grin on his face.

At a special community meeting an ingenious plan was devised. We would make Gladys and Gregory the most socially prominent couple in the community. They soon found their social calendar booked solid: dinners, breakfasts, buffets, picnics. . . . Gregory found himself seated down to tables groaning with carbohydrates. He was under constant surveillance. No sooner had he wiped the whipped cream from his lips, before a plate, mountain-high in ice cream, bristling with macaroons, was thrust before him. His mug of beer never reached the halfway mark before some vigilant wife refilled it for him.

At this time, ladies, I must point out that Gregory was in no way a conscious rebel, nor was he malicious or subversive. We must set aside his foolish notions of physical culture and regard him as he was—a charming man and an ideal husband: affable, reticent, and quite unintelligent. The militant fury of our community women soon gave way to a genuine solicitousness. And a beaming Gladys reported that he was wearing his belt out two notches.

A carefully coached Gladys waged psychological warfare. Magazines were left open about the house, all of them turned to calorie-rich advertisements. At parties she flirted openly with the heftiest husbands still allowed free.

By spring Gregory weighed an estimated 290. Bewildered, he still clung to his old notions. "Gotta get in shape for spring training," he would mumble, his mouth filled with chocolate mousse.

At 310 our cooperative spirit dwindled. The women, all

at once, realized what they had wrought and were horrified by the prospect.

Meanwhile Gladys, grown confident, moved swiftly and with brilliant technical strategy. She consulted a fortune-teller, who hinted to her that, given the chance, her Gregory would founder himself on brazil nuts. She bought a trial pound, and they were gone in five minutes.

Well, ladies, brazil nuts! It was the last straw. Calorie-filled brazil nuts. Community spirit turned to a hostile chill and then to virulent envy. He couldn't stop eating brazil nuts! Anxious eyes searched hopefully for the telltale signs of arrested development, the tight skin and fishy-eyed expression that signifies that a husband is nearing peak despite his apparent potential. We looked for hints of unsightly bloating. But at 325 Gregory was barely filling out. On his own he developed a taste for sweets.

The contest of that year was pure anticlimax. Jenny Schultz's Peter took a first at 423, but the prodigious Gregory was on the minds of all.

Shortly after, Gladys, contrary to expectation, put her Gregory into seclusion. It was the cause of hope. Certainly Gladys had overplayed her hand and had sacrificed strategy for youthful impetuosity. But her self-confidence incensed the ladies of our community.

For the first time in history our women banded together in an effort to counteract Gregory's impending victory. Surely the emotions that prompted this action were not entirely commendable, but, ladies, put yourself in our place. Would you be willing to undergo the heartache, the effort, even the expense of preparing a husband for a contest whose outcome was obvious in advance?

How long would it take her to prepare her Gregory? This was the burning question. The average husband takes three or four years, as we all know. Certainly Gregory was a special case. Four years for him would mean excess flab. Three years seemed most logical, but with Gregory two years did not seem impossible, and Gladys had already displayed eagerness and impatience. It was the studied opinion of our community that Gladys would enter Gregory in two years. Therefore, it was but a simple matter for the rest to hold their husbands for a different year. Should Gregory be the only entry, his would be a hollow victory.

Our solution was bold but strong. The women made an agreement to enter their husbands the following year despite the fact that many would not have reached peak. It was felt that should a three-year plan misfire (as it might through a slip of the tongue, chicanery, a thousand reasons), four or five years of seclusion would be unbearable for all wives concerned and of course with husbands, decline is most rapid after peak has been attained. Women whose husbands had been in seclusion under a year were permitted to breach the contract.

A period of curious tension ensued. Gladys's arrogance was hidden beneath a cover of interest in community affairs while the other women masked their complicity and hatred under the guise of camaraderie in the face of healthy competition.

Gladys took to having provisions delivered: quarter kegs of beer, bushels of potatoes, sacks of flour. Oh, yes! She would set a record in two years, but it would be a wasted triumph.

And then she could outdo herself. We all remembered Elizabeth Bent's Darius who, several years earlier, having had almost the potential of a Gregory, and eager to set a record, had allowed himself to be pushed too hard. He died six weeks before the contest; a sensational but disqualified 621.

With the contest a month away, Gregory was forgotten. True, this year's contest lacked the element of surprise. Everyone (but Gladys) knew which other husbands would be shown. The probable winner could be guessed with reasonable accuracy . . . but still, a contest is a contest, and the air was charged with the familiar bitter rivalry.

Contest day dawned hot and bright, and an excited crowd

gathered at the stadium. This year, of course, there was
little of that intense speculation: Who was entered by surprise; who was staying another year in seclusion?

But five minutes before the procession one question rippled through the audience. Has anyone seen Gladys? An
expectant audience became a feverish one. Necks craned.
Sharp eyes searched the crowd. She was not to be seen. A
murmur of anger swept the stands. Could she have prepared
her Gregory in a single year? No! No! It could not be done.

The band struck up, and slowly the gaily painted, bunt-
ing-draped trucks passed before the stand. Twenty-six in all.
How many women had entered the agreement to show their
husbands? Twenty-five? Twenty-six? No one remembered.

The trucks circled the field. Attention was divided between the parade and the entrance to catch Gladys's expected tardy arrival among the spectators.

The fanfare rose brassy and shrill, and the trucks halted.
The wives debouched from the cabs and stood before their
vehicles. We all know the tension of this moment, as the
audience takes in the line of wives at a glance, sees two
dozen or more women dressed in their best, tries at the
same time to remember those who might have been there
and are not. That tense moment when years of planning,
hoping, working, scheming, unfold too quickly . . . But in
this split-second all eyes focused on one person, and one
person alone. Gladys.

She stood before her truck, stunning in white organdy,
fresh as a daisy, showing nothing of what must have been
a tense and lonely ordeal, not a single wrinkle was visible,
not a strand of hair astray. I could feel hatred gathering in
a storm.

The other wives in the contest glared helplessly at Gladys.
The trumpet sounded, and the wives released the covers of
their trucks. It was the breathless instant when the husbands
stood revealed. But this time every eye focused on truck
seventeen: Gladys's Gregory.

There was no applause, none of the usual wild cheering,

nothing but an awed silence. In that single moment every wife present knew that her own small hopes were forever extinguished. They that never, never in their maddest daydreams had conceived of a Gregory.

He stood as though rooted to the back of the truck: monolithic. His face missed that bloated look usually found on the truly elephantine husbands; his brow was furrowed in thick folds of flesh; his cheeks, neither flabby nor swollen, hung in rich jowls like steaks. His neck was a squat cone leading unbroken into shoulders so gigantic that instead of easing into the inevitable paunch he seemed to drop sheer. He was perfect. A pillar, a block, a mountain, solid and immobile. He turned slowly, proudly. Front face, profile, rear view, front face. His weight was incalculable. He was bigger, heavier, more immense, more beautiful than anything we had ever witnessed. Hatred in the audience turned to despair. Our granddaughter might beg to hear about Gladys's Gregory, but *we* had seen him. For us there would be no more contests. Not a woman among us thought of Gladys's original torments; her years of social ostracism. But how could they?

The weighing began, and the audience cursed and fretted. Sixteen before Gregory. The winches lifted the husbands to the weighing platform and the results were announced: 345, 376, 268 (someone laughed), 417, 430 (someone clapped—a relative no doubt), 386, 344. Not a flurry of interest. The dismayed wives who had worked and schemed for years for this opportunity, who asked only for fair competition, wept openly. Then 403, 313. The wait seemed endless.

Gregory was next, but Gladys had a surprise in store. As the men went to adjust the slings on Gregory, Gladys waved them off. She attached a strong pipe ladder to the truck, and, ponderously, but without hesitation, Gregory descended.

He was still able to walk!

Shoulders thrown back to balance his magnificent bulk,

he swayed and lurched toward the stairs that led to the platform. He tested the frail banister, and it sundered. Using a section of the rail as a cane, he veered up the stairs while a breathless crowd waited for the sound of breaking planks. The stairs groaned but held, and Gregory made his own way to the scale.

Well, ladies, what difference does the actual figure make? It was all over. After seeing Gregory, cold statistics were irrelevant. The figure, however, was 743 pounds.

Gregory turned slowly, proudly, on the scale and smiled. There was no applause but, first singly, then in groups, then en masse the audience stood. Even jealousy and hatred were powerless in the presence of the contestant who would stand as a monument to Gladys and our community, and as an inspiration to the world.

Now, ladies, I wish, I only wish that I could finish this report on the note that such a performance deserves. Unfortunately, one incident marred the perfection of Gladys's Gregory's victory.

Our club, like all others, has always adhered to the tacit but traditional practice: *The contest winner is permitted to choose the manner in which he would like to be served.*

Gladys's Gregory, however, out of sheer spite (the argument still rages on this point), or hearkening back to some primitive instinct, demanded to be served raw.

Having no precedent to act upon, and fearing to break so time-honored a custom, we complied reluctantly with the request, creating acute physical discomfort for many and an acute physical revulsion in all. A motion is now under discussion in our community which will, in the future, relieve the contest winner of this responsibility. In view of our unfortunate experience, ladies, it is part of my mission here today to urge you and your club, and all other clubs, to pass a similar amendment at your earliest convenience.

I thank you for bearing with me, ladies.

BY THE RIVER, FONTAINEBLEAU

STEPHEN GALLAGHER

Stephen Gallagher's first credits in writing were for British radio and television. He then turned to fiction writing full-time; his first novel, *Chimera,* was published in the United States in 1982 by St. Martin's Press. *F & SF* has been fortunate enough to publish a number of his eerie and excellent short stories, among which we feel "By the River, Fontainebleau" is his best to date, and that means it is *very* good indeed. In it, Stephen Gallagher shares with us a horrific vision of infatuation. This surrealistic tale is perhaps the most frightening of the entire collection. It all depends, shall we say, on how you *look* at it.

We sheltered under the great oak for more than an hour, watching as the rain came down in sheets. The sky was as dark as old lead, and when the thunder came it seemed to shake the very soil of the forest. Even Antoine couldn't pretend that this was nothing more than a brief spring shower, and so we sat together in a bleak silence with our packs at our feet and our oilskin coats over our heads. It was then, I suppose, that I really came to my decision.

When the rain finally stopped, we shouldered our baggage and walked on. The lane had now mostly turned to mud, and a weak sun showed through the trees and raised a mist from the sodden ground. I wasn't in much of a mood to appreciate it, but after a while Antoine started to whistle. Ten minutes or so later we came to a shallow, fast-running river where the lane disappeared and reemerged over on the far side, and so wet and miserable was I by this time that I waded in to make the crossing without hesitation or complaint. Every step was taking me nearer to home, and this was all that I cared for.

But it soon became obvious that the track would take us no farther than the farm that stood on the opposite bank, as it led straight into a yard that had no exit. It was a mean-looking place, charmless and squalid even in the late afternoon sunlight, and my immediate impulse was to turn around and walk away. But Antoine, ever an optimist, said, "You think they'll take pity and feed us?"

"They're more likely to hit us over the head and rob us," I told him. "You stay here and look after the gear. I'll ask the way."

I left him and went on into the yard, looking for some sign of life. A few hens were picking over the barren ground close to where four scrawny goats stood in a makeshift pen, and a dog was barking somewhere over beyond the barn. The corner of the yard to my left was shaded by a large chestnut tree, and it was on the dry beaten earth in the shelter of this that I saw a terrible sight.

It was an underweight pig, trussed and made ready for slaughter; this was obviously the farm's regular spot for killing, because hooks had been fixed to the tree's lower branches for carcasses to be hung as they bled. What made the sight so terrible was the way in which the pig had been prepared. Each of its feet had been cut at the knuckle, sliced right back so that the bone showed bloodless and white. Those bound-together limbs were almost severed, but still the pig squirmed as it tried to stand.

I turned my head aside, and went on by. It was out in the open on the far side of the barn that I finally found the people that I was looking for; and an unwashed, surly crowd they turned out to be, a father and four brothers with narrow faces and dark, piercing stares. They were hauling logs for cutting, but all work stopped when they saw me. As I addressed myself to the older man, the others simply stood and watched, their mouths open and their hands hanging by their sides whilst a dim spark of intelligence burned in each pair of eyes. It went badly until I realized that money was the key that would unlock their patient and persistent misunderstanding, and then at the end of the process I learned nothing more than that the only way to regain the Paris road would be to return along the track by which we'd arrived. I thanked the farmer—feeling defeated and foolish because really I ought to have been cursing him—and trudged back to Antoine.

Antoine was where I'd left him. The packs with our easels and our brushes and our sketchbooks were at his feet, and he was leaning on the wall with a distant, thoughtful expression on his face. He was looking toward the chestnut tree. This was something that I'd avoided doing on my way back, but now I had to turn and see what it was that was affecting him so; and it was then that I realized that the trussed pig had been taken away at some time during my short absence, and that a different scene was now before him.

"I'm staying, Marcel," he said.

I didn't understand. "Staying where?"

"Right here. They must have a room or a loft or a barn, and they're not going to turn down good money. And it's late, and I'm tired. . . ."

"Any other reason?" I said, and I gave a pointed glance across to where, under the chestnut tree, a young girl was now standing and unselfconsciously brushing her hair. She was looking into a broken old mirror that she'd hung from one of the butchery hooks, and she didn't seem to be aware of us at all. She was barefoot, and in a cotton shift so damp and clinging that it was plain she wore nothing underneath. To my eyes she was nothing more than an ordinary farm girl, too heavy for grace and probably too dull for conversation . . . but who could say what she was to Antoine? I'd already learned, during the weeks of our walking tour, that his eyes and mine often seemed to see by a different light. Now, in answer to my question, he was smiling and saying nothing more.

"Then," I said, "you stay alone, Antoine."

This surprised him. "Are we going to argue over this?"

"No," I said, leaning on the wall beside him, "Not an argument. I simply don't want to get in your way. It's over for me, Antoine, and there's no point in me pretending otherwise. I've had enough of walking and sketching and being face-to-face with nature. I've yawned through sunrises and I've shivered through the rain, and if I died without ever seeing another tree or village or field of wheat, I'd be dying happy. What I'm trying to say is that I'm not an artist, Antoine. If these past few weeks have been the test, then I'm admitting that I've failed. I'm footsore and I'm aching, and I've got nothing left to prove. I'm going back to Paris tonight."

This had been my decision, back in the forest and under the oak. The excursion that had seemed so appealing to two young would-be painters had turned into a drudgery of patchy weather and drafty inns and a yearning for home; I'd carried on sketching only as a kind of dogged duty, something that I wouldn't have bothered with if Antoine hadn't been there. I hadn't looked back through the pages, and didn't care to. My artistic talent, I'd realized, wasn't strong enough to survive outside of the most pampered of drawing room conditions—which, I suppose, meant that it wasn't a real talent at all. A useful way of persuading young women to undress for me, perhaps, but not art.

"Oh, Marcel," Antoine said with sympathy. "Has it really been hell for you?"

"I'm going to be a dull citizen, Antoine," I told him. "I was *born* to be a dull citizen. It took a trip like this to make me realize how much I'd been looking forward to it."

He glanced across the yard again, to where the plain farm girl stood beneath the chestnut tree. For a moment it seemed that her eyes strayed from the mirror and met his, but her face betrayed nothing at all.

"I can't come with you," he said.

"I understand that."

I told him where to find the farmer, and while he was gone I transferred all of the pastels and the paints and the charcoal sticks from my luggage into his own. It was a strange feeling, the feeling of letting go of a dream. It was relief and regret, inextricably mixed. I also gave him my two untouched canvases in their carrying frame, and my fixing atomizer. When Antoine returned, he told me of the terms that the farmer had fixed for him to stay on; put simply, they were giving him two weeks in their barn with whatever meals the family could spare, in return for every franc that he carried. I was horrified, but Antoine was un-ruffled. He made me promise that I would go to his father and collect his monthly allowance, and that before the two weeks expired I would return with the money. Although I wouldn't have cared if I never saw the forest of Fontaine-bleau again, I was uneasy at the notion of leaving Antoine completely at the mercy of his new obsession. This way, at least, I'd be able to check on him.

He walked with me back to the river. There was little more than an hour of daylight left, and I had some way to go. Before I set out across the ford, I said, "What shall I tell your father?"

"Whatever you like," he said. "Whatever you think he needs to hear. But do it for me, Marcel."

I'd have said more, but he was already casting a longing look back toward the yard. A half hour's familiarity made it seem no less squalid to me than it had been at first sight . . . but, as I said, Antoine often seemed to see things with a different eye. An artist's eye, perhaps. My test had come and gone; and the next two weeks would be his.

I stayed that night in Barbizon, and made it back to Paris by the next evening. I entered the family home by the back door, partly because I was ashamed of what I saw as my failure, but mostly because I was aware that I looked like a tramp. The next few days saw the beginning of the process of my absorption into the family's business dealings, a strange world of ledger entries and manifests that somehow bore a relation to real ships that sailed somewhere out on real oceans. I was given a position as an apprentice clerk in order that I should be able to learn from the most fundamental of basic principles.

Even though I'd known what to expect, the long hours and the rigid timekeeping came as something of a shock to me. I'd sent out a note to Antoine's parents assuring them of his safety as soon as I'd arrived home, but it wasn't until the Friday that I was able to go and see them in the evening with his request.

The news was not good. My own father, to his credit, had been willing to let my preoccupations run themselves out; it was as if he'd foreseen the result and quietly made his preparations for when that time came around. Antoine's father had no such patience. All that he gave me was a message: There would be no allowance until Antoine abandoned his games and returned home.

Saturday was a half day, and as soon as my work was finished I set out for the railway station. It was late in the afternoon before I finally came into sight of the farm again. The place was much as I remembered it, although I dare say that I had changed in its eyes; I now wore my one decent suit and overcoat, and came prepared for the shallow river crossing.

It was a warm day. Spring was slipping toward summer, and the breeze no longer cut. The broken looking glass was still hanging under the chestnut tree, and it swung lightly back and forth as I stood in the doorway to the barn and called Antoine's name. He'd been sleeping *here*? Half of the place was taken up with hay, all the way to the upper loft, and there was nothing in the way of furniture. The slatted walls were badly fitted, and some of the gaps in the planking were a hand's width. But this was his lodging, all right, because over on the clear part of the floor I saw his easel and a stool and some of his materials laid out. Antoine's possessions, but no Antoine. I set out to search.

I finally found him in a clearing no more than two hundred meters from the barn. The girl, as I'd half expected, was with him. She was sitting on the ground with her hands clasped around her knees as Antoine sketched her, but on seeing me, with a cry of "Marcel!" he threw aside his pad and jumped up to greet me.

I'll confess that I was shocked, although I hid it well. In the space of less than a week he'd deteriorated like a man in the grip of a serious illness. He seemed thinner, and there were dark rings round his eyes that made them seem sunken and staring; but his manner was lively enough, and he seemed pleased to see me . . . although how much of this was genuine eagerness and how much of it was due to the money that he assumed I'd brought with me, I couldn't say.

They had a basket with them, and together we dined on cheese and rough wine and bread that had the texture of damp thatch. Antoine introduced the girl as Lise, short for Anneliese; I knew within a moment of hearing her speak that she was no native French girl, although her accent was one that I couldn't place. She seemed shy and ate nothing, and took only a little of the wine.

Antoine gave me his sketchbook to look through, just as we'd done at the end of each of our days together. As I'd expected, he'd been spending all of his time on the girl, switching between head studies and full-length portrayals, some of them hardly more than a few swift lines depicting the essence of some moment of motion. Although I didn't show it, I was disappointed. I was hoping that there would be some sign here, some showing-through of the vision that had motivated him, but each drawing seemed little more than a technical exercise. Perhaps there was nothing to envy here after all, I thought. Nothing other than a casual infatuation made practical by the artist-model relationship— a situation that I, at least, could understand, although I was strangely disappointed that I found nothing more.

Lise asked if Antoine was finished with his sketching for the day, and then excused herself. I noted a certain pain in Antoine's eyes as he watched her go.

"Who is she?" I said as soon as she was decently out of earshot.

"I don't know. She's an orphan, I think. The family just ignores her."

"Does she work on the farm?"

"I don't think so," he said, his face reflecting some of his uncertainty as if it were a question that he'd thought over a number of times in the past few days. "I can't be sure. She disappears for hours at a time, but . . . it's not important anyway. Did you speak to my father?"

I had no choice then but to give him the hard news. I saw his face fall, and the air of vague contentment that had offset the wasting of his features was replaced by a kind of desperation.

"Then I don't know what to do," he said. "They won't let me stay here without money. They've bled me white already. You don't understand these people."

"Not half as well as they seem to understand you," I told him. "It *is* because of the girl, isn't it?"

He looked down, and didn't answer.

"Then," I went on, "why don't you simply take her away?"

But he was dismissing the idea even before I'd finished suggesting it. "That's not possible," he said. "It pains her to walk any distance." And then, going on as if this minor quibble had been enough to put an end to the entire argument, he was getting to his feet and saying, "I can see only one way out. You'd better come with me."

He said nothing more as he led the way back toward the barn. Over by another of the outbuildings I saw one of the four sons watching us as we passed. He made no sign toward us, and Antoine didn't even glance his way.

Lise wasn't there when we arrived, nor did Antoine seem to expect her to be. He went over to the easel, and I followed; and then I waited as he hesitated for a moment before drawing away the paint-splashed cloth that had been draped to protect the canvas.

It was a painting, in full oils. I stood amazed. It was wonderful.

It showed that vision of the first moment in which Antoine had seen Lise under the chestnut tree. It was every detail that I'd seen, but transformed; I now realized that I'd been so preoccupied with my own discomfort that I'd been aware of almost nothing, nothing at all. Lise stood, hairbrush in hand, dappled in late afternoon sunlight with soft blue shadows behind her. In her plain features was a kind of quiet beauty as she studied her image in the glass; I knew instinctively that it was a sad picture, a celebration of the brevity of all experience and of life itself.

And as I looked, I felt something within me die. I thought of my own pretty, nondescript Fontainebleau landscapes and finally knew for sure that my decision had been a right one. My technique was as good as Antoine's, if not slightly better, but technique was only half the story. To paint, one first had to see. And I didn't, until led to it.

"You have to take it to Paris for me," he said. "Sell it for whatever you can get."

I nodded slowly. There was no question about it now, I

would help him however I could. "I'm envious, you know," I said.

"Don't be," he said, staring at his own canvas as if it disturbed him somehow. "The things we want most aren't always the things that make us happy."

I gave him most of the money that I had with me, including what I had set aside for a night's lodging before returning to the town. I sensed a certain reluctance in Antoine as we climbed a ladder and he showed me the upper loft where I could sleep, but I took it as a natural aversion to charity between friends. I didn't see it that way; if I was going to be a bourgeois, I thought ruefully, I might as well go the whole hog and become a patron of the arts.

A blanket in the hay was not my idea of comfort, but it was all that was available. I was warm enough, but the hay stuck at me through the thin wool from every angle; and though my overcoat, rolled, made a reasonable pillow, I couldn't help wondering what it would look like when I came to shake it out in the morning. No wonder Antoine was looking such a wreck, I thought, after a week of this.

I don't know what time it was when I awoke, but it must have been somewhere around two or three o'clock. I lay uneasy, looking at where the cloudy moonlit sky showed through the spaces in the walls, and I heard voices from below. They were whispering, but the night was so still that it was impossible not to hear.

"I remember leaving you and your friend," Lise was saying. "I was so tired after sitting for you this morning. But I don't remember where I went."

"You went where you always go," I heard Antoine say. "To the big stack of straw behind the house. You made yourself a space and you burrowed down inside."

"But the next thing that I knew, it was dark and I was standing out under the tree again. I was exhausted, and it was as if I'd been running. What had I been *doing*?"

"You were sleeping, that's all. Like you always do."

But Lise seemed scared, unable to accept so simple an

explanation. "But you know this?" she said insistently. "You've seen me?"

There was a long silence from Antoine. And then he said, "Yes."

I heard her moving slightly, making the hay rustle. She said, "I sometimes feel as if you're the only one who really sees me. As I am, I mean. As if, when you close your eyes, I no longer exist . . . because I didn't, in a way, before you came along."

Antoine said, "That's just foolish talk."

Her next question was one that I wouldn't have expected. She said, "Who am I, Antoine?" And she sounded lost and miserable, as if the answer would never be known.

"Sleep, now," he told her.

It was a good suggestion, and one that I wished I could follow; but further sleep seemed to elude me, and all that I could do was to squirm miserably in that itchy byre. Antoine's breathing became deep and noisy, which was of no help. And after a while I heard the sound below of somebody rising and making their way toward the door of the barn.

Moving as silently as I could, I crawled over to the trap by which I'd entered the loft, and peered down. Lise was at the doorway, framed in moonlight, and she was looking back at Antoine. I could not make out her expression, but her general attitude suggested a regretful leave-taking. Of Antoine himself I could see little more than the creamy blur of his shirt in the darkness. Then she turned and walked out into the yard.

A board creaked as I moved across to the unglazed window from where I'd be able to see down into the yard, but Antoine didn't stir. She was moving quickly now, a faint shape in a simple dress, and she was heading toward the back of the house as Antoine had said; and then as I watched, I saw another form rise from the shadows to meet her. This was, I guessed from his brutish outline, either the farmer or one of his four sons, and he seemed to have been waiting;

I saw him raise a rod or a switch of some kind, and to swipe at the air with it as if to speed her in the direction in which she was already going. He followed her through the gap between the buildings, and then bent to something that I couldn't see; but then I heard the scrape of a wooden gate across the rutted dirt, and the bang of it falling shut.

When they were gone from sight, Lise being casually driven ahead like some common farm animal, I returned to my blanket. It was obvious that she'd been expected, up and away the moment that Antoine was fully asleep, like a sheep being called to the fold at the end of the day. And having seen the way in which she'd been treated, I could only reflect that perhaps she'd been right: Antoine's vision of her differed so much from theirs that it was almost as if he'd actually created her beauty out of some more basic stuff, to which she could revert only when Antoine's attention moved elsewhere, as in sleep.

And sleep, unexpectedly, was what these idle and speculative thoughts led me to.

Breakfast was left outside for us in the morning. It was meager but decent. Antoine carefully packed the picture, wary of the paint that was still soft in the patches; he called it *La Jeune Fille au Miroir*, The Looking-Glass Girl. Lise sat aside and watched us; she'd returned to the barn some time before I'd woken, I didn't know when. She said little, and ate nothing. I now found it difficult to imagine how I could ever have thought her plain.

I suppose that to develop my fanciful thought from the night before, I now saw her as through Antoine's eyes. My own first impression now counted for nothing; it was not that I had simply changed an opinion to acquiesce to the views of another, but more that I'd found the actual fabric of my world transformed by the intensity of his vision. But it was an intensity that was draining him, I could see; he looked no better physically now than he had when I'd arrived, and seemed perhaps even a little worse. I wondered if a taste of success from the sale of the painting might nourish him.

I was on my way before ten, knowing that I had a long walk and a carriage drive ahead of me before I'd even reach the railway. My toughest boots had leaked a little during the river crossing the previous day, but they'd dried out overnight and Antoine went out to negotiate a ride of some kind so that I wouldn't be restarting the journey with a squelch. I didn't hear what was said or what was promised, but after ten minutes a dilapidated trap pulled by an even more dilapidated pony came rattling into the yard.

The morning sun struck a shimmering light from the river as we waved our good-byes and my transport jarred its way into the rutted crossing. My driver was one of the four brothers that I'd seen on my first visit to the farm, and I wondered if he might have been the one who had waited in the yard for Lise in the moonlight. I thought about asking . . . but he hadn't said one word to me so far, and seemed unlikely to. He sat with his shoulders hunched, and his eyes apparently fixed on the horse's rear end. I was half expecting to be set down on the opposite bank, but it soon became clear that Antoine's bargaining would take me farther as we continued, wheels dripping, down the lane. I turned for one last wave to Antoine's solitary figure, and then I faced front with *La Jeune Fille au Miroir* held protectively by my side.

I had a strange feeling of loss, as if I'd left a world that I might never be sure of reentering. The river was its boundary, the banks its borderland.

Ten minutes later, as we came into sight of the main crossroads, my coachman spoke.

"We've told your friend," he said suddenly and without any preamble, "we can't eat his pictures. When his money's gone, so's he."

It was a moment before I could be certain that I was the one being addressed; he hadn't lifted his eyes from the mare's backside. But when I was sure, I said, "Would you consider letting Lise come away with him?"

I watched for a reaction but saw none. He simply said, "Why?"

"She doesn't work for you, she isn't one of you . . . there's no future for her here. Antoine's family is very rich. He could set her up in apartments of her own and give her an income. She could send you money."

It was my boldest stroke, but it was having little effect; he was shaking his head slowly, and this angered me.

"It's rather late to start considering her moral welfare, isn't it?" I demanded. "Since you see fit to send her out to sleep in a barn with strangers."

"That doesn't matter," he said, reining the nag in so that we came to a halt at the empty crossroads. "She can't leave, that's all."

Such were my initial efforts on Antoine's behalf; and I now have to report that I had little more success in my new role as artist's agent. I gave my choice of dealer a lot of thought, and settled on one whom I believed would be sympathetic to the picture's fresh and quite modern approach to its subject; he had, I knew, recently made a buying trip to England and returned with several works of Constable that were considered to be almost revolutionary in their treatment of nature. I left the painting in his hands for several days, and then called on him to check on progress.

He'd found a buyer. But when I heard the sum on offer, my initial excitement died and went cold within me.

"So little?" I said. "But . . ."

"You might get more if you let it hang in the gallery for a few weeks, but I doubt it," he said. "And I wouldn't want to get a reputation for handling this kind of material." But then he conceded, "I'm not saying it isn't good."

"But if it's good, it *must* bring more."

"Not so. Good isn't what sells . . . fashionable is what

sells. We're talking about classical characters in idealized landscapes. Nature rearranged in the studio. Now, you tell me. How do I sell this little farm girl in a market like that?"

It was a good piece of work, I *knew* it; knew it with a greater confidence than I had ever brought to any work of my own. I said, "Are you telling me that this painting is at fault because there's too much of the truth in it?"

He shrugged delicately. "If you like. For what it's worth, I think your friend's very brave. But I can't sell his nerve, either . . . I just sell pictures."

What could I do? Antoine's tenure at the farm would last only as long as his ability to pay matched the greed of his landlords. The sum I'd been offered wouldn't buy him more than a few days grace at current rates, but any effort to find a better price for the picture would take time. Even then, there were no guarantees of any greater success. With a sense of defeat, I accepted the offer.

There had to come a point, I'd decided, where Antoine would have to get his obsession into some kind of perspective. He'd found himself in a situation that had made a conceptual breakthrough possible, but now it was time to give some consideration to the strategy of his new career. After all, hadn't he already made his first commercial sale? And if I was beginning to sound like his father in this way of thinking, I didn't dwell on the fact long enough for it to bother me.

I went out again on the following Sunday. Antoine was waiting for me, on the wrong side of the river.

He was sitting on a rock by the crossing, staring into the fast-running current. If I'd been shocked by his appearance before, I was horrified now. He was filthy and wretched, his skin gray with ill health under its ingrained surface of dirt; his hair was like old straw, and his entire body was hunched and bent. I saw what looked like dried wounds on his hands, and when he looked up at my approach, it was with the eyes of the starving.

For a moment I was unable to speak. To see a friend reduced so far, so fast! His bags, easel, and paints were beside him; they lay as if thrown there, the easel broken and the paints scattered and trampled into the riverside mud.

"Antoine!" I finally managed to say. "What happened here?"

"The money was gone, so they threw me out," he said simply. His voice was rough and weak. "I've been here for two days. When I tried to go back in, they set the dogs on me."

This, I assumed, would explain the wounds on his hands. "That's outrageous," I said. "I'm going to speak to them. Let them set the dogs on *me*, if they dare."

I stormed across the ford, not caring how much noise I made or how much spray I created. Antoine, after rising unsteadily from his rock, hesitated for a while and then began to follow me at a distance.

The yard was in silence, and to me seemed just as grim as it had on that first day. Lise's mirror no longer hung under the chestnut tree, and from the dark stains on the ground I'd have guessed that the butchery hooks had been put to recent use. With Antoine still trailing along behind, I took a look in the barn; some of the hay had been carted out, but there was no sign of anyone around.

"We're too late," Antoine said, but I paid him no attention and went out through the back doors of the barn. Out here, at least, I found a sign of life in the form of the remains of a recent fire; it was smoking still, and as I drew closer I saw that the smoke actually came from a scattering of almost-extinct coals in the bottom of a shallow pit. They lay on a bed of deep ash, and there was more ash and hay mingled in with the earth that had been spaded out onto the ground beside the excavation. Even without extending my hand, I could feel the heat.

I was not to be stopped. Antoine started to speak again, but I didn't wait to listen; I was already on my way toward the stone house with its steeply pitched roof and its inch-thick doors, as stolid and as resistant to inquiry as I knew the people inside it to be. I strode across a kitchen garden, where almost nothing grew, and hesitated at the side entrance; I could hear noises from inside, the sounds of a number of people together, and so without knocking I threw back the unbolted door before me and stepped through.

The noise ended as I entered, as sharply as if it had been cut by a blade. I saw a plain whitewashed room with a broad table down its center, around which at least a dozen people sat; it seemed that the same face turned toward me in twelve or thirteen slightly differing forms, from a child of three to a woman so old and pale that she seemed bloodless. One of them, a man of around thirty years, was bibbed like a baby and being fed with a spoon. All of their eyes save his were on me; he continued to look eagerly at his plate.

I'd interrupted a feast, and a strange feast it was; on the table stood nothing but meat and dishes of liquid fat, and more of this in one spread than such a family might normally expect to see in a year. I saw joints and ribs and bones already picked clean, and at the far end of the table a plate piled high with roasted offal. This, I didn't doubt, was all the product of the cooking pit that I'd seen behind the barn. The sight and the smell made me queasy at the excess on display; the faces that now studied me blankly were bloated and smeared with grease.

Nobody spoke. But in my mind I heard that voice from days before: *Tell your friend, we can't eat his pictures.*

And then came something that terrified me, as if the hooks that held the backcloth of my world had suddenly slipped in their holes and allowed a corner to fall, revealing the dark machinery that usually stood concealed. It happened as my gaze came to rest on one of the smaller serving dishes, runny with juices and melted fat. The joint that lay on it was charred around the edges, the skin scored and crisp; but for no more than a second it was recognizable, nails and all, as a human hand. I blinked and stared, and even as I did so, the joint seemed to shimmer and to change, becoming indistinct for a moment before being restored to my sight in a less obvious form. I might have called it an illusion, but I knew that it was not; it was, I am certain, the final demise of Antoine's vision, crushed by the presence of the same poverty and ignorance and need that had given it birth.

The retarded thirty-year-old began to wail and to drum on the table with his fists, and I took three halting steps back and grabbed at the door handle to pull it closed on that terrible scene.

Antoine hadn't followed me to the house. He'd stayed back, and now waited at some distance. He seemed to be hugging himself, his left arm holding his right as if he were nursing some half-healed bruise. I went across to him and turned him and began to usher him out of the yard, and he complied without protest. On the other side of the river we gathered up such of his things as were worth taking away; I gave him a few small pieces to carry, but the heaviest baggage I carried myself.

It was in this way that we walked down the lane, myself well laden and Antoine allowing himself to be hastened along. I couldn't take him onto the railway, not in a public compartment in his present state and condition, but there was enough money from the sale of the painting to be able to afford a horse and carriage to take us all the way back to Paris. We would arrive late and in darkness, but that would be no disadvantage.

I spoke on the subject only once as we left Corbeil after a half hour's rest. Antoine was huddled by the window, looking like a bundle of miserable sticks.

I said, "When you slept. Do you know where she went to?"

Antoine slowly turned his head so that his bleak eyes met mine. "I never wondered," he said.

And although I knew that he lied, I never asked him again.

PRIDE

CHARLES L. GRANT

Charles Grant is a congenial man with a deep, dark imagination, a force to be reckoned with in the field of horror. He first began publishing in the fields of science fiction and horror with his story, "The House of Evil," which appeared in *F & SF* in 1968. Since that time he has developed an entire town, Oxrun Station, in which many of his stories—including "Pride"—are set. It is an ordinary small town with a prediliction for certain "strange" happenings. "Pride" tells of one such event—the chance meeting of a man and a woman—the resultant love that occurs—and something else.

It was the middle of August when the nights changed in Oxrun Station. Some blamed it on the anticipation of a hurricane battering its way up the coast, its vanguard of ghost-clouds muting the stars; others blamed the two-week heat wave that had softened the tarmac, singed tempers and lawns; and still others accused the dying that robbed the evenings of their softness, filed edges on laughter, made walking the streets an exercise in silence.

As happened to me the night I left the Chancellor Inn and noted with a frown the empty porches, empty sidewalks. Usually there were strollers, creaking rockers, quiet whispers; usually the cars didn't move quite so fast. And usually I didn't have to listen to my heels on the pavement—flat, without echoes, as if I weren't there at all. The only sign of my passing were the shadows at my feet, darting ahead, sweeping back, teasing forward once again. I tried not to watch them, set reins on imagination, but I couldn't help jumping when a cat wailed behind a hedge.

A self-conscious grin as my left hand massaged the back of my neck while my right sought a trouser pocket. Nerves, I told myself; even the Lone Ranger would recheck his guns tonight. Nerves. It happened every time I fell into brooding, which today I suspected was working overtime.

First there'd been the letter from my former wife, Carole. After expressing her customary, and sometimes genuine concern for my welfare, she proceeded to extoll the therapeutic value of remarriage, in her case to a diplomat apparently drowning in money. I doubted the jibe was intended with malice, just as I'd doubted any of them over the years had been aimed at the jugular—but one can bleed to death by drops as well as gashes, and neither of us was weeping when the final papers were signed.

Then there was the slow and inexplicable erosion of my clients, and an unpleasant case which would be completed in the morning, a case that some had hoped would be the end of all the killing.

Late in April the first body had been discovered just

outside of Harley, twenty minutes from the Station. A young man, horribly mutilated, dismembered, partially devoured. Four more were uncovered at three- and four-week intervals, each one somewhat nearer. Then, last week, Syd Foster had been arrested, charged with all five brutal murders, and that of his nephew, right here in the village. It was shocking, it was scandal, and virtually no one believed it. The arrest had been a reflex, an unthinking reaction to the outcry for safety, and Syd was my client and I was going to set him free.

That did not make me the most popular man in some parts of the county, but for a change the unobserved technicalities were a pleasure to behold. Syd was fifty, a postman and a loner, and I'd known him for years. He was no more a cannibal than I was a Darrow.

So I walked, and I pondered, and I almost missed the woman.

She was leaning against a red maple between sidewalk and curb, one arm around the bole and her head slightly inclined as if sharing a lover's whisper. Not overwhelmingly beautiful, but certainly attractive enough: gold-brown hair that sifted down and away from a face of gentle curves, eyes wide-set and dark, thin lips, peaked chin, the rest of her willow slender in a print blouse and snug jeans.

She was humming.

I stopped, then, and I stared, finally cleared my throat falsely and found some faint courage. "Excuse me," I said in my best Samaritan voice, "but are you lost or something? Can I help you?"

She smiled, almost shyly. "No. I'm perfectly here, thanks."

I smiled back awkwardly and waited for inspiration to unleash the charm. But I could have waited all night for the silence I suffered. So I put a finger to my brow in a see-you salute and moved on. As far as the corner, where I stopped and glanced back. She was watching me, still smiling, finally pulling back her hair, away from her eyes, behind her ears. A hesitation, a quick look to either side, and she walked toward me, hands clasped behind her back, shoes silent on the pavement.

"Jean," she told me, "and to tell you the truth, yes, I do think I'm lost."

"Brian Farrell," I said, wondering about her perfume, rather odd and oddly compelling. "Where are you headed?"

She gave me an address on Woodland Avenue, three blocks to our right and four blocks up. I started to point, then drew back my arm. "If you like, I'll walk you," I said. "It's on my way, and I wouldn't mind, really." I grinned, feeling foolish.

"Well, I wouldn't mind either," she said, put a hand to my elbow, and allowed me to lead her.

And as we walked she questioned me about the dark houses, the lack of pedestrian traffic, and I told her about the dying—and the inevitable conclusion that if Syd Foster was innocent, the killer was still free. She shuddered and hugged my arm; I straightened, and tried not to smile.

"That's really . . . horrid," she said as we came to her street. "You sound like you know an awful lot about it, though. I mean, more than what you read in the *Herald*."

"I should," I said, after debating the answer. "I'm Syd Foster's lawyer."

There was no response. Instead, she scratched idly the back of my hand until we reached her front gate, set in a privet hedge that surrounded her home. Then, before I could say anything, she thanked me graciously for the escort, shook my hand, and left me standing alone, in front of a bulky gray Victorian caged by willow and beech, with a station wagon in the driveway and a yellow light on the porch. I blinked when the front door closed, blinked when the light died, stood for a long moment thinking I'd said something wrong. A shrug, then, and I walked away, turned around, and walked back to double-check the address with a squint and a nod. What I would do with it I didn't know, but the fancies that came with it took my mind off Foster as I moved on home.

To dreams. Swirling, red-coated dreams I'd been having for weeks. Tangled sheets, a lost pillow, and several times waking to wonder why I'd wakened. Oversleeping at last and rushing late to the office to learn that Foster's hearing had been postponed to Friday. I was annoyed, and felt reprieved, and the relief on my face not soon enough hidden.

"You still go in two days," my partner told me stiffly.

Chester Frazier and I had been affiliated for just four years that month, an association instigated by Carole, who had ambitions I didn't, and who'd hoped some of Chet's drive would somehow rub off. Unfortunately for her (and I'm not sure about me), he had come to resent strongly my less than wholehearted devotion to the concept of the flamboyant. Not that there was all that much opportunity for it in Oxrun, but by the nature of the village there was a great deal of money and lots of connections to be made. He dogged them avidly. I ducked them quietly, preferring instead the relatively uncomplicated. For me, that meant wills and small suits and handling the estates of the far-from-wealthy. Chet called it charity work; I figured somebody had to do it, and it might as well be me. To save me from myself, then—and because he liked me, really cared—it was he who'd talked the judge into appointing me Foster's counsel. Small wonder he was put off when I wasn't enraged at the delay.

"No big deal," I said when he finally stopped his grousing. "All it means, for crying out loud, is two more nights in a cell. And if you believe him, he doesn't want to leave anyway."

"He could be out on bail, you know."

"He doesn't want it, Chet," I said patiently, marching over familiar ground. "Whoever, whatever's out there doing this has scared him to death. He thinks he's safer behind bars than in his own home."

"Brian, there are times . . ."

He stopped and shook his head in weary resignation, left my office for the deserted reception area out front. I watched him from my desk, rose, and stood at the door. Frowned. He was a large man, girth and height, with curled blond hair and hand-tailored suits, and generally he moved like a man with a mission. Today, however, he almost shambled across the carpet.

"You look tired," I said.

He turned away from the plate-glass window overlooking Centre Street and made his slow way back to me, leaned against the wall that separated our rooms. "I am," he confessed. "Elizabeth needs braces, Amy's heart murmur isn't clearing, and for the past three days Alice has had me up four or five times a night to check on prowlers she keeps hearing in the yard." His smile was one-sided. "It's amazing," he said, "how the mundane can kill you."

I would have tried wit to lighten his mood, but he'd inadvertently taken one of Carole's favorite lines. So I tried to change the subject.

"I met a girl last night. Lives over on Woodland. Nice girl. Pretty." I grinned. "I think I'm in lust."

"Oh, great, Brian, just great. Your practice is seeping away through the baseboard, and you say you're in love."

"Lust," I corrected him. "I don't know her that well."

He didn't appreciate the joke. Instead, he grunted sourly and ducked into his office. It was just as well. At that moment my phone rang—another client moving out, thanks to all this killing going on. It was an old woman with seven cats and little money, and I didn't bother to argue because I knew she wouldn't handle the shadows stalking their homes—but I wished it would happen to Chet for a change. I was getting tired of it, just as I'd grown tired of Carole not understanding that comfort to me didn't have to mean rich.

When that ended, however, I had only been relieved; the call I'd just taken was making me scared.

Worse. At the end of the day Chet hinted rather strongly he was seriously considering finally going it alone. He had expenses, he told me, and he couldn't carry me much longer unless I got off the mark.

It was a long walk home, then, and a tasteless short dinner. I couldn't read, couldn't watch television, couldn't find the nerve to walk over to Jean's. The way things were going, she'd probably not know me.

The porch was the best place I'd discovered for self-pity, watching the neighbors enjoying their lives, watching the children enjoying their living. A good dose of maudlin now and then, I thought, was good for the soul, but that, too, was denied me the moment I stepped out.

The humidity had turned to fog, the air touched with ice, and some blocks away I heard a police siren screaming. It was the wrong sound for the night, the wrong sound for the times. I shuddered and went in, would have gone straight to bed but the telephone rang.

"Brian? Brian Farrell?"

I gasped, and I grinned, and since the telephone table was right in the hallway, I sat at the bottom of the staircase and aimed my feet toward the door. "Jean? Is that you, Jean?" Brilliant, I thought; you should write for the theater.

"Am I bothering you?"

A bitter laugh. "Anything but."

She paused, and I heard a faint rustling on the line. "I hope you're not mad, but when I heard that siren I thought about what you told me last night and . . ." She laughed, sounded breathless. "Well, I scared myself is what I did. I needed a friendly voice."

"At your disposal," I said gallantly, and hoped Carole's ears were smarting.

We talked for almost an hour, most of it, I realized later, about my own problems, not hers, and when I rang off with a promise for dinner, I was virtually whistling.

But the dreams came again, not over till dawn.

And when I got to the office, Chet wasn't there.

Puzzled, but not worried, I left a message on his desk and went to see Foster. He wasn't talking, however, and I was gone in ten minutes. He bothered me, I supposed, more than he should have, a concern not helped by the change in the weather—the clouds had thickened, had grayed, and a drizzle started falling. Strong enough to streak dust on windows and darken the curbs, but not enough to wash them or to warrant a coat. Dismal, I decided, was the perfect word for the day.

When I returned from lunch, Chet was waiting. Impatiently, close to anger. His hair was unkempt and his shirt-front was wrinkled.

"Jesus," I said. "Chet, did something happen to—"

He shut me off with a slash of his hand, turned, and went into my office, where he poured himself a whiskey from my bottle on the sideboard. His hands were trembling, and just at his temple a tic pulled at his eye.

"I've been to the police," he said. "I talked to Fred Borg."

I didn't know what to say. So I said nothing. Just sat.

"Last night—"

"The siren," I said quickly.

He nodded after a moment, after draining his glass. "I was walking around the house from the garage after taking out the garbage. Bunch of kids had been cutting through the yard, I think I mentioned it yesterday. Alice's prowler. Anyway, I heard something, so I went back to have a look. Intrepid husband stalks wily teenager, or an alley cat, you know?" His smile was grotesque. "It was something, but I don't know what the hell it was. It stayed under the trees, growling at me." He poured another drink. "When I tried to get to the back door, it came after me."

"My God," I said softly, more stunned by his look than by what he was saying—it was almost as if he were ready to cry.

"I don't know what made me do it," he continued, "but I grabbed my lighter from my pocket and lit it. I wanted to see what it was, but I scared it off instead. But it was big, Brian. Christ, it was big."

"Well, what did they find? Some kind of dog?"

His look turned to disgust. "Nothing. Not a goddamned thing. I could tell Borg thought I was drinking or something.

If it hadn't been for the, uh . . . any other time he probably would've made me blow up the balloon. As it is, he told me about a dozen other calls he gets every night. Trying to make me feel better. A member of the loony club." Then he looked at his glass and tried a weak smile. "Alice is having a fit. She wants me to sell the place today and move to New York. That's why I came in, to get a few papers and do some work at home. She . . . well, if anybody calls . . ."

"Sure, of course," I said quickly.

He nodded as he set his glass down. "And you're ready for Foster this afternoon?"

"Chet, for God's sake, give me some credit, all right?"

It was the wrong thing to say, an against-the-grain stroking of his already frayed temper.

"Credit? You want credit? For what, Brian? For pissing away a great chance to set yourself up as a damned fine lawyer? For fucking up a perfectly good marriage? For screwing around with some woman while your life goes down the tubes?" He shoved a trembling hand back through his hair, raised a fist, and dropped it. "I don't understand people like you, Brian." An apology of sorts. "I swear to God, I don't understand."

He left before I could respond, but by the time the front door slammed shut, I realized I had nothing to say. The language we spoke was English, but somewhere along the line all the communications broke down and what came to our ears was little more than gibberish.

Nevertheless, I was angry. So much so that by the time I reached Judge Ford's chambers in the courthouse, my manner had become brusque, my words clipped, my presentation aimed not only at freeing Syd but flaying the prosecution and police as cold-bloodedly as I could. No histrionics here, just a marching out of statements placing Syd miles away from each of the first four killings, a few tart reminders about Constitutional law and Miranda, and not a few acid comments about damages done to my client's reputation.

When I was through, the prosecution folded— as he would have done if I'd only smiled and told him his case was full of shit. But he was also perspiring, and Judge Ford couldn't help the admiration in his voice as he dismissed the case, sent us home, and gave me a look that wondered what the hell kind of pills I'd been taking since I'd seen him last.

It was, admittedly, an excellent job, one Chet would have been proud of had he seen it. Syd, on the other hand, only thanked me curtly and left me standing on the courthouse steps, trying hard not to run as he headed for home. I returned to the empty office and filed all the papers, straightened up my desk, wandered about for nearly an hour before realizing I was pacing. I should have been pleased with myself, and in a way I was. But it was a desperate, cold, emotionless sort of pleasure, a combination of the residue of ash my anger had left me and the understanding that, unlike Chet, I could never become addicted to something like this.

I ate at the Chancellor Inn.

I drank at the Chancellor Inn.

I wondered what was wrong with me that I couldn't exult over my victory. After all, an innocent man was free, and the police were free to find the real killer.

I wanted to call Jean, and I didn't know her last name.

I stepped outside, and it was dark. Cool. The wind working at the trees and the drizzle hardening to rain. I lifted my collar and shoved my hands into my pockets, thinking I'd stop by Chet's and see how he was doing. Instead, I found myself outside Foster's house, blinking water from my eyelids as I tried to form the question that would get Syd to tell me just what it was, specifically, that had frightened him so much.

The front door was locked, no response to my knocking. I stepped off the porch and made my way around back, noting as I went that all the lights were on, top floor and bottom.

As I reached the corner, I heard someone grunting.

I stopped, ignoring the dampness that crawled down my back and clung to my cheeks. I listened, knowing I'd heard that sound somewhere before. Then the grunting was replaced by a snarling, the snarling by feet running across wet grass. A single stride, and I was in the tiny backyard, staring through the soft glare of the kitchen lights reaching out to the dark. I could see nothing, though something told me there was movement out there. A swirling, receding movement that had me moving after it until I saw the open back door.

My hesitation stalled me, swerved me, had me on the concrete stoop and inside, one hand up to shade my eyes from the overhead light.

Syd was lying partway beneath a small table, the chairs shoved back against the cabinets, two of them on their sides. There was red all over the tiled floor, bright red, running red, most of it pooled by the stumps where Syd's arms and legs used to be.

It was a fever dream then: the air filled with black motes, and all motion was studied. I fell into a calm and called the police, then fell into the yard and vomited my dinner. Blue lights, and flashlights, and a hand on my shoulder, an arm around my waist. Chet materializing and sitting with me in the station while I told my story and swallowed back the tears. He offered me a ride home. I declined; I needed to walk. I needed to breathe. I needed to drive that grunting from my head—like the softly deep sound of a contented animal feeding.

It never occurred to me that I might be in danger.

Nor did I head for anyplace in particular until I found myself on Woodland Avenue and nearly ran to Jean's gate, pulled it open, and raced to the front door. She answered my knocking in moments, saw my face, and pulled me slowly into the living room, murmuring and stroking until I was seated on a couch, knees together and hands clasped in my lap. When she left I almost stood, but there was no strength left in my legs; when she returned I must have

looked at her like a lost puppy finally found by its mistress.
She smiled, knelt beside me, and pushed me back. A towel
to my hair, my face; she took off my shoes and socks and
dried my feet, until, at her urging, I told her what had
happened, what I'd found.

She said nothing, and I kept on talking. She kissed my
cheek, and I closed my eyes. And kept on talking.

She stripped off my jacket and shirt, dried my chest and
back. And I kept on talking. Taking in the touch of her,
the smell of her, feeling her breath against my ear as she
whispered sympathies and soothings and a number of other
things I did not hear because I finally told her how afraid
I was—not of the nightcreature stalking the Station, but of
the glass partitions that had been slamming down around
me one by one, cutting me off from wife, work, and the
last of my friends.

"As if," I said as I stared at the ceiling, "I'm turning into
a ghost. Life goes on, but not around me. I'm not there
anymore."

"No," she said gently, tracing a sharp nail along my jaw.
"No, but you're here."

I smiled, grateful, and looked around the room at the
furniture heavy and heavily padded, at the fringed floor
lamps, at the floral carpet, the floral wallpaper. Not clut-
tered, not spare.

"You live here alone." Not really a question.

"For the time being," she said. She gestured at the room
and at the rooms beyond. "Mother left it to us, me and my
sisters. I came to see if it was all right, worth keeping or
worth selling." She sighed lightly and lay her cheek against
my shoulder, reminding me it was bare. "It's big, though."

I shifted slightly. "It's late."

She said, "Stay."

I neither grinned like a rake nor silently thanked my lucky
stars; I merely followed her upstairs, where she made love
to me, slept beside me, fixed me breakfast in the morning,
and pushed me out laughing, sending me home for some

fresh clothes for the weekend. I very nearly ran, almost didn't answer the phone as I was leaving with my suitcase.

It was Chet, come to a decision.

"Don't say it," I told him, not really caring, thinking about Jean, the way she looked at me, the way she listened. "And you don't have to explain, either. I understand."

"You always understand," he said wearily. "I think that's part of your problem, Brian. You understand so goddamned well . . . ah, the hell with it. Look, there'll be formalities and things—I'll call you later and we can—"

"I'll be at Jean's," I said. "Don't bother to call, I'll talk to you on Monday."

"Jean," he said flatly. I could almost see him shaking his head. "You never learn, do you."

"About what? Christ, Chet, you haven't even met her."

"I don't have to, pal. Unless she's into submission, she'll eat you alive." A pause. "Just don't be stupid, Brian," he said more softly, more concerned. "You've had a hell of a week."

I rang off without saying good-bye, locked the door behind me, and just did beat the next spate of rainfall to Jean's porch. When I burst inside, however, all grinning and foolish, the house was empty. I called, felt cold, hurried from room to room praying aloud I hadn't been wrong. Then I heard her calling my name, found a partially open door in the kitchen and went through to the garage, where she was working under the hood of the station wagon.

"Damned thing's gone again," she said, straightening and wiping her hands on a greasy rag. "She has a zillion miles on her, but I was hoping she'd last at least until fall." She grinned and slammed the hood down, punched at it and mimed a wince.

"How long has it been giving you trouble?" I tried to sound knowledgeable, though it sounded pompous.

"Since I got here, in April."

I nodded and returned to the kitchen, stood at the back

door and watched the rain slant in on the back of the wind.
A cold wind now that flayed the trees and churned puddles
in the grass. It was dusk at noon, and felt like midnight.

She was moving about the garage, shifting things, heavy
and awkward.

April, she'd said—yet she'd told me she hadn't known
about the killings, or my involvement with Syd, or my
profession at all.

April, she'd said—when I'd first started fading.

*The rain and Syd Foster's and something running through
the dark; the kitchen and the blood and—*

She grunted softly as she came into the room, and suddenly there was ice lodged deep in my throat.

When I turned she was standing in the doorway, the
living room behind her. No lights had been turned on, and
her face and figure were in shadow, pale shadows that had
me squinting to keep her form from shifting. The wind
keened in the eaves and across the mouth of the chimney;
a gust, and the panes rattled. I looked to the floor and saw
my shadow framed by the door window behind me, dark
serpents and worms writhing down toward my shoulders.

Then she spoke my name lovingly and I moved around
the room because I couldn't stand still; she began to talk
quietly and I tried through the wind and the cold and the
images of blood to listen and understand, without having
to scream: about how people thought of this animal and
that, how cats were female and dogs were male, women
were feline and men were bestial, and with roles these days
so swiftly blurring—

I opened the refrigerator; it was empty.

—wouldn't it be fascinating to think about what new
mythic creatures would have to conform to new dreams,
what extraordinary night-things would have to fill in the
void; but it wasn't all that bad because people wouldn't
believe any more than they used to, and with violence still
growing—

The cupboards, the cabinets, the drawers were all empty.

—who'd know the difference between two types of nightmare, as long as there was care taken in the hunting.

I leaned over the sink and thought of Chet's warning.

"Who are you?" I said, and wished I'd been drinking.

"Jean," she said simply.

"What . . . what are you?" I said, and wished I were dreaming.

"Your lover, a friend—"

"You know what I mean," I said harshly, spun around, and she was still standing there, in the doorway, in the shadow. I wanted to be afraid, the most natural reaction, but first there was the anger of what I thought was betrayal.

"Someone," she said, "who's been looking for someone like you. Not weak in the old sense, but not always strong enough to fight his own battles. A wonderful streak of feminine sensitivity, plus a little masculine posturing he knows is a sham. A man, Brian, who was more alone than he knew."

"You drove them away," I said weakly.

"There are times, like now, when vulnerability breeds belief."

I should have argued, but I couldn't. The wind was too noisy, and I couldn't focus my anger, and when she started to move toward me, I was too frightened to run.

"We have needs too," she said when she reached me, tilting her head and looking up at me sideways. "Physical"—her hands on my hips—"emotional"—that smile she first gave me—"and the practical, Brian. In the smaller towns we like I think they still call it respectability, a lot easier to get with a solid man in the house. Like a lawyer, for instance. A low-keyed man who never rocks the boat."

"You drove them away."

"You do what you have to."

Then a word caught me, and echoed. "You said . . . we?"

"Why, my sisters," she said, and her expression turned

bemused. "A small lie. There's no mother. I came here looking, and one day I found you."

The house trembled at a blow, and rain crashed against the windows.

Her bemusement grew. "Why . . . why don't you think of yourself as something like the king of beasts, Brian, with five lovely mates to choose from, who'll keep you warm, make you content, keep the world from intruding and making you sad. You'll work, of course, because a man like you has to. But so will we, until it's time to move on." She touched my chin with a finger. "Think about it, darling, don't be rash. I know what you're thinking, you know, what you'd like to do now."

I shook my head, once.

"Of course you want to run," she said sternly. "You wouldn't be human if you didn't. And you're wondering how you could ever live with my sisters and me." She shrugged. "Well, sometimes it works and sometimes it doesn't."

I watched and said nothing when she started to leave me. It was too much, and it wasn't enough, and she had all my feelings pegged down to the last. And worse—she knew I almost believed and, in almost believing, was tempted.

I followed her into the front hall. She opened the front door and helped me into my coat. Then she smiled warmly, and sadly. "Go ahead," she said. "It's all right, believe me: But as a favor to me, please stay on the porch."

I nodded dumbly, shivering at the wind that clutched wildly at my jacket and my hair, crossed the threshold with my arms folded tightly over my chest. But before I could even begin to wonder about madness and nightmares and the perfect reality of the storm in spite of its fury, she whispered my name as she closed the door behind me. I turned and she was shadow, she was shimmering, she was Jean and she was smiling.

"Two things to consider," she said, "just to help you out. The most important is this: you'll never, ever, have to be alone again. We'll give you more pride than any man's ever had."

Oh, Jesus, I thought; for God's sake, stop smiling!

She did. Abruptly. Expressionless now.

"The other thing is . . ." and she glanced to the street, to the storm, back to me. "They won't believe you if you decide you have to run."

And she left me alone as she closed the door, grunting.

LONGTOOTH

EDGAR PANGBORN

Edgar Pangborn (1909–1976) will be remembered by longtime readers of science fiction and fantasy for his fine stories about Davy, which showed the triumph of art and scholarship against religious oppression; these were combined into a novel, *Davy*, published in 1964. Although Edgar Pangborn was best known for his science fiction stories, he also was the creator of such taut, literate tales of horror as "Longtooth." "Longtooth" takes place in rural Maine, and concerns something frightening that is born, lives—and kills—briefly in the peaceful forest.

My word is good. How can I prove it? Born in Darkfield, wasn't I? Stayed away thirty more years after college, but when I returned I was still Ben Dane, one of the Darkfield Danes, Judge Marcus Dane's eldest. And they knew my word was good. My wife died and I sickened of all cities; then my bachelor brother Sam died, too, who'd lived all his life here in Darkfield, running his one-man law office over in Lohman—our nearest metropolis, pop. 6437. A fast coronary at fifty; I had loved him. Helen gone, then Sam—I wound up my unimportances and came home, inheriting Sam's housekeeper Adelaide Simmons, her grim stability and celestial cooking. Nostalgia for Maine is a serious matter, late in life: I had to yield. I expected a gradual drift into my childless old age playing correspondence chess, translating a few of the classics. I thought I could take for granted the continued respect of my neighbors. I say my word is good.

I will remember again that middle of March a few years ago, the snow skimming out of an afternoon sky as dirty as the bottom of an old aluminum pot. Harp Ryder's back road had been plowed since the last snowfall; I supposed Bolt-Bucket could make the mile and a half in to his farm and out again before we got caught. Harp had asked me to get him a book if I was making a trip to Boston, any goddamn book that told about Eskimos, and I had one for him, De Poncins's *Kabloona*. I saw the midget devils of white running crazy down a huge slope of wind, and recalled hearing at the Darkfield News Bureau, otherwise Cleve's General Store, somebody mentioning a forecast of the worst blizzard in forty years. Joe Cleve, who won't permit a radio in the store because it pesters his ulcers, inquired of his Grand Inquisitor who dwells ten yards behind your right shoulder: "Why's it always got to be the worst in so-and-so many years, that going to help anybody?" The bureau was still analyzing this difficult inquiry when I left, with my cigarettes and as much as I could remember of Adelaide's grocery list after leaving it on the dining table. It wasn't yet three when I turned in on Harp's back road, and a gust slammed at Bolt-Bucket like death with a shovel.

I tried to win momentum for the rise to the high ground, swerved to avoid an idiot rabbit and hit instead a patch of snow-hidden melt-and-freeze, skidding to a full stop from which nothing would extract me but a tow.

I was fifty-seven that year, my wind bad from too much smoking and my heart (I now know) no stronger than Sam's. I quit cursing—gradually, to avoid sudden actions—and tucked *Kabloona* under my parka. I would walk the remaining mile to Ryder's, stay just to leave the book, say hello, and phone for a tow; then, since Harp never owned a car and never would, I could walk back and meet the truck.

If Leda Ryder knew how to drive, it didn't matter much after she married Harp. They farmed it, back in there, in almost the manner of Harp's ancestors of Jefferson's time. Harp did keep his two hundred laying hens by methods that were considered modern before the poor wretches got condemned to batteries, but his other enterprises came closer to antiquity. In his big kitchen garden he let one small patch of weeds fool themselves for an inch or two, so he'd have it to work at; they survived nowhere else. A few cows, a team, four acres for market crops, and a small dog Droopy, whose grandmother had made it somehow with a dachshund. Droopy's only menace in obese old age was a wheezing bark. The Ryders must have grown nearly all vital necessities except chewing tobacco and once in a while a new dress for Leda. Harp could snub the twentieth century, and I doubt if Leda was consulted about it in spite of his obsessive devotion for her. She was almost thirty years younger, and yes, he should not have married her. Other side up just as scratchy; she should not have married him, but she did.

Harp was a dinosaur perhaps, but I grew up with him, he a year the younger. We swam, fished, helled around together. And when I returned to Darkfield growing old, he was one of the few who acted glad to see me, so far as you can trust what you read in a face like a granite promontory. Maybe twice a week Harp Ryder smiled.

I pushed on up the ridge, and noticed a going-and-coming set of wide tire tracks already blurred with snow. That would be the egg truck I had passed a quarter hour since on the main road. Whenever the west wind at my back lulled, I could swing around and enjoy one of my favorite prospects of birch and hemlock lowland. From Ryder's Ridge there's no sign of Darkfield two miles southwest except one church spire. On clear days you glimpse Bald Mountain and his two big brothers, more than twenty miles west of us.

The snow was thickening. It brought relief and pleasure to see the black shingles of Harp's barn and the roof of his Cape Codder. Foreshortened, so that it looked snug against the barn; actually house and barn were connected by a two-story shed fifteen feet wide and forty feet long—woodshed below, hen loft above. The Ryders' sunrise-facing bedroom window was set only three feet above the eaves of that shed roof. They truly went to bed with the chickens. I shouted, for Harp was about to close the big shed door. He held it for me. I ran, and the storm ran after me. The west wind was bouncing off the barn; eddies howled at us. The temperature had tumbled ten degrees since I left Darkfield. The thermometer by the shed door read fifteen degrees, and I knew I'd been a damn fool. As I helped Harp fight the shed door closed, I thought I heard Leda, crying.

A swift confused impression. The wind was exploring new ranges of passion, the big door squawked, and Harp was asking: "Ca' break down?" I do still think I heard Leda wail. If so, it ended as we got the door latched and Harp drew a newly fitted two-by-four bar across it. I couldn't understand that: the old latch was surely proof against any wind short of a hurricane.

"Bolt-Bucket never breaks down. Ought to get one, Harp—lots of company. All she did was go in the ditch."

"You might see her again come spring." His hens were

scratching overhead, not yet scared by the storm. Harp's eyes were small gray glitters of trouble. "Ben, you figure a man's getting old at fifty-six?"

"No." My bones (getting old) ached for the warmth of his kitchen-dining-living-everything room, not for sad philosophy. "Use your phone, okay?"

"If the wires ain't down," he said, not moving, a man beaten on by other storms. "Them loafers didn't cut none of the overhang branches all summer. I told 'em of course, I told 'em how it would be . . . I meant, Ben, old enough to get dumb fancies?" My face may have told him I thought he was brooding about himself with a young wife. He frowned, annoyed that I hadn't taken his meaning. "I meant, *seeing* things. Things that can't be so, but—"

"We can all do some of that at any age, Harp."

That remark was a stupid brushoff, a stone for bread, because I was cold, impatient, wanted in. Harp had always a tense one-way sensitivity. His face chilled. "Well, come in, warm up. Leda ain't feeling too good. Getting a cold or something."

When she came downstairs and made me welcome, her eyes were reddened. I don't think the wind made that noise. Droopy waddled from her basket behind the stove to snuff my feet and give me my usual low passing mark.

Leda never had it easy there, young and passionate with scant mental resources. She was twenty-eight that year, looking tall because she carried her firm body handsomely. Some of the sullenness in her big mouth and lucid gray eyes was sexual challenge, some pure discontent. I liked Leda; her nature was not one for animosity or meanness. Before her marriage the Darkfield News Bureau used to declare with its customary scrupulous fairness that Leda had been covered by every goddamn thing in pants within thirty miles. For once the bureau may have spoken a grain of truth in the malice, for Leda did have the smoldering power that draws men without word or gesture. After her abrupt marriage to Harp—Sam told me all this; I wasn't living in

Darkfield then and hadn't met her—the garbage-gossip went hastily underground: enraging Harp Ryder was never healthy.

The phone wires weren't down, yet. While I waited for the garage to answer, Harp said, "Ben, I can't let you walk back in that. Stay over, huh?"

I didn't want to. It meant extra work and inconvenience for Leda, and I was ancient enough to crave my known safe burrow. But I felt Harp wanted me to stay for his own sake. I asked Jim Short at the garage to go ahead with Bolt-Bucket if I wasn't there to meet him. Jim roared: "Know what it's doing right now?"

"Little spit of snow, looks like."

"Jesus!" He covered the mouthpiece imperfectly. I heard his enthusiastic voice ring through cold-iron echoes: "Hey, old Ben's got that thing into the ditch again! Ain't that something . . . ? Listen, Ben, I can't make no promises. Got both tow trucks out already. You better stop over and praise the Lord you got that far."

"Okay," I said. "It wasn't much of a ditch."

Leda fed us coffee. She kept glancing toward the landing at the foot of the stairs where a night-darkness already prevailed. A closed-in stairway slanted down at a never-used front door; beyond that landing was the other ground floor room-parlor, spare, guestroom—where I would sleep. I don't know what Leda expected to encounter in that shadow. Once when a chunk of firewood made an odd noise in the range, her lips clamped shut on a scream.

The coffee warmed me. By that time the weather left no loophole for argument. Not yet 3:30, but west and north were lost in furious black. Through the hissing white flood I could just see the front of the barn forty feet away. "Nobody's going no place into that," Harp said. His little house shuddered, enforcing the words. "Leda, you don't look too brisk. Get you some rest."

"I better see to the spare room for Ben."

Neither spoke with much tenderness, but it glowed openly in him when she turned her back. Then some other need bent his granite face out of its normal seams. His whole gaunt body leaning forward tried to help him talk. "You wouldn't figure me for a man'd go off his rocker?" he asked.

"Of course not. What's biting, Harp?"

"There's something in the woods, got no right to be there." To me that came as a letdown of relief: I would not have to listen to another's marriage problems. "I wish, b' Jesus Christ, it would hit somebody else once, so I could say what I know and not be laughed at all to hell. I *ain't* one for dumb fancies."

You walked on eggs, with Harp. He might decide any minute that *I* was laughing. "Tell me," I said. "If anything's out there now, it must feel a mite chilly."

"Ayah." He went to the north window, looking out where we knew the road lay under white confusion. Harp's land sloped down the other side of the road to the edge of mighty evergreen forest. Katahdin stands more than fifty miles north and a little east of us. We live in a withering shrink-world, but you could still set out from Harp's farm and, except for the occasional country road and the rivers—not many large ones—you could stay in deep forest all the way to the tundra, or Alaska. Harp said, "This kind of weather is when it comes."

He sank into his beat-up kitchen armchair and reached for *Kabloona*. He had barely glanced at the book while Leda was with us. "Funny name."

"Kabloona's an Eskimo word for white man."

"He done these pictures . . . ? Be they good, Ben?"

"I like 'em. Photographs in the back."

"Oh." He turned the pages hastily for those, but studied only the ones that showed the strong Eskimo faces, and his interest faded. Whatever he wanted was not here. "These people, be they—civilized?"

"In their own way, sure."

"Ayah, this guy looks like he could find his way in the woods."

"Likely the one thing he couldn't do, Harp. They never see a tree unless they come south, and they hate to do that. Anything below the Arctic is too warm."

"That a fact . . . ? Well, it's a nice book. How much was it?" I'd found it second-hand; he paid me to the exact penny. "I'll be glad to read it." He never would. It would end up on the shelf in the parlor with the Bible, an old almanac, a Longfellow, until someday this place went up for auction and nobody remembered Harp's way of living.

"What's this all about, Harp?"

"Oh . . . I was hearing things in the woods, back last summer. I'd think, fox, then I'd know it wasn't. Make your hair stand right on end. Lost a cow, last August, from the north pasture acrosst the rud. Section of board fence tore out. I mean, Ben, the two top boards was *pulled out from the nail holes*. No hammer marks."

"Bear?"

"Only track I found looked like bear except too small. You know a bear wouldn't *pull* it out, Ben."

"Cow slamming into it, panicked by something?"

He remained patient with me. "Ben, would I build a cow-pasture fence nailing the crosspieces from the outside? Cow hit it with all her weight she might bust it, sure. And kill herself doing it, be blood and hair all over the split boards, and she'd be there, not a mile and a half away into the woods. Happened during a big thunderstorm. I figured it had to be somebody with a spite ag'inst me, maybe some son of a bitch wanting the prop'ty, trying to scare me off that's lived here all my life and my family before me. But that don't make sense. I found the cow a week later, what was left. Way into the woods. The head and the bones. Hide tore up and flang around. Any *person* dressing off a beef, he'll cut whatever he wants and take off with it. He don't sit down and chaw the meat off the *bones*, b'Jesus Christ. He don't tear the thighbone out of the joint. . . . All right, maybe bear. But no bear did that job on that fence and then driv old Nell a mile and a half into the woods to kill her. Nice little Jersey, clever's a kitten, Leda used to make over her, like she don't usually do with the stock. . . . I've looked plenty in the woods since then, never turned up anything. Once and again I did smell something. Fishy, like bear-smell but—*different*."

"But Harp, with snow on the ground—"

"Now you'll really call me crazy. When the weather is clear, I ain't once found his prints. I hear him then, at night, but I go out by daylight where I think the sound was, there's no trail. Just the usual snow tracks. I know. He lives in the trees and don't come down except when it's storming, I got to believe that? Because then he does come, Ben, when the weather's like now, like right now. And old Ned and Jerry out in the stable go wild, and sometimes we hear his noise under the window. I shine my flashlight through the glass—never catch sight of him. I go out with the ten gauge if there's any light to see by, and there's prints around the house—holes filling up with snow. By morning there'll be maybe some marks left, and they'll lead off to the north woods, but under the trees you won't find it. So he gets up in the branches and travels thataway? . . . Just once I have seen him, Ben. Last October. I better tell you one other thing first. A day or so after I found what was left of old Nell, I lost six roaster chickens. I made over a couple box stalls, maybe you remember, so the birds could be out on range and roost in the barn at night. Good doors, and I always locked 'em. Two in the morning, Ned and Jerry go crazy. I got out through the barn into the stable, and they was spooked, Ned trying to kick his way out. I got 'em quiet, looked all over the stable—loft, harness room, everywhere. Not a thing. Dead quiet night, no moon. It had to be something the horses smelled. I come back into the barn, and found one of the chicken-pen doors open—*tore* out from the lock. Chicken thief would bring along something to pry with—wouldn't he be a Christly idjut if he didn't . . . ? Took six birds, six nice eight-pound roasters, and left the heads on the floor—bitten off."

"Harp—some lunatic. People *can* go insane that way. There are old stories—"

"Been trying to believe that. Would a man live the winter out there? Twenty below zero?"

"Maybe a cave—animal skins."

"I've boarded up the whole back of the barn. Done the same with the hen-loft windows—two-by-fours with four-inch spikes driv slantwise. They be twelve feet off the ground, and he ain't come for 'em, not yet. . . . So after that happened I sent for Sheriff Robart. Son of a bitch happens to live in Darkfield, you'd think he might've took an interest."

"Do any good?"

Harp laughed. He did that by holding my stare, making no sound, moving no muscle except a disturbance at the eye corners. A New England art; maybe it came over on the *Mayflower*. "Robart he come by, after a while. I showed him that door. I showed him them chicken heads. Told him how I'd been spending my nights out there on my ass, with the ten gauge." Harp rose to unload tobacco juice into the range fire; he has a theory it purifies the air. "Ben, I might've showed him them chicken heads a shade close to his nose. By the time he got here, see, they wasn't all that fresh. He made out he'd look around and let me know. Mid-September. Ain't seen him since."

"Might've figured he wouldn't be welcome?"

"Why, he'd be welcome as shit on a tablecloth."

"You spoke of—seeing it, Harp?"

"Could call it seeing . . . All right. It was during them Indian summer days—remember? Like June except them pretty colors, smell of windfalls—God, I like that, I like October. I'd gone down to the slope acrosst the rud where I mended my fence after losing old Nell. Just leaning there, guess I was tired. Late afternoon, sky pinking up. You know how the fence cuts acrosst the slope to my east wood lot. I've let the bushes grow free—lot of elder, other stuff the birds come for. I was looking down toward that little break between the north woods and my wood lot, where a bit of

old growed-up pasture shows through Pretty spot. Painter
fella come by a few years ago and done a picture of it, said
the place looked like a coro, dunno what the hell that is,
he didn't say."

I pushed at his brown study. "You saw it there?"

"No. Off to my right in them elder bushes. Fifty feet
from me, I guess. By God, I didn't turn my head. I got it
with the tail of my eye and turned the other way as if I
meant to walk back to the rud. Made like busy with something in the grass, come wandering back to the fence some
nearer. He stayed for me, a brownish patch in them bushes
by the big yellow birch. Near the height of a man. No gun
with me, not even a stick . . . Big shoulders, couldn't see
his goddamn feet. He don't stand more'n five feet tall. His
hands, if he's got real ones, hung out of my sight in a tangle
of elder bushes. He's got brown fur, Ben, reddy-brown fur
all over him. His face, too, his head, his big thick neck.
There's a shine to fur in sunlight, you can't be mistook.
So—I did look at him direct. Tried to act like I still didn't
see him, but he knowed. He melted back and got the birch
between him and me. Not a sound." And then Harp was
listening for Leda upstairs. He went on softly: "Ayah, I ran
back for a gun, and searched the woods, for all the good it
did me. You'll want to know about his face. I ain't told
Leda all this part. See, she's scared, I don't want to make
it no worse, I just said it was some animal that snuck off
before I could see it good. A big face, Ben. Head real human
except it sticks out too much around the jaw. Not much
nose—open spots in the fur. Ben, the—the *teeth!* I seen
his mouth drop open and he pulled up one side of his lip
to show me them stabbing things. I've seen as big as that
on a full-growed bear. That's what I'll hear, I ever try to
tell this. They'll say I seen a bear. Now, I shot my first bear
when I was sixteen and Pa took me over toward Jackman.
I've got me one maybe every other year since then. I know
'em, all their ways. But that's what I'll hear if I tell the
story."

I am a frustrated naturalist, loaded with assorted facts. I know there aren't any monkeys or apes that could stand our winters except maybe the harmless Himalayan langur. No such beast as Harp described lived anywhere on the planet. It didn't help. Harp was honest; he was rational; he wanted a reasonable explanation as much as I did. Harp wasn't the village atheist for nothing. I said, "I guess you will, Harp. People mostly won't take the—unusual."

"Maybe you'll hear him tonight, Ben."

Leda came downstairs, and heard part of that. "He's been telling you, Ben. What do you think?"

"I don't know what to think."

"Led', I thought, if I imitate that noise for him—"

"No!" She had brought some mending and was about to sit down with it, but froze as if threatened by attack. "I couldn't stand it, Harp. And—it might bring them."

"Them?" Harp chuckled uneasily. "I don't guess I could do it that good he'd come for it."

"Don't *do* it, Harp!"

"All right, hon." Her eyes were closed, her head drooping back. "Don't git nerved up so."

I started wondering whether a man still seeming sane could dream up such a horror for the unconscious purpose of tormenting a woman too young for him, a woman he could never imagine he owned. If he told her a fox bark wasn't right for a fox, she'd believe him. I said, "We shouldn't talk about it if it upsets her."

He glanced at me like a man floating up from underwater. Leda said in a small, aching voice: "I wish to God we could move to Boston."

The granite face closed in defensiveness. "Led', we been over all that. Nothing is going to drive me off of my land. I got no time for the city at my age. What the Jesus would I do? Night watchman? Sweep out somebody's back room, b'Jesus Christ? Savings'd be gone in no time. We been all over it. We ain't moving nowhere."

"I could find work." For Harp, of course, that was the

worst thing she could have said. She probably knew it from his stricken silence. She said clumsily, "I forgot something upstairs." She snatched up her mending and she was gone.

We talked no more of it the rest of the day. I followed through the milking and other chores, lending a hand where I could, and we made everything as secure as we could against storm and other enemies. The long-toothed furry thing was the spectral guest at dinner, but we cut him, on Leda's account, or so we pretended. Supper would have been awkward anyway. They weren't in the habit of putting up guests, and Leda was a rather deadly cook because she cared nothing about it. A Darkfield girl, I suppose she had the usual twentieth-century mishmash of television dreams until some impulse or maybe false signs of pregnancy tricked her into marrying a man out of the nineteenth. We had venison treated like beef and overdone vegetables. I don't like venison even when it's treated right.

At six Harp turned on his battery radio and sat stone-faced through the day's bad news and the weather forecast —"a blizzard which may prove the worst in forty-two years. Since three P.M., eighteen inches have fallen at Bangor, twenty-one at Boston. Precipitation is not expected to end until tomorrow. Winds will increase during the night with gusts up to seventy miles per hour." Harp shut it off, with finality. On other evenings I had spent there he let Leda play it after supper only kind of soft, so there had been a continuous muted bleat and blatter all evening. Tonight Harp meant to listen for other sounds. Leda washed the dishes, said an early good night, and fled upstairs.

Harp didn't talk, except as politeness obliged him to answer some blah of mine. We sat and listened to the snow and the lunatic wind. An hour of it was enough for me; I said I was beat and wanted to turn in early. Harp saw me to my bed in the parlor and placed a new chunk of rock maple in the pot-bellied stove. He produced a difficult granite smile, maybe using up his allowance for the week, and pulled out a bottle from a cabinet that had stood for many years below a parlor print—George Washington, I think, concluding a treaty with some offbeat sufferer from hepatitis who may have been General Cornwallis if the latter had two left feet. The bottle contained a brand of rye that Harp sincerely believed to be drinkable, having charred his gullet forty-odd years trying to prove it. While my throat healed, Harp said, "Shouldn't've bothered you with all this crap, Ben. Hope it ain't going to spoil your sleep." He got me his spare flashlight, then let me be, and closed the door.

I heard him drop back into his kitchen armchair. Under too many covers, lamp out, I heard the cruel whisper of the snow. The stove muttered, a friend, making me a co-coon of living heat in a waste of outer cold. Later I heard Leda at the head of the stairs, her voice timid, tired, and sweet with invitation: "You comin' up to bed, Harp?" The stairs creaked under him. Their door closed; presently she cried out in that desired pain that is brief release from trouble.

I remembered something Adelaide Simmons had told me about this house, where I had not gone upstairs since Harp and I were boys. Adelaide, one of the very few women in Darkfield who never spoke unkindly of Leda, said that the tiny west room across from Harp and Leda's bedroom was fixed up for a nursery, and Harp wouldn't allow anything in there but baby furniture. Had been so since they were married seven years before.

Another hour dragged on, in my exasperations of sleep-lessness.

Then I heard Longtooth.

The noise came from the west side, beyond the snow-hidden vegetable garden. When it snatched me from the edge of sleep, I tried to think it was a fox barking, the ringing, metallic shriek the little red beast can belch dragonlike from his throat. But wide awake, I knew it had been much deeper, chestier. Horned owl?—no. A sound that belonged to an-cient times when men relied on chipped stone weapons and had full reason to fear the dark.

The cracks in the stove gave me firelight for groping back into my clothes. The wind had not calmed at all. I stumbled to the west window, buttoning up, and found it a white blank. Snow had drifted above the lower sash. On tiptoe I could just see over it. A light appeared, dimly illuminating the snowfield beyond. That would be coming from a lamp in the Ryders' bedroom, shining through the nursery room and so out, weak and diffused, into the blizzard chaos.

Yaaarrhh!

Now it had drawn horribly near. From the north windows of the parlor I saw black nothing. Harp squeaked down to my door.

" 'Wake, Ben?"

"Yes. Come look at the west window."

He had left no night-light burning in the kitchen, and only a scant glow came down to the landing from the bedroom. He murmured behind me, "Ayah, snow's up some. Must be over three foot on the level by now."

Yaaarrhh!

The voice had shouted on the south side, the blinder side of the house, overlooked only by one kitchen window and a small one in the pantry where the hand pump stood. The view from the pantry window was mostly blocked by a great maple that overtopped the house. I heard the wind shrilling across the tree's winter bones.

"Ben, you want to git your boots on? Up to you—can't ask it. I might have to go out." Harp spoke in an undertone as if the beast might understand him through the tight walls.

"Of course." I got into my knee boots and caught up my parka as I followed him into the kitchen. A .30-caliber rifle and his heavy shotgun hung on deerhorn over the door to the woodshed. He found them in the dark.

What courage I possessed that night came from being shamed into action, from fearing to show a poor face to an old friend in trouble. I went through the Normandy invasion. I have camped out alone, when I was younger and healthier, and slept nicely. But that noise of Longtooth stole courage. It ached along the channel of the spine.

I had the spare flashlight, but knew Harp didn't want me to use it here. I could make out the furniture, and Harp reaching for the gun rack. He already had on his boots, fur cap, and mackinaw. "You take this'n," he said, and put the ten gauge in my hands. "Both barrels loaded. Ain't my way to do that, ain't right, but since this thing started—"

Yaaarrhh!

"Where's he got to now?" Harp was by the south window. "Round this side?"

"I thought so. . . . Where's Droopy?"

Harp chuckled thinly. "Poor little shit! She come upstairs at the first sound of him and went under the bed. I told Led' to stay upstairs. She'd want a light down here. Wouldn't make sense."

Then, apparently from the east side of the hen loft and high, booming off some resonating surface: *Yaaarrhh!*

"He can't! Jesus, that's twelve foot off the ground!" But Harp plunged out into the shed, and I followed. "Keep your light on the floor, Ben." He ran up the narrow stairway. "Don't shine it on the birds, they'll act up."

So far the chickens, stupid and virtually blind in the dark, were making only a peevish tut-tutting of alarm. But something was clinging to the outside of the barricaded east window, snarling, chattering teeth, pounding on the two-by-fours. With a fist?—it sounded like nothing else. Harp snapped, "Get your light on the window!" And he fired through the glass.

We heard no outcry. Any noise outside was covered by the storm and the squawks of the hens scandalized by the shot. The glass was dirty from their continual disturbance of the litter; I couldn't see through it. The bullet had drilled the pane without shattering it, and passed between the two-by-fours, but the beast could have dropped before he fired. "I got to go out there. You stay, Ben." Back in the kitchen he exchanged rifle for shotgun. "Might not have no chance to aim. You remember this piece, don't y'?—eight in the clip."

"I remember it."

"Good. Keep your ears open." Harp ran out through the door that gave on a small paved area by the woodshed. To get around under the east loft window he would have to push through the snow behind the barn, since he had blocked all the rear openings. He could have circled the house instead, but only by bucking the west wind and fighting deeper drifts. I saw his big shadow melt out of sight.

Leda's voice quavered down to me: "He—get it?"

"Don't know. He's gone to see. Sit tight. . . ."

I heard that infernal bark once again before Harp returned, and again it sounded high off the ground; it must have come from the big maple. And then moments later —I was still trying to pierce the dark, watching for Harp— a vast smash of broken glass and wood, and the violent bang of the door upstairs. One small wheezing shriek cut short, and one scream such as no human being should ever hear. I can still hear it.

I think I lost some seconds in shock. Then I was groping up the narrow stairway, clumsy with the rifle and flashlight. Wind roared at the opening of the kitchen door, and Harp was crowding past me, thrusting me aside. But I was close behind him when he flung the bedroom door open. The blast from the broken window that had slammed the door had also blown out the lamp. But our flashlights said at once that Leda was not there. Nothing was, nothing living.

Droopy lay in a mess of glass splinters and broken window sash, dead from a crushed neck—something had stamped on her. The bedspread had been pulled almost to the window—maybe Leda's hand had clenched on it. I saw blood on some of the glass fragments, and on the splintered sash, a patch of reddish fur.

Harp ran back downstairs. I lingered a few seconds. The arrow of fear was deep in me, but at the moment it made me numb. My light touched up an ugly photograph on the wall, Harp's mother at fifty or so, petrified and acid-faced before the camera, a puritan deity with shallow, haunted eyes. I remembered her.

Harp had kicked over the traces when his father died, and quit going to church. Mrs. Ryder "disowned" him. The farm was his; she left him with it and went to live with a widowed sister in Lohman, and died soon, unreconciled. Harp lived on as a bachelor, crank, recluse, until his strange marriage in his fifties. Now here was Ma still watchful, pucker-faced, unforgiving. In my dullness of shock I thought: Oh, they probably always made love with the lights out.

But now Leda wasn't there.

I hurried after Harp, who had left the kitchen door to bang in the wind. I got out there with rifle and flashlight, and over across the road I saw his torch. No other light, just his small gleam and mine.

I knew as soon as I had forced myself beyond the corner of the house and into the fantastic embrace of the storm that I could never make it. The west wind ground needles into my face. The snow was up beyond the middle of my thighs. With weak lungs and maybe an imperfect heart I could do nothing out here except die quickly to no purpose. In a moment Harp would be starting down the slope of the woods. His trail was already disappearing under my beam. I drove myself a little farther, and an instant's lull in the storm allowed me to shout: "Harp! I can't follow!"

He heard. He cupped his mouth and yelled back: "Don't try! Git back to the house! Telephone!" I waved to acknowledge the message and struggled back.

I only just made it. Inside the kitchen doorway I fell flat, gun and flashlight clattering off somewhere, and there I stayed until I won back enough breath to keep myself living. My face and hands were ice blocks, then fires. While I worked at the task of getting air into my body, one thought continued, an inner necessity: *There must be a rational*

cause. I do not abandon the national cause. At length I
hauled myself up and stumbled to the telephone. The line
was dead.

I found the flashlight and reeled upstairs with it. I stepped
past poor Droopy's body and over the broken glass to look
through the window space. I could see that snow had been
pushed off the shed roof near the bedroom window; the
house sheltered that area from the full drive of the west
wind, so some evidence remained. I guessed that whatever
came must have jumped to the house roof from the maple,
then down to the shed roof and then hurled itself through
the closed window without regard for it as an obstacle.
Losing a little blood and a little fur.

I glanced around and could not find that fur now. Wind
must have pushed it out of sight. I forced the door shut.
Downstairs, I lit the table lamps in kitchen and parlor. Harp
might need those beacons—if he came back. I refreshed
the fires, and gave myself a dose of Harp's horrible whiskey.
It was nearly one in the morning. If he never came back?

It might be days before they could plow out the road.
When the storm let up I could use Harp's snowshoes, maybe
. . .

Harp came back at 1:20, bent and staggering. He let me
support him to the armchair. When he could speak he said,
"No trail. No trail." He took the bottle from my hands and
pulled on it. "Christ Jesus! What can I do? Ben . . . ? I got
to go to the village, get help. If they got any help to give."

"Do you have an extra pair of snowshoes?"

He stared toward me, battling confusion. "Hah? No, I
ain't. Better you stay anyhow. I'll bring yours from your
house if you want, if I can git there." He drank again and
slammed in the cork with the heel of his hand. "I'll leave
you the ten gauge."

He got his snowshoes from a closet. I persuaded him to
wait for coffee. Haste could accomplish nothing now; we
could not say to each other that we knew Leda was dead.

When he was ready to go, I stepped outside with him into
the mad wind. "Anything you want me to do before you
get back?" He tried to think about it.

"I guess not, Ben . . . God, ain't I *lived* right? No, that
don't make sense? God? That's a laugh." He swung away.
Two or three great strides and the storm took him.

That was about two o'clock. For four hours I was alone
in the house. Warmth returned, with the bedroom door
closed and fires working hard. I carried the kitchen lamp
into the parlor, and then huddled in the nearly total dark
of the kitchen with my back to the wall, watching all the
windows, the ten gauge near my hand, but I did not expect
a return of the beast, and there was none.

The night grew quieter, perhaps because the house was
so drifted in that snow muted the sounds. I was cut off from
the battle, buried alive.

Harp would get back. The seasons would follow their
natural way, and somehow we would learn what had happened to Leda. I supposed the beast would have to be something in the human pattern—mad, deformed, gone wild,
but still human.

After a time I wondered why we had heard no excitement
in the stable. I forced myself to take up gun and flashlight
and go look. I groped through the woodshed, big with the
jumping shadows of Harp's cordwood, and into the barn.
The cows were peacefully drowsing. In the center alley I
dared to send my weak beam swooping and glimmering
through the ghastly distances of the hayloft. Quiet, just
quiet; natural rustling of mice. Then to the stable, where
Ned whickered and let me rub his brown cheek, and Jerry
rolled a humorous eye. I suppose no smell had reached
them to touch off panic, and perhaps they had heard the
barking often enough so that it no longer disturbed them.
I went back to my post, and the hours crawled along a ridge
between the pits of terror and exhaustion. Maybe I slept.

No color of sunrise that day, but I felt paleness and
change; even a blizzard will not hide the fact of dayshine

somewhere. I breakfasted on bacon and eggs, fed the hens,
forked down hay, and carried water for the cows and horses.
The one cow in milk, a jumpy Ayrshire, refused to concede
that I meant to be useful. I'd done no milking since I was
a boy, the knack was gone from my hands, and relief seemed
less important to her than kicking over the pail; she was
getting more amusement than discomfort out of it, so for
the moment I let it go. I made myself busy work shoveling
a clear space by the kitchen door. The wind was down, the
snowfall persistent but almost peaceful. I pushed out beyond
the house and learned that the stuff was up over my hips.

Out of that, as I turned back, came Harp in his long,
snowshoe stride, and down the road three others. I recognized Sheriff Robart, overfed but powerful; and Bill Hastings, wry and ageless, a cousin of Harp's and one of his
few friends; and last, Curt Davidson, perhaps a friend to
Sheriff Robart but certainly not to Harp.

I'd known Curt as a thickwitted loudmouth when he was
a kid; growing to man's years hadn't done much for him.
And when I saw him I thought, irrationally perhaps: Not
good for our side. A kind of absurdity, and yet Harp and I
were joined against the world simply because we had experienced together what others were going to call impossible, were going to interpret in harsh, even damnable ways;
and no help for it.

I saw the white thin blur of the sun, the strength of it
growing. Nowhere in all the white expanse had the wind
and the new snow allowed us any mark of the visitation of
the night.

The men reached my cleared space and shook off snow.
I opened the woodshed. Harp gave me one hopeless glance
of inquiry and I shook my head.

"Having a little trouble?" That was Robart, taking off his
snowshoes.

Harp ignored him. "I got to look after my chores." I told
him I'd done it except for that damn cow. "Oh, Bess, ayah,

she's nervy. I'll see to her." He gave me my snowshoes that he had strapped to his back. "Adelaide, she wanted to know about your groceries. Said I figured they was in the ca'."

"Good as an icebox," says Robart, real friendly.

Curt had to have his pleasures too. "Ben, you sure you got hold of old Bess by the right end, where the tits was?" Curt giggles at his own jokes, so nobody else is obliged to. Bill Hastings spat in the snow.

"Okay if I go in?" Robart asked. It wasn't a simple inquiry: He was present officially and meant to have it known. Harp looked him up and down.

"Nobody stopping you. Didn't bring you here to stand around, I suppose."

"Harp," said Robart pleasantly enough, "don't give me a hard time. You come tell me certain things has happened, I got to look into it is all." But Harp was already striding down the woodshed to the barn entrance. The others came into the house with me, and I put on water for fresh coffee. "Must be your ca' down the rud a piece, Ben? Heard you kind of went into a ditch. All's you can see now is a hump in the snow. Deep freeze might be good for her, likely you've tried everything else." But I wasn't feeling comic, and never had been on those terms with Robart. I grunted, and his face shed mirth as one slips off a sweater. "Okay, what's the score? Harp's gone and told me a story I couldn't feed to the dogs, so what about it? Where's Mrs. Ryder?"

Davidson giggled again. It's a nasty little sound to come out of all that beef. I don't think Robart had much enthusiasm for him either, but it seems he had sworn in the fellow as a deputy before they set out. "Yes, sir," said Curt, "that was *really* a story, that was."

"Where's Mrs. Ryder?"

"Not here," I told him. "We think she's dead."

He glowered, rubbing cold out of his hands. "Seen that window. Looks like the frame is smashed."

"Yes, from the outside. When Harp gets back you'd better look. I closed the door on that room and haven't opened it. There'll be more snow, but you'll see about what we saw when we got up there."

"Let's look right now," said Curt.

Bill Hastings said, "Curt, ain't you a mite busy for a dep'ty? Mr. Dane said when Harp gets back." Bill and I are friends; normally he wouldn't mister me. I think he was trying to give me some flavor of authority.

I acknowledged the alliance by asking: "You a deputy too, Bill?" Giving him an opportunity to spit in the stove, replace the lid gently, and reply: "Shit no."

Harp returned and carried the milk pail to the pantry. Then he was looking us over. "Bill, I got to try the woods again. You want to come along?"

"Sure, Harp. I didn't bring no gun."

"Take my ten gauge."

"Curt here'll go along," said Robart. "Real good man on snowshoes. Interested in wild life."

Harp said, "That's funny, Robart. I guess that's the funniest thing I heard since Cutler's little girl fell under the tractor. You joining us too?"

"Fact is, Harp, I kind of pulled a muscle in my back coming up here. Not getting no younger neither. I believe I'll just look around here a little. Trust you got no objection? To me looking around a little?"

"Coffee's dripped," I said.

"Thing of it is, if I'd've thought you had any objection, I'd've been obliged to get me a warrant."

"Thanks, Ben." Harp gulped the coffee scalding. "Why, if looking around the house is the best you can do, Sher'f, I got no objection. Ben, I shouldn't be keeping you away from your affairs, but would you stay? Kind of keep him company? Not that I got much in the house, but still—you know—"

"I'll stay." I wished I could tell him to drop that manner; it only got him deeper in the mud.

Robart handed Davidson his gun belt and holster. "Better have it, Curt, so to be in style."

Harp and Bill were outside getting on their snowshoes; I half heard some remark of Harp's about the sheriff's aching back. They took off. The snow had almost ceased. They passed out of sight down the slope to the north, and Curt went plowing after them. Behind me Robart said, "You'd think Harp believed it himself."

"That's how it's to be? You make us both liars before you've even done any looking?"

"I got to try to make sense of it is all." I followed him up to the bedroom. It was cruelly cold. He touched Droopy's stiff corpse with his foot. "Hard to figure a man killing his own dog."

"We get nowhere with that kind of idea."

"Ben, you got to see this thing like it looks to other people. And keep out of my hair."

"That's what scares me, Jack. Something unreasonable did happen, and Harp and I were the only ones to experience it—except Mrs. Ryder."

"You claim you saw this—animal?"

"I didn't say that. I heard her scream. When we got upstairs this room was the way you see it." I looked around, and again couldn't find that scrap of fur, but I spoke of it, and I give Robart credit for searching. He shook out the bedspread and blankets, examined the floor and the closet. He studied the window space, leaned out for a look at the house wall and the shed roof. His big feet avoided the broken glass, and he squatted for a long gaze at the pieces of window sash. Then he bore down on me, all policeman personified, a massive, rather intelligent, conventionally honest man with no patience for imagination, no time for any fact not already in the books. "Piece of fur, huh?" He made it sound as if I'd described a Jabberwock with eyes of flame. "Okay, we're done up here." He motioned me downstairs—all policemen who'd ever faced a crowd's dangerous stupidity with their own.

As I retreated I said, "Hope you won't be too busy to have a chemist test the blood on that sash."

"We'll do that." He made move-along motions with his slab hands. "Going to be a pleasure to do that little thing for you and your friend."

Then he searched the entire house, shed, barn, and stable. I had never before watched anyone on police business; I had to admire his zeal. I got involved in the farce of holding the flashlight for him while he rooted in the cellar. In the shed I suggested that if he wanted to restack twenty-odd cords of wood he'd better wait till Harp could help him; he wasn't amused. He wasn't happy in the barn loft either. Shifting tons of hay to find a hypothetical corpse was not a one-man job. I knew he was capable of returning with a crew and machinery to do exactly that. And by his lights it was what he ought to do. Then we were back in the kitchen, Robart giving himself a manicure with his jackknife, and I down to my last cigarette, almost the last of my endurance.

Robart was not unsubtle. I answered his questions as temperately as I could—even, for instance: "Wasn't you a mite sweet on Leda yourself?" I didn't answer any of them with flat silence; to do that right you need an accompanying act like spitting in the stove, and I'm not a chewer. From the north window he said: "Comin' back. It figures." They had been out a little over an hour.

Harp stood by the stove with me to warm his hands. He spoke as if alone with me: "No trail, Ben." What followed came in an undertone: "Ben, you told me about a friend of yours, scientist or something, professor—"

"Professor Malcolm?" I remembered mentioning him to Harp a long while before; I was astonished at his recalling it. Johnny Malcolm is a professor of biology who has avoided too much specialization. Not a really close friend. Harp was watching me out of a granite despair as if he had asked me to appeal to some higher court. I thought of another acquaintance in Boston, too, whom I might consult—Dr. Kahn, a psychiatrist who had once seen my wife, Helen, through a difficult time. . . .

"Harp," said Robart, "I got to ask you a couple, three

things. I sent word to Dick Hammond to get that goddamned
plow of his into this road as quick as he can. Believe he'll
try. Whiles we wait on him, we might's well talk. You know
I don't like to get tough."

"Talk away," said Harp, "only Ben here he's got to get
home without waiting on no Dick Hammond."

"That a fact, Ben?"

"Yes. I'll keep in touch."

"Do that," said Robart, dismissing me. As I left he was
beginning a fresh manicure, and Harp waited rigidly for the
ordeal to continue. I felt morbidly that I was abandoning
him.

Still—corpus delicti—nothing much more would happen until Leda Ryder was found. Then if her body were
found dead by violence, with no acceptable evidence of
Longtooth's existence—well, what then?

I don't think Robart would have let me go if he'd known
my first act would be to call Short's brother Mike and ask
him to drive me into Lohman, where I could get a bus for
Boston.

Johnny Malcolm said, "I can see this is distressing you,
and you wouldn't lie to me. But, Ben, as biology it won't
do. Ain't no such animile. You know that."

He wasn't being stuffy. We were having dinner at a quiet
restaurant, and I had, of course, enjoyed the roast duckling
too much. Johnny is a rock-ribbed beanpole who can eat
like a walking famine with no regrets. "Suppose," I said,
"just for argument and because it's not biologically inconceivable, that there's a basis for the yeti legend."

"Not inconceivable. I'll give you that. So long as any
poorly known corners of the world are left—the Himalayan
uplands, jungles, tropic swamps, the tundra—legends will
persist and some of them will have little gleams of truth.
You know what I think about moon flights and all that?"
He smiled; privately I was hearing Leda scream. "One of
our strongest reasons for them, and for the biggest flights

we'll make if we don't kill civilization first, is a hunt for new legends. We've used up our best ones, and that's dangerous."

"Why don't we look at the countries inside us?" But Johnny wasn't listening much.

"Men can't stand it not to have closed doors and a chance to push at them. Oh, about your yeti—he might exist. Shaggy anthropoid able to endure severe cold, so rare and clever the explorers haven't tripped over him yet. Wouldn't have to be a carnivore to have big ugly canines—look at the baboons. But if he was active in a Himalayan winter, he'd have to be able to use meat, I think. Mind you, I don't believe any of this, but you can have it as a biological not-impossible. How'd he get to Maine?"

"Strayed? Tibet—Mongolia—Arctic ice."

"Maybe." Johnny had begun to enjoy the hypothesis as something to play with during dinner. Soon he was helping along the brute's passage across the continents, and having fun till I grumbled something about alternatives, extraterrestrials. He wouldn't buy that, and got cross. Still hearing Leda scream, I assured him I wasn't watching for little green men.

"Ben, how much do you know about this—Harp?"

"We grew up along different lines, but he's a friend. Dinosaur, if you like, but a friend."

"Hardshell Maine bachelor picks up dizzy young wife—"

"She's not dizzy. Wasn't. Sexy, but not dizzy."

"All right. Bachelor stewing in his own juices for years. Sure he didn't get up on that roof himself?"

"Nuts. Unless all my senses were more paralyzed than I think, there wasn't time."

"Unless they were more paralyzed than you think."

"Come off it! I'm not senile yet. . . . What's he supposed to have done with her? Tossed her into the snow?"

"Mph," said Johnny, and finished his coffee. "All right. Some human freak with abnormal strength and the endurance to fossick around in a Maine blizzard stealing women.

I liked the yeti better. You say you suggested a madman to Ryder yourself. Pity if you had to come all the way here just so I could repeat your own guesswork. To make amends, want to take in a bawdy movie?"

"Love it."

The following day Dr. Kahn made time to see me at the end of the afternoon, so polite and patient that I felt certain I was keeping him from his dinner. He seemed undecided whether to be concerned with the traumas of Harp Ryder's history or those of mine. Mine were already somewhat known to him. "I wish you had time to talk all this out to me. You've given me a nice summary of what the physical events appear to have been, but—"

"Doctor," I said, "it *happened*. I heard the animal. The window *was* smashed—ask the sheriff. Leda Ryder did scream, and when Harp and I got up there together, the dog had been killed and Leda was gone."

"And yet, if it was all as clear as that, I wonder why you thought of consulting me at all, Ben. I wasn't there. I'm just a headshrinker."

"I wanted . . . Is there any way a delusion could take hold of Harp *and* me, disturb our senses in the same way? Oh, just saying it makes it ridiculous."

Dr. Kahn smiled. "Let's say, difficult."

"Is it possible Harp could have killed her, thrown her out through the window of the *west* bedroom—the snow must have drifted six feet or higher on that side—and then my mind distorted my time sense? So I might've stood there in the dark kitchen all the time it went on, a matter of minutes instead of seconds? Then he jumped down by the shed roof, came back into the house the normal way while I was stumbling upstairs? Oh, hell."

Dr. Kahn had drawn a diagram of the house from my description, and peered at it with placid interest. "Benign" was a word Helen had used for him. He said, "Such a distortion of the time sense would be—unusual. . . . Are you feeling guilty about anything?"

"About standing there and doing nothing? I can't seriously believe it was more than a few seconds. Anyway, that would make Harp a monster out of a detective story. He's not that. How could he count on me to freeze in panic? Absurd. I'd've heard the struggle, steps, the window of the west room going up. Could he have killed her and I known all about it at the time, even witnessed it, and then suffered amnesia for that one event?"

He still looked so patient, I wished I hadn't come. "I won't say any trick of the mind is impossible, but I might call that one highly improbable. Academically, however, considering your emotional involvement—"

"I'm not emotionally involved!" I yelled that. He smiled, looking much more interested. I laughed at myself. That was better than poking him in the eye. "I'm upset, Doctor, because the whole thing goes against reason. If you start out knowing nobody's going to believe you, it's all messed up before you open your mouth."

He nodded kindly. He's a good joe. I think he'd stopped listening for what I didn't say long enough to hear a little of what I did say. "You're not unstable, Ben. Don't worry about amnesia. The explanation, perhaps some human intruder, will turn out to be within the human norm. The norm of possibility does include such things as lycanthropic delusions, maniacal behavior, and so on. Your police up there will carry on a good search for the poor woman. They won't overlook that snowdrift. Don't underestimate them, and don't worry about your own mind, Ben."

"Ever seen our Maine woods?"

"No, I go away to the Cape."

"Try it sometime. Take a patch of it, say about fifty miles by fifty, that's twenty-five hundred square miles. Drop some eager policemen into it, tell 'em to hunt for something they never saw before and don't want to see, that doesn't want to be found."

"But if your beast is human, human beings leave traces. Bodies aren't easy to hide, Ben."

"In those woods? A body taken by a carnivorous animal? Why not?" Well, our minds didn't touch. I thanked him for his patience and got up. "The maniac responsible," I said. "But whatever we call him, Doctor, he was *there*."

Mike Short picked me up at the Lohman bus station and told me something of a ferment in Darkfield. I shouldn't have been surprised. "They're all scared, Mr. Dane. They want to hurt somebody." Mike is Jim Short's younger brother. He scrapes up a living with his taxi service and occasional odd jobs at the garage. There's a droop in his shaggy ringlets, and I believe thirty is staring him in the face. "Like old Harp, he wants to tell it like it happened and nobody buys. That's sad, man. You been away what, three days? The fuzz was pissed off. You better connect with Mr. Sheriff Robart like soon. He climbed all over my ass just for driving you to the bus that day, like I should've known you shouldn't."

"I'll pacify him. They haven't found Mrs. Ryder?"

Mike spat out the car window, which was rolled down for the mild air. "Old Harp he never got such a job of snow-shoveling done in all his days. By the c'munity, for free. No, they won't find her." In that there was plenty of I-want-to-be-asked, and something more, a hint of the mythology of Mike's generation.

"So what's your opinion, Mike?"

He maneuvered a fresh cigarette against the stub of the last and drove on through tiresome silence. The road was winding between ridged mountains of plowed, rotting snow. I had the window down on my side, too, for the genial afternoon sun, and imagined a tang of spring. At last Mike said, "You prob'ly don't go along . . . Jim got your ca' out, by the way. It's at your place. . . . Well, you'll hear 'em talking it all to pieces. Some claim Harp's telling the truth. Some say he killed her himself. They don't say how he made her disappear. Ain't heard any talk against you, Mr. Dane, nothing that counts. The sheriff's peeved, but that's just on account you took off without asking." His vague, large eyes watched the melting landscape, the ambiguous messages of spring. "Well, I think, like, a demon took her, Mr. Dane. She was one of his own, see? You got to remember, I knew that chick. Okay, you can say it ain't scientific, only there is a science to these things, I read a book about it. You can laugh if you want."

I wasn't laughing. It wasn't my first glimpse of the contemporary medievalism and won't be my last if I survive another year or two. I wasn't laughing, and I said nothing. Mike sat smoking, expertly driving his twentieth-century artifact while I suppose his thoughts were in the seventeenth, sniffing after the wonders of the invisible world, and I recalled what Johnny Malcolm had said about the need for legends. Mike and I had no more talk.

Adelaide Simmons was dourly glad to see me. From her I learned that the sheriff and state police had swarmed all over Harp's place and the surrounding countryside, and were still at it. Result, zero. Harp had repeatedly told our story and was refusing to tell it anymore. "Does the chores and sets there drinking," she said, "or staring off. Was up to see him yesterday, Mr. Dane—felt I should. Couple days they didn't let him alone a minute, maybe now they've eased off some. He asked me real sharp, was you back yet. Well, I redd up his place, made some bread, least I could do."

When I told her I was going there, she prepared a basket while I sat in the kitchen and listened. "Some say she busted that window herself, jumped down, and run off in the snow, out of her mind. Any sense in that?"

"Nope."

"And some claim she deserted him. Earlier. Which'd make you a liar. And they say whichever way it was, Harp's made up this crazy story because he can't stand the truth." Her clever hands slapped sandwiches into shape. "They claim Harp got you to go along with it, they don't say how."

"Hypnotized me, likely. Adelaide, it all happened the way Harp told it. I heard the thing too. If Harp is ready for the squirrels, so am I."

She stared hard, and sighed. She likes to talk, but her mill often shuts off suddenly, because of a quality of hers which I find good as well as rare: I mean that when she has no more to say she doesn't go on talking.

I got up to Ryder's Ridge about suppertime. Bill Hastings was there. The road was plowed slick between the snow ridges, and I wondered how much of the litter of tracks and crumpled paper and spent cigarette packages had been left by sight-seers. Ground frost had not yet yielded to the mud season, which would soon make normal driving impossible for a few weeks. Bill let me in, with the look people wear for serious illness. But Harp heaved himself out of that armchair, not sick in body at least. "Ben, I heard him last night. Late."

"What direction?"

"North."

"You hear it, Bill?" I set down the basket.

My pint-size friend shook his head. "Wasn't here." I couldn't guess how much Bill accepted of the tale.

Harp said, "What's the basket?—oh. Obliged. Adelaide's a nice woman." But his mind was remote. "It was north, Ben, a long way, but I think I know about where it would be. I wouldn't've heard it except the night was so still, like everything had quieted for me. You know, they been a-deviling me night and day. Robart, state cops, mess of smart little buggers from the papers. I couldn't sleep, I stepped outside like I was called. Why, he might've been the other side of the stars, the sky so full of 'em and nothing stirring. Cold . . . You went to Boston, Ben?"

"Yes. Waste of time. They want it to be something human—anyhow, something that fits the books."

Whittling, Bill said neutrally, "Always a man for the books yourself, wasn't you, Ben?"

I had to agree. Harp asked, "Hadn't no ideas?"

"Just gave me back my own thoughts in their language. We have to find it, Harp. Of course some wouldn't take it for true even if you had photographs."

Harp said, "Photographs be goddamned."

"I guess you got to go," said Bill Hastings. "We been talking about it, Ben. Maybe I'd feel the same if it was me. . . . I better be on my way or supper'll be cold and the old woman raising hellfire." He tossed his stick back in the woodbox.

"Bill," said Harp, "you won't mind feeding the stock couple, three days?"

"I don't mind. Be up tomorrow."

"Do the same for you sometime. I wouldn't want it mentioned anyplace."

"Harp, you know me better'n that. See you, Ben."

"Snow's going fast," said Harp when Bill had driven off. "Be in the woods a long time yet, though."

"You wouldn't start this late."

He was at the window, his lean bulk shutting off much light from the time-seasoned kitchen where most of his indoor life had been passed. "Morning, early. Tonight I got to listen."

"Be needing sleep, I'd think."

"I don't always get what I need," said Harp.

"I'll bring my snowshoes. About six? And my carbine— I'm best with a gun I know."

He stared at me awhile. "All right, Ben. You understand, though, you might have to come back alone. I ain't coming back till I get him, Ben. Not this time."

At sunup I found him with Ned and Jerry in the stable. He had lived eight or ten years with that team. He gave Ned's neck a final pat as he turned to me and took up our conversation as if night had not intervened. "Not till I get him. Ben, I don't want you drug into this ag'inst your inclination."

"Did you hear it again last night?"

"I heard it. North."

The sun was at the point of rising when we left on our snowshoes, like morning ghosts ourselves. Harp strode ahead down the slope to the woods without haste, perhaps with some reluctance. Near the trees he halted, gazing to his right, where a red blaze was burning the edge of the sky curtain; I scolded myself for thinking that he was saying good-bye to the sun.

The snow was crusted, sometimes slippery even for our web feet. We entered the woods along a tangle of tracks, including the fat tire marks of a snow scooter. "Guy from Lohman," said Harp. "Hired the goddamn thing out to the state cops and hisself with it. Goes pootin' around all over hell, fit to scare everything inside eight, ten miles." He cut himself a fresh plug to last the morning. "I b'lieve the thing is a mite farther off than that. They'll be messing around again today." His fingers dug into my arm. "See how it is, don't y'? They ain't looking for what we are. Looking for a dead body to hang on to my neck. And if they was to find her the way I found—the way I found—"

"Harp, you needn't borrow trouble."

"I know how they think," he said. "Was I to walk down the road beyond Darkfield, they'd pick me up. They ain't got me in shackles because they got no—no body, Ben. Nobody needs to tell me about the law. They got to have a body. Only reason they didn't leave a man here overnight, they figure I can't go nowhere. They think a man couldn't travel in three, four foot of snow. . . . Ben, I mean to find that thing and shoot it down. . . . We better slant off this-away."

He set out at a wide angle from those tracks, and we soon had them out of sight. On the firm crust our snowshoes left no mark. After a while we heard a grumble of motors far back, on the road. Harp chuckled viciously. "Bright and early like yesterday." He stared back the way we had come. "They'll never pick that up without dogs. That son of a bitch Robart did talk about borrying a hound somewhere, to sniff Leda's clothes. More likely give 'em a sniff of mine, now."

We had already come so far that I didn't know the way back. Harp would know it. He could never be lost in any woods, but I have no mental compass such as his. So I followed him blindly, not trying to memorize our trail. It was a region of uniform old growth, mostly hemlock, no recent lumbering, few landmarks. The monotony wore down native patience to a numbness, and our snowshoes left no more impression than our thoughts.

An hour passed, or more; after that the sound of motors faded. Now and then I heard the wind move peacefully overhead. Few bird calls, for most of our singers had not yet returned. "Been in this part before, Harp?"

"Not with snow on the ground, not lately." His voice was hushed and careful. "Summers. About a mile now, and the trees thin out some. Stretch of slash where they were taking out pine four, five years back and left everything a christly pile of shit like they always do."

No, Harp wouldn't get lost here, but I was well lost, tired, sorry I had come. Would he turn back if I collapsed? I didn't think he could, now, for any reason. My pack with blanket roll and provisions had become infernal. He had said we ought to have enough for three or four days. Only a few years earlier I had carried heavier camping loads than this without trouble, but now I was blown, a stitch beginning in my side. My wristwatch said only nine o'clock.

The trees thinned out as he had promised, and here the land rose in a long slope to the north. I looked up across a tract of eight or ten acres, where the devastation of stupid lumbering might be healed if the hurt region could be let alone for sixty years. The deep snow, blinding out here where only scrub growth interfered with the sunlight, covered the worst of the wreckage. "Good place for wild ras'berries," Harp said quietly. "Been time for 'em to grow back. Guess it was nearer seven years ago when they cut here and left this mess. Last summer I couldn't hardly find their logging road. Off to the left—"

He stopped, pointing with a slow arm to a blurred gray line that wandered up from the left to disappear over the rise of ground. The nearest part of that gray curve must have been four hundred feet away, and to my eyes it might have been a shadow cast by an irregularity of the snow surface; Harp knew better. Something had passed there, heavy enough to break the crust. "You want to rest a mite, Ben? Once over that rise I might not want to stop again."

I let myself down on the butt of an old log that lay tilted toward us, cut because it had happened to be in the way, left to rot because they happened to be taking pine. "Can you really make anything out of that?"

"Not enough," said Harp. "But it could be him." He did not sit by me but stood relaxed with his load, snowshoes spaced so he could spit between them. "About half a mile over that rise," he said, "there's a kind of gorge. Must've been a good brook, former times, still a stream along the bottom in summer. Tangle of elders and stuff. Couple, three caves in the bank at one spot. I guess it's three summers since I been there. Gloomy goddamn place. There was foxes into one of them caves. Natural caves, I b'lieve. I didn't go too near, not then."

I sat in the warming light, wondering whether there was any way I could talk to Harp about the beast—if it existed, if we weren't merely a pair of aging men with disordered minds. Any way to tell him the creature was important to the world outside our dim little village? That it ought somehow to be kept alive, not just shot down and shoveled aside? How could I say this to a man without science, who had lost his wife and also the trust of his fellow men?

Take away that trust and you take away the world.

Could I ask him to shoot it in the legs, get it back alive? Why, to my own self, irrationally, that appeared wrong, horrible, as well as beyond our powers. Better if he shot to kill. Or if I did. So in the end I said nothing, but shrugged my pack into place and told him I was ready to go on.

With the crust uncertain under that stronger sunshine, we picked our way slowly up the rise, and when we came at length to that line of tracks, Harp said matter-of-factly, "Now you've seen his mark. It's him."

Sun and overnight freezing had worked on the trail. Harp estimated it had been made early the day before. But wherever the weight of Longtooth had broken through, the shape of his foot showed clearly down there in its pocket of snow, a foot the size of a man's but broader, shorter. The prints were spaced for the stride of a short-legged person. The arch of the foot was low, but the beast was not actually flat-footed. Beast or man. I said, "This is a man's print, Harp. Isn't it?"

He spoke without heat. "No. You're forgetting, Ben. I seen him."

"Anyhow, there's only one."

He said slowly, "Only one set of tracks."

"What d'you mean?"

Harp shrugged. "It's heavy. He could've been carrying something. Keep your voice down. That crust yesterday, it would've held me without no web feet, but he went through, and he ain't as big as me." Harp checked his rifle and released the safety. "Half a mile to them caves. B'lieve that's where he is, Ben. Don't talk unless you got to, and take it slow."

I followed him. We topped the rise, encountering more of that lumberman's desolation on the other side. The trail crossed it, directly approaching a wall of undamaged trees that marked the limit of the cutting. Here forest took over once more, and where it began, Longtooth's trail ended. "Now you seen how it goes," Harp said. "Anyplace where he can travel above ground he does. He don't scramble up the trunks, seems like. Look here—he must've got aholt of that branch and swung hisself up. Knocked off some snow, but the wind knocks off so much, too, you can't tell nothing.

See, Ben, he—he figures it out. He knows about trails.
He'll have come down out of these trees far enough from
where we are now so there ain't no chance of us seeing the
place from here. Could be anywhere in a half circle, and
draw it as big as you please."

"Thinking like a man."

"But he ain't a man," said Harp. "There's things he don't
know. How a man feels, acts. I'm going on to them caves."
From necessity, I followed him. . . .

I ought to end this quickly. Prematurely I am an old
man, incapacitated by the effects of a stroke and a damaged
heart. I keep improving a little—sensible diet, no smoking,
Adelaide's care. I expect several years of tolerable health on
the way downhill. But I find, as Harp did, that it is even
more crippling to lose the trust of others. I will write here
once more, and not again, that my word is good.

It was noon when we reached the gorge. In that place
some melancholy part of night must always remain. Down
the center of the ravine between tangles of alder, water
murmured under ice and rotting snow, which here and
there had fallen in to reveal the dark brilliance. Harp did
not enter the gorge itself but moved slowly through tree
cover along the left edge, eyes flickering for danger. I tried
to imitate his caution. We went a hundred yards or more
in that inching advance, maybe two hundred. I heard only
the occasional wind of spring.

He turned to look at me with a sickly triumph, a grimace
of disgust and of justification too. He touched his nose and
then I got it also, a rankness from down ahead of us, a
musky foulness with an ammoniacal tang and some smell
of decay. Then on the other side of the gorge, off in the
woods but not far, I heard Longtooth.

A bark, not loud. Throaty, like talk.

Harp suppressed an answering growl. He moved on until
he could point down to a black cave mouth on the opposite
side. The breeze blew the stench across to us. Harp whispered, "See, he's got like a path. Jumps down to that flat

rock, then to the cave. We'll see him in a minute." Yes, there were sounds in the brush. "You keep back." His left palm lightly stroked the underside of his rifle barrel.

So intent was he on the opening where Longtooth would appear, I may have been first to see the other who came then to the cave mouth and stared up at us with animal eyes. Longtooth had called again, a rather gentle sound. The woman wrapped in filthy hides may have been drawn by that call or by the noise of our approach.

Then Harp saw her.

He knew her. In spite of the tangled hair, scratched face, dirt, and the shapeless deer pelt she clutched around herself against the cold, I am sure he knew her. I don't think she knew him, or me. An inner blindness, a look of a beast wholly centered on its own needs. I think human memories had drained away. She knew Longtooth was coming. I think she wanted his warmth and protection, but there were no words in the whimper she made before Harp's bullet took her between the eyes.

Longtooth shoved through the bushes. He dropped the rabbit he was carrying and jumped down to that flat rock snarling, glancing sidelong at the dead woman who was still twitching. If he understood the fact of death, he had no time for it. I saw the massive overdevelopment of thigh and leg muscles, their springy motions of preparation. The distance from the flat rock to the place where Harp stood must have been fifteen feet. One spear of sunlight touched him in that blue-green shade, touched his thick red fur and his fearful face.

Harp could have shot him. Twenty seconds for it, maybe more. But he flung his rifle aside and drew out his hunting knife, his own long tooth, and had it waiting when the enemy jumped.

So could I have shot him. No one needs to tell me I ought to have done so.

Longtooth launched himself, clawed fingers out, fangs exposed. I felt the meeting as if the impact had struck my own flesh. They tumbled roaring into the gorge, and I was cold, detached, an instrument for watching.

It ended soon. The heavy brownish teeth clenched in at the base of Harp's neck. He made no more motion except the thrust that sent his blade into Longtooth's left side. Then they were quiet in that embrace, quiet all three. I heard the water flowing under the ice.

I remember a roaring in my ears, and I was moving with slow care, one difficult step after another, along the lip of the gorge and through mighty corridors of white and green. With my hard-won detached amusement I supposed this might be the region where I had recently followed poor Harp Ryder to some destination or other, but not (I thought) one of those we talked about when we were boys. A band of iron had closed around my forehead, and breathing was an enterprise needing great effort and caution, in order not to worsen the indecent pain that clung as another band around my diaphragm. I leaned against a tree for thirty seconds or thirty minutes, I don't know where. I knew I mustn't take off my pack in spite of the pain, because it carried provisions for three days. I said once: "Ben, you are lost."

I had my carbine, a golden bough, staff of life, and I recall the shrewd management and planning that enabled me to send three shots into the air. Twice.

It seems I did not want to die, and so hung on the cliff edge of death with a mad stubbornness. They tell me it could not have been the second day that I fired the second burst, the one that was heard and answered—because they say a man can't suffer the kind of attack I was having and then survive a whole night of exposure. They say that when a search party reached me from Wyndham Village (eighteen miles from Darkfield), I made some garbled speech and fell flat on my face.

I woke immoblized, without power of speech or any motion except for a little life in my left hand, and for a long time memory was only a jarring of irrelevancies. When that cleared, I still couldn't talk for another long deadly while. I recall someone saying with exasperated admiration that with cerebral hemorrhage on top of coronary infarction, I had no damn right to be alive; this was the first sound that gave me any pleasure. I remember recognizing Adelaide and being unable to thank her for her presence. None of this matters to the story, except the fact that for months I had no bridge of communication with the world; and yet I loved the world and did not want to leave it.

One can always ask: What will happen next?

Sometime in what they said was June my memory was (I think) clear. I scrawled a little, with the nurse supporting the deadened part of my arm. But in response to what I wrote, the doctor, the nurses, Sheriff Robart, even Adelaide Simmons and Bill Hastings, looked—sympathetic. I was not believed. I am not believed now, in the most important part of what I wish I might say: that there are things in our world that we do not understand, and that this ignorance ought to generate humility. People find this obvious, bromidic—oh, they always have!—and therefore they do not listen, retaining the pride of their ignorance intact.

Remnants of the three bodies were found in late August, small thanks to my efforts, for I had no notion what compass direction we took after the cut-over area, and there are so many such areas of desolation I couldn't tell them where to look. Forest scavengers, including a pack of dogs, had found the bodies first. Water had moved them, too, for the last of the big snow melted suddenly, and for a couple of days at least there must have been a small river raging through that gorge. The head of what they are calling the "lunatic" got rolled downstream, bashed against rocks, partly buried in silt. Dogs had chewed and scattered what they speak of as "the man's fur coat."

It will remain a lunatic in a fur coat, for they won't have it any other way. So far as I know, no scientist ever got a look at the wreckage, unless you glorify the coroner by that title. I believe he was a good vet before he got the job.

When my speech was more or less regained, I was already through trying to talk about it. A statement of mine was read at the inquest—that was before I could talk or leave the hospital. At this ceremony society officially decided that Harper Harrison Ryder, of this township, shot to death his wife, Leda, and an individual, male, of unknown identity, while himself temporarily of unsound mind, and died of knife injuries received in a struggle with the said individual of unknown, and so forth.

I don't talk about it because that only makes people more sorry for me, to think a man's mind should fail so, and he not yet sixty.

I cannot even ask them: "What is truth?" They would only look more saddened, and I suppose shocked, and perhaps find reasons for not coming to see me again.

They are kind. They will do anything for me, except think about it.